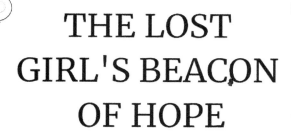

THE LOST GIRL'S BEACON OF HOPE

Emma Hardwick

BOOK CARD

Other books by Emma Hardwick

The Urchin of Walton Hall

Forging the Shilling Girl

The Scullery Maid's Salvation

The Widow of the Valley

The Christmas Songbird

The Slum Lady

The Vicar's Wife

COPYRIGHT

Title: The Lost Girl's Beacon of Hope

First published in 2021

Copyright © 2021 Emma Hardwick

ISBN: 9798528677415 (Paperback)

CONTENTS

1

EMMY'S SHAME

Five-year-old Tilda Sterling stood with her snotty nose and grubby face pushed up against the gates outside the cotton mill. It was cold and wet, but she didn't feel it. Hot air radiated from the bustling factory, making it a haven for the homeless who cluttered the adjacent streets. Tilda was fascinated as the golden courtyard gas lights reflected millions of minute pieces of cotton fluff drifting through the air. The devious cotton fibre created the magical image of thousands of fairies floating peacefully—but the fairies were deadly, lodging themselves in the mill workers' lungs and gradually smothering them to death.

It wasn't this which had killed Tilda's mother four years ago, but rather a fire which had ravaged the mill. The dry cotton fibres that drifted through the air would combust with the slightest flame, exploding into floating fireballs, setting off a chain reaction throughout the factory.

Mavis Sterling had been standing in the path of one of these explosions when her dress caught alight. Witnesses said she tore through the factory like a Catherine wheel, trying to outrun the fatal flames that clung to her clothing.

Ultimately, she collapsed. With the fire quickly extinguished by terrified onlookers, there had been minor damage to her body. Sadly, poor Mavis had inhaled the red-hot air, which in turn scorched her delicate lung tissue, suffocating her to death.

Embeth was older than her sister Tilda, old enough to work. Emmy had no choice but to seek employment at the same cotton mill which had killed her mother. Her father, Jimmy Sterling, didn't have a permanent job, and Emmy had to help the miserable, feckless man keep the family financially afloat. Emmy could no longer attend the meagre excuse of a school that the government provided, and thus her education was stunted.

Forty years prior, Tilda would have been working at the tender age of four but the laws had changed so, thank the Lord, Tilda was protected from the harsh factory environment. Now, she was legally obliged to attend school until she turned ten years old.

Of course, all this meant nothing to the tiny tot. The highlight of her day was standing at the factory's wrought-iron gates and watching the magic show performed by the glittering fairies every night. Brimming with glee at the spectacle, she always went to fetch her sister Emmy, whom she adored.

"Emmy! Emmy, can you see them? They're fairies, Emmy!"

Tilda smiled and pointed at the cotton drifting in the light. Emmy understood that the cotton fluff was treacherous but would nod her head, not wanting to spoil Tilda's fun.

"One day, I'm going to work with the fairies," said a grinning Tilda, her overactive imagination getting the best of her.

"No, you are not Tilda, not if I can help it," chided Emmy. "You can write stories about fairies, but you will never work in a cotton mill."

Tilda was quiet for the entire walk home, knowing that she'd made Emmy angry again, and still not understanding why.

Their first stop on their return was at Mrs Dunberry's shop, a small bakery. Although she made them pay a stale loaf price, she always gave them a fresh one. Mrs Dunberry was an angel who did this for the most impoverished families.

"C'mon now, you two. Let me pack ye in some fresh farm butter. I got it in a fresh delivery this morning, I did. Ah, and some cheese too. The cheesemaker delivered far too much."

Mrs Dunberry would spoil them every evening. They were oblivious that it was given from the private stock in her kitchen. The old woman felt desperately sorry for the two young girls, particularly Embeth, who was left to care for her tiny sister.

"Thank ye, Mrs Dunberry," chirruped the ragged-looking girls.

"Go on with yer now. The night is bitter, and that little one is already shivering."

Then Mrs Dunberry would wrap the hot, fresh bread in some paper and shove them out of the bakery to ensure that they got home as fast as their legs could carry them. The protective wrapper didn't last long. The crisp bread smelled so enticing that Emmy and Tilda would break off pieces of the crust and nibble on the loaf all the way home.

Home was a room with two beds, a grimy coal stove, and their despicable father, Jimmy Sterling. Jimmy was a charming, manipulative man with an overdeveloped sexual appetite. Every night he would sit in front of the fire, drinking tankard after tankard of beer. As soon as his sobriety left him, he would try and lure his young daughters to sit on his knee or sleep in his bed.

During the occasional spell of good weather, Jimmy would prance around the room in his underwear, urging the little girls to do the same. Emmy and Tilda's instincts warned them to stay away from him, and the sisters would escape to the streets and play with their friends instead.

Emmy wasn't lucky enough to permanently escape her ever leering father, and by the age of thirteen, Jimmy Sterling was using the young girl as a wife.

Tilda was seven when she realised that her father was taking Emmy into his bed. She had an awareness that sleeping in a man's bed was terrible, having heard the women in the building gossiping about other ladies who had laid with men at night. Jimmy's youngest daughter didn't appreciate the gravity of the situation, because Emmy had done her best to preserve the girl's innocence.

Tilda remembered how, on Emmy's thirteenth birthday, Jimmy Sterling fetched her sister from their bed. He blew out the lamp and waited for half an hour until he thought young Tilda was asleep.

Life had become expensive. Jimmy knew that he was close to landing himself in the debtors' prison if he continued to spend money as he did. He'd chalked up some almighty debts gambling with the vicious Italians. Eventually, he sold the treasured watch he inherited from his father to pay his debt. Alas, the timepiece didn't raise enough money to settle the outstanding balance, and the Italians threatened to break his legs and drive a stiletto blade through his ribs if he tried to outwit them.

As with all compulsive gamblers, Jimmy believed he could win from Peter to pay Paul—but that wasn't how it worked out for him. Lady Luck didn't shine her benevolent face upon him, and he began to pawn everything he owned, irrespective of how humble the item was. All that was left over in the single room was a buckled pot and the two beds. He would've sold the coal stove if it wasn't bolted to the floor. Fortunately, for the girls, it was a fixture. His two young daughters had to be content to wear the same dress day in and day out. When it rained for weeks, they were forced to turn their dresses inside out and often wore wet clothes for days. When Jimmy wasn't in the flat, they dared to take off their sodden rags and dry them over the stove.

Until recently, Jimmy had enough money to frequent a brothel, and he even took a lover for a short while. When he ran out of money, he had to curb his exotic tastes and settle for 'any old whore off the street'. Eventually, he realised the solution to his woes was right in front of him—his thirteen years old eldest daughter. His decision was easy to justify.

It's not my fault my wife died. All men needed a physical outlet.

"For crying out loud, go and play bloody football if yer frustrated, Jimmy," said his friend Martin Blackburn, astounded when Sterling mentioned the idea. "The right thing to do is leave the girl alone!"

Although Martin was no saint himself, he found Jimmy's suggestion despicable. As long as Jimmy never mentioned it again, though, Martin didn't pry.

In her sleepy haze, Tilda saw Jimmy touch her sister's shoulder and give her a gentle shake. He whispered in Emmy's ear, his hot and stale tobacco breath against her skin.

"Come lass, wake up. Yer Da is cold. Come lie with me and warm me up a little," coaxed Jimmy in his best sing-song, oh-so-charming voice.

Drowsily, Emmy shrugged his hand off her shoulder and rolled over.

"Yer ol' Da isn't feeling too grand, cold shivers it is. C'mon now, lass. Yer dunna want yer old Da sick now, do yer? Where will you get grub for Tilda?"

Still half-asleep, Emmy got up and stumbled to Jimmy Sterling's bed.

Tilda heard a lot of tossing and turning in the gloom, later accompanied by her sister's low, harsh voice.

"No, Da! No! Stop—stop—you're hurting me!"
protested Emmy.

"Quiet now, girl, or you will wake yer sister."

Emmy tried to scream but gave a muffled cry instead as her brute of a father clapped his hand over her open mouth. For an ecstatic Jimmy Sterling, it was his time to perform. His groaning filled the air, and the floorboards creaked in time with his undulating bulk. Then the movement stopped, and a nauseating silence followed.

"Now, lass," said her father's sickly-sweet voice,
"that wasn't so bad then, was it?"

Beneath him, he noticed Emmy's eyes filling with stinging hot tears.

"Now, now luvvie, don't yer cry. Next, time, will be better, you'll see. It got better for yer Ma. So, you must be a brave little girl like yer dear old mother was. She would be very proud of you."

2

SAMUEL'S LOVES

Samuel Hudson, the self-made industrialist, reclined in the worn leather chair. He wore no tie, his shirt collar was open, and his sleeves were rolled up to his elbows. Samuel was still a handsome man for his years, his hair short and streaked with grey, his eyes bright and lively reflecting a keen sense of humour. He had his usual wit and feisty temper, accompanied by a determined mind.

He protected his family and household like a ferocious lion, challenging anyone who dared to destroy the happiness of his beloved pride.

Since Samuel's retirement, he and his wife, Annabelle, spent more and more time at their country home, close to Birmingham and his successful foundry. Samuel stabled some fine horses, which they enjoyed riding and walking across their beautiful estate. He forbade any form of hunting on his land, and refused to participate in the annual fox hunt, declaring blood sport illegal on his property. This aggravated the local aristocracy and gentry no end. Samuel also forbade them to jump his fences, thus diminishing his popularity even further.

For people with money, his behaviour rubbed them up the wrong way, making them wonder at his reasoning. *Who does he think he is, laying down the law like that? This is an age-old tradition? How dare he!*

"This isn't a place of death," he snapped on one occasion when criticised." Trespass onto my property, and I'll shoot your dogs and your horse."

Nobody dared challenge Samuel Hudson.

Samuel's beautiful thirty-something daughter, Shilling, sat in front of him, trying to get his attention.

"Papa, I've received a letter from a Mr Adamson in Manchester."

Samuel grunted.

"He has asked for a meeting at the foundry. They're improving the canal system from Liverpool to Manchester and need an eyewatering amount of materials. He wants us to supply them."

"Where is my granddaughter?" asked Samuel, not in the least bit interested in canals linking to the filthy river.

"Oh, Papa! Can't we for once have a conversation that excludes Tanner, please? She's in the library reading."

"Annabelle and I have planned to take her to France with us," said Samuel, adding with persistence, "that child needs more free time, and she needs to visit me more often."

"Papa! You see her three or four times a week, and you overindulge her."

Seeing her father's face fall, her voice dropped, her expression softened.

"Really, Shilling? I do not recall it being that often. And as for overindulgence—."

Samuel clasped his hands behind his head, a mischievous, exasperating twinkle in his eye. Shilling shook her head at her father affectionately before reprimanding him again.

"If you are not at our home, she is visiting here. Your demands to spend more time with her are unreasonable"

Samuel was undeterred.

"—and now you are subjecting my granddaughter to Mrs Wallace, your old governess. You were always fighting with the old dragon. Now you have appointed her to teach Tanner!"

"Father, Mrs Wallace is an excellent governess."

"Hmph! If I do not keep a finger on what you are doing, Tanner will end up in one of those ghastly boarding schools, designed to torture the very souls of children."

Shilling sighed.

"No, Papa. Miss Wallace is perfect. Although, perhaps Tanner does need a new mathematics and physics teacher."

"Shilling, it's time to give up the hope that Tanner will follow in your footsteps," argued Samuel. "She wants to be a writer, and she will change the world in her own way. She could be the next Mrs Beeton!"

"Mathematics and physics are the most important subjects for a woman these days, not how to make a sponge cake. At least Tanner will know the difference between a circle, and a square."

"The pen is mightier than the sword!" insisted Samuel stubbornly, "and I will support her."

"The pen is only mighty if you can read, write and share powerful points, Papa."

Shilling had a point. Samuel tried a different tack.

"Did I ever stop your dreams of becoming an engineer, Shilling? Did I ever stand in your way when you decided to follow a career akin to men?"

"Do not tell me how to raise my daughter, Papa."

"Tanner is my granddaughter, and you must allow her to determine her own future, not the one you deem fit for her."

"Papa, she can be anything she wishes, but she needs a broad education, please respect that."

Samuel nodded begrudgingly as his anger dissipated as fast as it had flared. He walked to Shilling and kissed her on the forehead.

"Tanner is going to make us very proud someday, Shilling."

"Yes, she is, Papa, now, will you please stop complaining about her lessons!"

Samuel found he couldn't ignore Shilling's earlier mention of the canals. His curiosity was getting the better of him, and he waited for her to calm down sufficiently before he broached the subject.

"By the way, what were you saying about the canals in Manchester?" asked Samuel casually. "I thought railways were the future for goods transportation?"

"Aha! so, you are interested after all," Shilling muttered. "The city is planning to improve the shipping canal system in the North West, and Hudson Engineering has been invited to a meeting to discuss the project."

Samuel grimaced as he nodded.

"It's about bloody time they did something to help the steamers get to the Liverpool docks. The rivers up there are filthy."

"We'll need to do extensive research if we want to get the business, of course, but I think the gamble will pay off."

"Well, it sounds lucrative," Samuel mused. "Miles of new infrastructure, bridges, props, docks, cranes, winches, moorings—."

"—and I want the Hudson Forge stamp on every piece of metal they use."

Samuel smiled at his ambitious daughter.

"Are you taking your husband with you?"

"Of course not. Benjamin's a financier!"

"So, who will accompany you?"

"I would like you to come with me, Papa. I'm also inviting Baxter Lee."

"What? Baxter Lee? Does your husband know?" roared Samuel.

"Not this again! Benjamin is a banker, not an engineer. He has nothing to contribute in such a meeting except money."

Samuel barely allowed her to finish the sentence.

"Baxter Lee," he thundered. "Why would you want to take that swine with you?"

"Papa, stop it. Baxter is a brilliant engineer, and I trust him."

"You trust him?"

"Yes, Papa. And I trust myself."

"How can you rely on that man after what he did you?" Samuel ranted.

Their yelling was so loud that neither one heard the study door open. Miss Annabelle stood in the doorway, listening to the argument between father and daughter. Poised and graceful, Samuel's beautiful wife was unperturbed by the commotion. Anyone else would have been dismayed by the fiery debate under their roof, yet Annabelle was well accustomed to such outbursts.

"Papa, we are not going on a romantic engagement. We are going to a business meeting."

Annabelle walked over to Samuel and put her arm around him.

"Furthermore, I expect you to be cordial,"

"You're asking too bloody much of me," Samuel hissed through his teeth.

"Papa, I'm an adult. I do not have to explain this to you."

"Of course, you do!"

"—Samuel. Samuel, quieten down. You're lifting the roof off the house," interrupted Annabelle.

"Thank you," said Shilling.

Samuel looked at his wife, his heart melting, and his temper dissipating. He put his arm around her and kissed her unashamedly on the mouth.

"I'm sorry, my love, but Shilling does the most exasperating things."

"Of course, she does." answered Annabelle, "She's just like you."

"Can you believe, not only does she employ that dubious character, Baxter Lee, but now she includes him in our business trips?" Samuel hissed.

"Now, Samuel, we have discussed this many times before. What happened between them was a lifetime ago. It's in the past. And— it's none of your concern."

"Baxter Lee has been in love with her since she was eighteen, Annabelle. He was her tutor, and he had romanced her. He'd a wife and son in Dorset, who knew nothing of his antics. The man has no honour. I should've put him in his place while I'd the opportunity."

"No, Papa! That is enough!"

Shilling shook her beautiful head. Her black hair was pulled back off her face, and her green eyes flashed the same colour as the emerald pendant at her throat. A scar ran from her temple to her jaw, and it reminded Samuel that his daughter was fearless.

"You're going too far, Samuel. If you say another word, Shilling, Tanner, and I will have tea without you. You can stay here and sulk by yourself," Annabelle reprimanded.

The words sobered Samuel somewhat. The threat of missing a moment with his cherished granddaughter was the worst punishment he could anticipate.

"Alright, alright," he muttered in surrender.

There was a soft knock at the door, and Socrates wafted in.

"Your tea is ready, Sir. Are you still going to have it with Miss Tanner?"

"Of course, I bloody am!"

Everyone grimaced at the outburst, compelling Samuel to calm down. A tight smile spread across his face.

"I'll discuss the canals with you later, Shilling."

"Thank you, Papa."

Miss Annabelle watched Samuel kiss Shilling on the top of her head, knowing that for all their arguing, they couldn't live without each other. Annabelle was always the voice of reason between them. She defended Shilling to Samuel many times when he was unreasonable and overdemanding. When he eventually calmed down, he would agree with what she said. Annabelle understood how Samuel felt about Baxter Lee and the heartache he caused, but he had no right to remind Shilling of the experience for the rest of her life.

"Grandpa," called Tanner and ran straight into her grandfather's arms.

Miss Annabelle led her to the table where Socrates had set out the tea. Samuel pulled a chair out for Annabelle, and then for Tanner. He looked at the beautiful girl, who was the image of her mother. He thought back fondly to her birth, then was struck that Tanner was no longer a child. The passage of time had made her a young woman. *I wonder how long it will be before she makes her own way in life and I have to share her with others?* He snapped out of the reverie with a question.

"Now, what have you been studying with that dreadful Wallace woman, Tanner?"

"Mrs Wallace is forcing me to do maths and science. I find it boring, of course, but I'm persevering and making progress."

"Are you allowed to have any fun?" Samuel asked behind his hand in a mock whisper.

Shilling glared as Tanner continued.

"Grandmother Fischer is insisting that I attend a function at the French ambassador's residence one year. It's the annual charity ball."

Samuel raised an eyebrow at Shilling.

"We are all invited, Papa, including you and Miss Annabelle."

"I hate these bloody socialite functions," he muttered under his breath. "I'd be delighted to be your escort for the evening," teased Samuel.

"Thank you, Grandpa! You will be the most handsome man there."

Annabelle chuckled to herself. —*And also, the most grumpy, Tanner!*

"You're right, Tanner. Grandpa is the most handsome man wherever he goes."

"You had better not look too pretty, Tanner. I do not want those snooty, sissy boys looking at you."

Tanner giggled.

Socrates caught Samuel's glinting eye and gave a knowing nod.

Annabelle kicked Samuel's leg under the table and gave him one of her severe 'do not interfere' stares.

Tanner heard the footsteps of her father Benjamin Fisher in the entrance hall, who opened the door and let himself in.

When he saw everybody assembled in the drawing-room, he smiled broadly.

"Papa," yelled Tanner, rushing into his arms.

Benjamin embraced his jubilant daughter.

"Calm down, Tanner! Good day, Miss Annabelle, Samuel," said Benjamin as he fought to escape her grasp.

"Papa, Grandpa, says he will escort me to the French Embassy charity dinner one day," said Tanner loudly.

"He did, did he? I'm very fussy about who escorts my daughter, so I'll have to have a word with your grandfather," chortled Benjamin.

Samuel knew that he was in trouble with Benjamin when the man referred to him as 'grandfather'. Most of the time, Samuel was endearing, and Benjamin loved him dearly except for one infuriating habit.

His only wish was that his father-in-law stopped interfering in how he and Shilling raised Tanner. Benjamin knew Samuel didn't want to attend the embassy's pompous function, yet Samuel would happily go to please his granddaughter. Plus, he insisted on putting ideas in her head that she should pursue her career as a writer, rather than more heavyweight academic subjects.

The Fischer family were tantamount to royalty worldwide, and their endorsement of the annual charity event was an institution. Socialising was their life blood. It was these competing needs that caused Benjamin guilt when he occasionally confronted Samuel.

"Samuel," Benjamin would say in private, "leave us to raise Tanner. She needs discipline."

Samuel would put his head back and laugh in delight.

"What has that got to do with me, Ben?"

"She has a brilliant mind, Samuel. We must prepare her for all facets of life, not only the things that interest her. It's called a broad education."

Samuel's brow wrinkled as a frown formed.

"You mean she has to prepare for marriage, homemaking, society and childbearing," he said, in a steely voice.

Benjamin shook his head. He'd heard this all before.

"Not at all, Sam. Give us some credit."

"I refuse to allow Tanner to be turned into some society hostess who breeds like a thoroughbred mare to satisfy a family dynasty."

In an instant, Samuel regretted his harsh words.

"I'm sorry, Ben, that was callous of me."

"Yes, it was Sam."

With a softer tone, Samuel finished getting his point across.

"Ben, you and Shilling have raised Tanner in a home where she has witnessed your care and benevolence toward the working classes. Shilling has instigated great social change with her sponsorship of the industrial school. Do you think Tanner will be any different to you? You have created a firebrand, and the child is going to achieve greatness. Leave her alone to find her own outlet for her talents. She doesn't have to be limited to engineering or finance."

Samuel watched his wife tilt her head to one side and glare. It was her silent warning to discontinue the conversation.

Samuel avoided her eyes. He knew he was being cantankerous. To spare himself a lecture, he began discussing the Manchester ship canal.

Benjamin Fischer was captivated with Shilling Hudson from the first moment he saw her. The raven-haired, green-eyed beauty with the scar down the side of her face. She intrigued him from the instant she stepped into his office. Instead, of the wound detracting from her beauty, it enhanced it. The mark would go on to become a trademark. If someone mentioned 'the woman with the scar', everyone knew that they were referring to Shilling Hudson, the woman brave enough to fight for a better world.

Many years before Benjamin met Shilling, she'd taken a severe lashing across the face from a riding crop. Shilling remembered the horrendous event clearly. On a cold wintery night, she and Socrates witnessed a young boy being beaten outside a Birmingham factory. When she dived on top of the child to protect him from his boss, the deranged man brought the weapon down upon her, slashing her face from temple to jaw. Although she'd saved the boy, she would have the scar forever.

Instead of the event and the disfigurement destroying her confidence, it had further impassioned her to protect the weak, and the poor. Her dedication to the common workers made her unpopular with the upper class and industrialists. She was branded a trouble maker, and a threat. Shilling was even accused of being a socialist, and a traitor, but she argued that the unions were powerful because they were doing the state's work. It was the government's duty to protect the working class from exploitation, and yet, time and again, it had failed them.

Politicians, and the aristocracy knew that Shilling Hudson wasn't intimidated by men or politics, making them reluctant to confront her. They didn't want her dragged before a parliamentary committee to explain herself in case she gained support from the Liberal Party or sympathy from honourable men in the ruling class. Worse still for her detractors, not only was she beautiful, brilliant, and fearless, she was also the daughter of Samuel Hudson, a self-made man who didn't answer to society and also a man who would protect his daughter—at any cost.

Later that night, Benjamin and Shilling lay in bed and discussed the day.

"My darling, I'm tempted to ban your father from this house, even though he owns it! If I were not so fond of him, I would've done it years ago. He causes mayhem, and he takes nothing seriously. Samuel is fiercely loyal to us, but he still treats us like we are children," Benjamin lamented.

What he'd observed was true. Samuel was his own man. Shilling burst into fits of giggles as a solemn and confused Benjamin frowned. Noticing his frustration, she gazed into his dark, smouldering eyes and stroked his hair.

"My father had his hands full raising me. Let him enjoy Tanner. He adores her."

"My life was quite simple before I met you," Benjamin said wistfully. "Work, sleep, work, sleep. There was nothing complicated about it."

Shilling giggled.

"You have to admit you were bored to death before you met me."

"Yes, I suppose I was—but I never thought marrying Shilling Hudson would be like living in an eternal hurricane," Benjamin teased.

"Stop complaining. You love the liveliness in the house."

"Since Tanner was born, I've no control over anything that happens in this house," he continued. "I'm a highly regarded banker from one of the wealthiest dynasties in the world. I control billions of pounds all over the globe, but I have no hope of controlling the two women in my life."

"Don't exaggerate, Benjamin. You're being melodramatic. Besides, we can't function without your level head to steady us," laughed Shilling.

"Just like that," Benjamin snapped his fingers, "my life became chaotic. I'm not the man I was before. You and Tanner have defeated me."

"Oh, darling, we adore you," Shilling said, playfully.

"I've a vague idea Tanner is going to be like you." Benjamin sighed. "I'm exhausted just thinking of the future."

"Will it be so bad if she is like me?" asked Shilling.

Benjamin kissed her and pulled her toward him.

"Of course not, my darling. I may grow old before my time, but you know I'll never look at another woman. I adore you."

Benjamin rolled over and kissed her, running his hand along the front of her thigh.

The Mayfair house was still once more. The staff were in their quarters, except for Socrates, who never seemed to sleep. Samuel loved the tranquillity of the night when he was left to his thoughts without any distractions.

Annabelle lay in the crook of Samuel's arm, with her head on his chest. He'd waited years to tell her that he was in love with her, and his only regret was that he should've told her sooner. He cherished the time they had alone together.

"Annabelle, I'm afraid that Shilling and Benjamin will force Tanner into a future she does not care for."

"Tanner is young, Sam, and she has a strong character. She will be fine. All you need to do is trust her." said Annabelle, stroking his face gently.

Samuel kissed the top of her forehead, lingering to feel her soft skin against his lips.

"I'm sure that she will be strong enough to deal with her parents when she reaches twenty."

"If she is like Shilling, she will not wait until twenty."

"I'm getting old, Annabelle. I'll not always be here to protect her."

"You do not need to protect her, Sam."

"I'm not getting any younger—"

"—don't talk that way," said Annabelle, clipping the discussion topic short.

"Tanner has a wonderful mother and father to protect her, Sam. You have to learn to let go."

"But Tanner is like Shilling. She's headstrong."

"And Shilling is just like you— capable," smiled Annabelle, running her fingers through his greying hair.

"Annabelle, I'm surrounded by people I love. I don't want to lose any of you. I thank God every day. How much more heaven can a man ask for? You, my dear, you have been my lover, companion, confidante, and best friend. You have fulfilled me."

"Samuel, are you becoming sentimental?" whispered Annabelle.

"Yes, I'm sentimental tonight. You're the love of my life," he said, stroking her cheek and blinking his watering eyes.

Annabelle ran her hand over Samuel's chest. As a young woman, she was crushed by the pain of losing her first husband, and their beloved baby. She'd believed she would never be happy, never find love ever again—until she met Samuel. He indulged and protected her as if she were a precious gem. Over the years, she learned to open her heart once more.

Samuel put out the bedside lamp, and Annabelle fell asleep almost immediately. He, however, lay awake for a long time mulling over the past, the future, and the people he loved, as he began to consider his own mortality.

These days, his joints ached in the cold, his memory wasn't what it used to be and he had to wear reading spectacles. Yet, Samuel still had energy.

Life had served Samuel both joy and sorrow.

He thought about his first marriage to the fiery and exotic Catherine, and their twin sons, all of whom he'd lost in childbirth. The tragedy would all but destroy Samuel, and for quite some time his life meant nothing to him after the trio died. He threw his energy into his work, making a hopeless attempt to forget the past. Samuel almost lost his mind. Empty and lost, he questioned God. In the dark winter gloom, he raged, wept, and cursed. Samuel felt he had nothing to live for, and the only person who kept him from taking his own life was Socrates. He'd stationed himself at Samuel's side day after day. The loyal valet even dozed in a Chesterfield chair outside his master's bedroom door every night, snatching only a few moments of rest.

The miracle of Shilling arrived without warning.

Samuel remembered the street in Wapping as clear as day. Socrates had turned the cab into a narrow road when they came upon a commotion in the middle of a filthy lane. A woman had died giving birth to a child in the gutter. Samuel saw the body of the beautiful young lass, and grief consumed him. He wondered what cruel god would expose him to the same tragedy.

An old woman had picked up the baby, hidden it under her coat, planning to sell her to the highest bidder. Samuel recalled her grimy face, and her wild, carrot-orange hair. His temper still flared at the memory. In his melancholic mood, if Socrates had not been in attendance, he would've throttled the heartless woman and happily faced the gallows.

Maggie Carrot's plan was simple. If the infant died, she would sell it to an anatomist at the medical school. Otherwise, she planned to sell it to a desperate, infertile couple. If that failed, a greedy baby farmer would snap up the opportunity.

Samuel remembered the rage he felt when old Maggie pulled the naked child from under her coat like some sort of commodity.

Instinctively, he knew he was going to take the child home with him. The toothless woman could sense Samuel's fury. Maggie had to save her pride in front of the large crowd and spitefully demanded a shilling from him in exchange for the tot. Socrates dropped the coin into the hag's outstretched hand.

From the moment that Samuel held the little girl in his hands, Alexandria Hudson became his daughter; and from that day on, he called her 'Shilling'.

Samuel had no hope of keeping the child alive without help, so he and Socrates combed the streets of Wapping, desperate to find a wet nurse. A woman at the Salvation Army recommended a young mother who had recently lost her child. Annabelle's eyes reflected the same desolation that Samuel had in his heart. After Socrates had gently explained the circumstances, Annabelle left her dingy room without a backward glance.

She got into Samuel's cab with a small bag, and the clothes on her back. In their later conversations, Samuel understood that Annabelle had suffered the same loss as him.

To the outside world, he was ferocious, but with Annabelle, he was tender and gentle. Even if there had been no romance between them, he would never have insisted she left his house. He would rather have her as a friend than lose her forever.

Samuel remembered how he had dedicated himself to his child and his household. He fell in love with Annabelle, and he would never forsake her, but he couldn't tell her, afraid he would scare her away. His life was whole once more and he didn't want to upset that with a careless comment or foolish fumble.

Many years later, when Samuel held his granddaughter for the first time, he knew that there was no end to his blessings. As he watched the perfect little creature, he fell in love with her and rejoiced in her perfection. True to his sense of humour, Samuel nicknamed the child 'Tanner', slang for half-a-shilling.

Samuel looked at Annabelle, sleeping peacefully. His heart leapt in his chest, and he felt melancholy. He would never love a woman as he loved her. He was filled with dread when he allowed himself to ponder their inevitable deaths. The feelings he had for Annabelle were so great that he wanted to spend more than one lifetime with her. His love for her was eternal.

3

THE BROKEN BABY

Manchester's River Irwell flowed sluggishly past the cotton mill where Emmy Sterling worked. It was infused with the poisonous effluent cast off by all the factories along the river. There were no signs of life in the brown sludge, whereas fifty years earlier, there were fish in abundance.

Emmy, and her sister lived in a tenement, close to the foul waterway. Leaving their humble room was a challenge. Emmy had to navigate the stairs down to the filthy street. She always sidestepped the puddles of human waste, but often, a cart would trundle past and splash her and ruin her efforts to protect herself.

She did her best to hold her breath when she walked past Chillingworth's tannery, where the stench of flayed animal hides, bobbing in steaming cauldrons of urine, was utterly overbearing. It was the smell of hell itself. Sometimes, if her lungs where wheezy that day, she would pull her shawl over her nose to stave off the foul odour. Even so, the thought of her breathing in the rot through her mouth made her wretch.

Recently, Emmy was aware she felt weak and ill. She didn't know that she was pregnant. How would she? Nobody had ever told her how babies were made, and Emmy was only too glad when she didn't suffer the dreaded 'curse' for three months. She put it down to a lack of proper food.

Emmy was a slight girl, and it wasn't long before the older women in the factory and tenement became suspicious of her growing belly.

"Bloody Jimmy Sterling," muttered Mary Dobson.

"What ye saying?" asked Sheila Moore. "Ye are not saying he is the father are ye?"

"I dunna want to speak out of turn, Sheila, but I believe Jimmy has been fiddlin' with his daughter since his wife died," answered Mary.

"Pull the other one, Mary! Jimmy's a bit of a wrong'un, but he wouldn't try it on with his own daughter, surely?"

"I thought ye would know? Everybody in the rows knows about it. Martin says Jimmy was almost bragging about it." said Mary glumly.

"Someone must put Sterling right, the scoundrel."

"Quite, Sheila. She's no more than a wee girl. I'm sure she doesn't even know what has happened to her because of that foul man's uncontrollable urges."

"Yer must talk to her, Mary. She needs help with no mother to take care of the problem."

"I'd rather send my Billy to break Jimmy's legs, than just 'talk'. Sterling's a monster."

Mary Dobson was filled with pity for Emmy. The next evening, after her long shift was over, she made sure she was walking alongside Emmy when they passed through the gates.

"How ye doing then, Emmy?"

"I'm feeling a tad ill of late, Mary," murmured the forlorn girl weakly. "It must be the water. My belly's bloated. I hope it's not the cholera."

"Don't say that, lass. We don't need that now, do we?"

"I've been tired like, and me stomach is upset. In the morning, even if I just have a mug of black tea, I want to bring it straight back up."

Mary took a deep breath. She was a gentle woman, and didn't want to frighten Emmy off with the inevitable truth she felt compelled share.

"Emmy, lass," Mary said gently. "I see year belly is a bit round."

"'Tis the sickness, I swear. 'Tis the cholera."

"Is yer Da or Tilda sick as well?"

"No, they're both right as rain," answered Emmy, wondering why Mary was taking such a sudden interest in her welfare.

"If yer had the cholera, we'd all be sick lass. Everyone in this godforsaken hole called Salford would be dying."

"Then what is it, Mary? I don't have money for Dr Ellis."

Mary's heart broke for the girl. How was she going to tell her that she was pregnant? How was she going to tell Emmy that her father was doing unnatural things to her?

"Emmy, when last were you on the rag, sweetheart?" Mary whispered, keen to keep the matter private.

Emmy blushed and, eventually, answered her.

"Last Shrove Tuesday," said Emmy. "I remember couldn't eat any pancakes cos my stomach was lurching."

Mary's face blanched. *Oh, dear God. That was four months ago.*

"I don't think you are sick with cholera, Emmy. I think you are going to have a bairn."

Emmy looked at Mary with large innocent eyes.

"How do you get a bairn in yer tummy, Mary?"

It was Mary's turn to blush.

"Does—er—does yer Da ever take you into his bed?"

Ashamed, Emmy looked at her feet and then nodded her head.

"And does he—?"

Mary couldn't finish the sentence, but Emmy knew what she was going to ask her.

"Da told me that all the lasses slept in their Da's beds if they loved them. And if they really loved their Da, they would do more."

"More?"

Emmy had instinctively known that what they were doing was wrong, but if she didn't lie with him, he would threaten to put Tilda in his bed instead. Besides, it didn't hurt her anymore. Alone, in the darkness, she bit her lip and allowed it to happen, praying the ordeal would soon be over.

"Yeah, Mary," answered Emmy, "I sleep wiv Da like he says me Ma used to."

Emmy confirmed Mary's worst fears, but she didn't know what to do with the information. She had nobody to confide in except Sheila, who could be trusted to keep her gob shut, even if she wouldn't be able to offer Mary any help.

Jimmy Sterling learned of his daughter's pregnancy in the pub.

"Ah, Jimmy! Congratulations mate, we have heard that yer to be a grandpa," shouted someone at the bar.

"Me? Nah, ye have the wrong fella, mate."

"My Sheila told me!"

"Well, Rory, yer missus is off about that, lad. No bairns under my roof except me own."

"Yeah, right! A little dickie bird told me things have changed in the Sterling household," answered the man snidely. "Now, you've definitely got three nippers."

Sterling's drunken mind was all over the place as it tried to unravel what was said to him. The disdain in Rory Moore's voice was palpable.

Jimmy's friend Martin Blackburn had been watching the exchange from the other side of the pub. Most of the patrons of the Lancashire Arms lived in the housing rows close to the mill, and everybody was familiar with each other.

Martin sidled over and sat down next to him.

"I hear that Emmy has got 'erself knocked up," goaded Blackburn.

"Ah, give it a rest, will ye? I ain't heard nothing, and I ain't seen nothing."

Martin became serious.

"Yer did a bad thing by her, Jimmy."

"I swear down, I never touched 'er," said Jimmy, sheepishly.

"Do not come running to me when the whole row is after yer blood."

"I ain't done nowt wrong. Buy me a scoop or peg it."

Martin stared at a defiant Jimmy Sterling. The sight of the despicable fellow filled him with disgust. From the first moment Jimmy had mentioned Emmy, he knew Sterling had terrible intentions that he would have no qualms to execute.

"And what if I bloody did, anyway?" grizzled Jimmy. "Now she's used to it, the girl is always mad for some."

Martin's jaw dropped at Jimmy's casual confession. Blackburn knew that if he stayed in the pub any longer, he would give Jimmy a good hiding, so he settled his tab and left quietly. Martin wasn't a saint, but he would never condone fiddling with a young girl—especially if he was related to her. The thought of it made him sick.

Jimmy remained at the pub long enough to allay any suspicions that he was worried about his daughter, but his mind was awash with ideas. Knowing he would have to find a way to get rid of the problem, he left the pub with an outward devil-may-care attitude, but underneath the façade was an anxious man.

Sterling got home in a sombre mood. Emmy heard the doorknob rattle. Jimmy walked to the bed where she and Tilda slept and looked down upon his two daughters. Emmy kept her eyes closed and pretended to be asleep. Jimmy ran his fingers through his fringe, brushing it off his face, and then lay on his bed fully clothed.

Emmy's young mind was in turmoil, this time because Jimmy had not come directly to her. *I think he knows! What will happen now? Would he send me away? What if I have to leave Tilda behind? I can't allow that. She'll be next in line for Da's attentions.*

Mary Dobson was surprised to see Jimmy at her door so early in the morning.

"Jimmy," Mary greeted, with an awkward nod.

Jimmy nodded back. Mary knew exactly why he was there. It was the first time she witnessed the smooth, manipulative Jimmy at a loss for words.

"What brings you about?" asked Mary.

"Can we chat over a brew, Mary?"

"No, Jimmy, I don't have time for chit-chat this morning. What's bothering you?"

Jimmy fidgeted, unable to look Mary in the eye.

"I swear down, I never touched her. Can yer help—us—her, like?"

"Getaway, Jimmy, you cad. I wish the child would go to the courts. You should be in gaol for cruelty."

"I swear down, I never went near her," repeated Jimmy.

"Get out of my kitchen, Jimmy. Billy is home soon, and there is no telling what he might do to ya."

"Everybody does it, Mary. There is no law against it, and courts will never do anything to me. What is that fancy word they use? Consent? She did consent, Mary, honest to God she did!"

"Get out of my house, now!"

Mary was disgusted as she watched Jimmy slink out of her kitchen. She wanted to take Sheila and wring her neck. Mary would have been able to keep the whole affair quiet for the sake of the girl, but it was clear Sheila had told everyone in the row, confirming their dark suspicions.

Emmy continued to work at the cotton mill. The conditions were appalling, and the hours long. She was a piecer who twisted broken threads together. It meant she was on her feet for sixteen hours a day. Thankfully, Emmy was young and energetic now. In the past few weeks, the morning sickness had abated, and the spinner liked working with her once more. Although she was pregnant, Emmy still performed her duties well.

Tommy Holmes, the foreman, felt sorry for the girl, and he was even more upset when he learned that she was having a baby by her father. Tommy was a man who had young daughters of his own and felt an overwhelming desire to protect Emmy. Within a short while, he'd taught her what to do, and she was the most efficient piecer that would ever work with him.

It was on her shift with Tommy that her waters broke.

Tommy ran to fetch Mary. Emmy had no grasp of what was happening to her.

"Don't look! I've wet meself!" she wailed.

Her face matched the crimson cotton she'd been collecting. Mary dashed up the steps to where Emmy was standing above a puddle.

"Now, now, lass!" Mary said kindly. "Do not ye go into a panic, it's just a little water, and it means the baby is on its way. It's all perfectly normal."

Guilt wracked her as the reassuring words tumbled out. Emmy's situation was anything but normal.

"I think you need to take her home, Mary," ordered Tommy. "I'll cover for you, and I'll make sure that they don't dock yer wages."

Tommy watched the girl leave, and he was beside himself with fear and fury. Tommy's wife had given birth to four children, and he knew what pain the girl was about to suffer. He wanted to murder Jimmy Sterling for what he'd done to his daughter.

Everyone in the mill stopped to stare, then began whispering to each other as Mary marched Emmy through the factory. The girl's dress and shoes were soaked, and she was starting to feel severe discomfort in her lower stomach. She cupped her belly in her hands, but it provided no relief.

"Stop ye bloody gawping at her," hollered Mary.

"Can I help you any?" asked Sheila.

"You've done enough, Sheila, go back to yer work."

Mary took Emmy back to the rows. Tilda stood in the corner of the room, silently taking in the scene around her, as Mary had demanded money from Jimmy to pay for a midwife.

"Come now, Mary, ye know I do not have two ha'pennies to rub together."

"You swine," yelled Mary. "You got the child in the family way, and you're happy to do nothing to help. Do you want her to die? I'll see ye in the courts for murder yet. So, get on with it."

Jimmy kept quiet. He was smart enough to know that no amount of charm would get him out of the mess that he'd got himself into.

Jimmy was forced to borrow money from the old Jewish clockmaker to whom he sold his watch. Jimmy told Yakov Weiner a long shaggy dog story: a young lad had impregnated Emmy. She was in labour, and he needed money for a midwife.

Knowing it was a pack of lies, the only reason that Yakov helped the rogue was because he took pity upon young

Emmy. He thought of her as an honest, polite girl when he chatted to her in the bakery queue.

Fuming about Jimmy's blatant yarn, Yakov didn't say anything to Sterling. He fumbled in his pocket for the money to cover the midwife's fee, then slid it across the counter.

"Thank you kindly, Sir," said Jimmy as he skipped out of the shop.

Rachel Weiner was a fiery woman who went into full action-stations at Yakov's news.

"We need to say Tehillim for the girl, Yakov. And we need to ask Hashem to protect her."

Yakov fetched the giant bible and placed it on the old dining-room table. He opened it at the Book of Psalms and began to pray.

Nothing would've prepared Emmy for the excruciating pain that she was suffering. Her agony was first recognised in her moaning, and reinforced by the crying, and finally screaming. The midwife struggled to keep Emmy calm. She considered calling the chemist for laudanum, but she knew it would make the baby lazy, and the birth more difficult.

Tilda covered her ears and sat in the corner, disturbed by what she saw. Mary had forgotten that the younger sister was there, and when she saw the troubled child, she took her outside and told her to go off and play. Tilda soon became engrossed in a skipping rope, and soon Emmy's screams stopped haunting her. Jimmy Sterling looked on, puffing anxiously on a cigarette, unable to face the music upstairs.

Emmy writhed in pain for hours. Eventually, she was too exhausted to move, and with every contraction, her body spasmed, her head and limbs twisting out of control. The midwife would never experience such a difficult birth again.

Most youthful wives knew what they could expect in childbirth, learning from their elders. Sadly, young motherless Emmy, little more than a girl herself, knew nothing of the practicalities that were to follow.

In the cold, candlelit gloom, she felt her legs being ripped apart by the midwife. Her private parts were exposed for everyone to see as the woman set to work trying to save the child.

In a final spasm, Emmy felt something slither out of her body as it expelled the infant into the hands of the midwife. Without looking at the baby, she beckoned Mary, who was waiting with a grubby grey blanket.

As the midwife began slicing at the umbilical cord trailing out of Emmy, and the baby made no sound. Mary opened the blanket to examine the infant. She stared down in horror and screamed.

The midwife spun around and looked at the child. The baby was severely deformed. The head was enlarged, and a strange shape. There was no differentiation between its head and its abdomen. Everything was welded together by flesh. The legs were footless, and the only perfect thing was the two little pink hands.

"Cut it! Cut the cord," cried Mary, "Get it away from her. Get it away."

"Is it alive?" asked the midwife.

Mary put her ear to its mouth. Just then, the child made a low sound that sent chills down her spine. She wanted to throw the horrible creature on the ground and run. It took all her resolve not to.

"Yes," answered Mary, taking deep breaths in a futile attempt to keep calm.

It only took a second glance for the midwife to know how to deal with the thing.

"Strangle it," ordered the midwife.

"I can't. I can't," screamed Mary.

Keen to escape the horror, the midwife tied off the sliced cord.

"Give it to me," she said firmly.

Mary handed the child over. The midwife took it and held it in the crook of her arm as she would any other newborn. She put her hand where she thought the windpipe would be, and she squeezed until the child began turning blue. It eventually went limp in her arms.

"I've seen it before," muttered the midwife as she shook the dangling child by an arm to make sure it was dead. "It's the only way to deal with it."

Shocked, Mary had not experienced anything like that before and she was a bag of nerves at the spectacle.

"Stay with the girl. She will need friends and family around her now. I am sorry for the loss."

Mary focused her attention on a distraught Emmy, mopping her brow and lowering her dress down to cover her modesty one more.

The midwife wrapped the child up, went down the steps to the street, and gave it to Jimmy Sterling. Mary was happy to sacrifice the blanket. She didn't want to see or touch it ever again.

"A son," the woman sneered.

"What do ye want me to do with him?"

"Bury him," she said with hatred in her voice.

Jimmy felt a surge of relief as he took the swaddled corpse from the midwife, then casually tucked it under his arm as if it were a parcel.

He headed toward the Salford Old Bridge, crossed over it onto the other bank, and then continued to walk upstream until he was out of sight. He found an isolated spot and started to dig up the smooth clay soil with his bare hands. Eventually, the hole was large enough to take the tiny corpse.

Curiosity got the better of Jimmy Sterling, and he began to unwrap the blanket. The sun was low, and it cast an eerie glow across the brown river. Putrid water and faeces floated past him.

He looked down at the horrific creature in his arms, the abomination that he'd created with his daughter. His heart lurched in his chest, and it began to beat faster and faster as if something was squeezing it to bursting point. Struggling to breathe, he wanted to scream.

He couldn't bear to hold the thing any longer, and he threw it into the hole, and scrabbled with his blackened fingernails to scrape the thick, stinking clay back over it in a bid to make it disappear for good.

Once he thought the layer of earth was thick enough, he stamped on the mound as hard as he could, terrified that the monster would rise out of the earth and harm him.

Jimmy Sterling started to run, but the horrific image was imprinted upon his mind. Fifty yards further, he fell to his knees and began to retch.

Above their watchmaker's shop, Yakov and Rachel Weiner sat at their old table reading Tehillim, the Hebrew Book of Psalms.

'Behold, children are a heritage from the Lord.
The Fruit of the Womb. A Reward.'

4

SHILLING'S LOSS

Shilling Hudson stood at St. Pancras station waiting for the train that would take her to Manchester. A striking woman, many people turned to look at her as she passed by. Socrates paced alongside Shilling, and the tall and lovely Tanner followed on, two paces behind.

Shilling paid attention to everything mechanical, but Tanner was more interested in observing the people, fascinated by the buzz of humanity around her. Noting facial expressions, body language, hair, clothes, she could discern people's moods, attitudes, and feelings, and sometimes, if they were close enough, even hear their conversations.

Despite her youth, Tanner was unusually astute for her age, so when she saw something that impressed her, she grabbed her journal and felt compelled to document the experience.

Samuel had given his granddaughter a luxurious leather-bound notebook at the beginning of every year, since she learned to read and write. The year was embossed in gold on each cover.

The books formed a comprehensive record of her life since the age of five. Her early journals were childlike, with sentences written in crooked handwriting. Now, she documented noteworthy incidents with vibrant detail in delicate copperplate flourishes. As the trio sat at the platform, Tanner scribbled her observations at length, with Shilling and Socrates chuckling quietly as they watched the gold nib of her fountain pen dance along the feint ruled lines.

"I'm glad my father allowed you to come with me, Socrates" Shilling said with a smile.

"We have been on many adventures, Shilling. Perhaps this will be less dramatic than some of the others," he joked.

They both giggled like naughty school children on the back row.

"Papa is rather suspicious of Baxter," whispered Shilling. "That is the only reason that he has allowed you to accompany me."

"Yes, I can understand your father's concern when it comes to that man," said Socrates with a knowing look.

"That was a long time ago, Socrates, and I do not need another person reminding me about it."

"I'm sorry, Shilling. You must remember that I found you distraught and alone in the coach house at Mayfair after he left you, so I've even more reason to dislike him than Samuel."

Shilling blushed. It wasn't a night she wanted to reminisce about.

"Ah, there comes Mr Lee as we speak."

Shilling watched Baxter approach. A handsome man, he turned as many heads as she did. They would've made a fine couple. Baxter was as tall as Samuel, with the rugged physique of a labourer, despite devoting his life to science.

"Hello, Shilling," he greeted, outstretching his hand.

Tanner received a broad smile. Socrates ignored Lee's arrival.

"Have you arranged for my baggage to be loaded?" Baxter said, gazing at Socrates.

"No, Sir. Please feel free to hail a porter."

Shilling sensed the still simmering tension between the two men and chose to ignore it.

"Did you have to bring him with us?" muttered Baxter when Socrates was out of earshot.

"My father insisted he accompanies me."

Baxter frowned, taking it all personally.

"I'm an adult. I do not need anyone to look after me."

"Actually, he is here to look after me," corrected Shilling.

"He is mistaken. I'm not the man I used to be," he mumbled.

Shilling ignored his remark. He was precisely the man he used to be, and she wanted no reminders of the past.

A shrill whistle blew, and the conductor shouted 'all aboard' in a broad cockney accent. Socrates happily assisted Shilling and Tanner into the coach, but he would have been delighted to leave Baxter Lee on the platform, as Samuel had suggested. Baxter tried and failed to hail a porter and ended up struggling to load all the bags himself, huffing, puffing and clanking his way into the carriage with his oversized suitcases. Socrates smirked as he watched him fight to get the luggage in the tiny overhead rack too.

When Shilling heard the groaning of the colossal steam engine, a thrill coursed through her body. Her engineering brain could imagine all the machinery in her mind's eye. She understood each component and its function.

As she stared out of the window, she was dreaming about cogs and pistons, not the comings and goings on the platform. She'd seen the water running from the overhead tank into the boiler. She envisioned the stoker carefully shovelling coal into the furnace to create as much heat as possible. The engineer was checking his gauges and valves, waiting for the boiler to reach the correct pressure. Only then would he loosen the brake.

The great steel wheels, just like those that the Hudson Foundries forged, began to move on the rails. It created a screeching, squealing sound as metal ground upon metal, and steam poured out from under the locomotive.

The magnificent hunk of iron and steel began to move, slowly at first, but soon gathered speed as it left the station and thundered towards its destination.

Manchester's Victoria Station Hotel was a tribute to the masons, architects, and decorators who had built it, as much as the queen. Tanner was accustomed to living in grand houses, but the beauty she witnessed there took her breath away.

"Oh, Mama," she whispered, "It's magnificent."

Majestic chandeliers dripped from plaster rosettes. The delicate crystals illuminated the foyer. Light reflected from the white marble floors and walls, showcasing the lavishly upholstered furniture. Arched windows stretched from floor to ceiling and were dressed in pale blue velvet curtains. Large gilt wall sconces supported magnificent planters which contained the most exotic orchids that Tanner had ever seen. The hotel's energy and beauty was a pleasant change from the dark and cluttered Victorian décor she'd seen in other hotels.

Shilling smiled at Tanner, grateful that her daughter could still appreciate the privilege of living in such splendour.

"I wish Papa could see this," smiled Tanner, "he would love it."

Shilling agreed but chose not to tell the girl that Benjamin Fischer had lived in hotels like this all over the world. These days the extravagance would wash over him as he thought about how much he preferred to be back with his family at home.

"Your Papa will be here at the end of the week,
and then you can show him all the exciting things
that you have seen."

"Where is he, Mama?"

"He has gone to do some business at a mine in
Durham. You'd better write down what you see.
He will want to know everything."

Shilling smiled down at the beautiful young lady. She was acutely aware of Tanner's delicate innocence. Now that she was a mother, she understood why Samuel had been so protective of her.

The hotel served dinner at seven o'clock sharp every evening. Their table was set perfectly. Delicate crystal, fine porcelain and glistening silver stood upon the crisp Egyptian linen. A vase of fragrant white roses stood proudly in the centre.

Shilling and Tanner caused quite a stir when they walked into the dining room. Tanner seldom appeared in public, and her likeness to Shilling was astounding. Baxter Lee studied Shilling, and then his eyes travelled to Tanner. *She is already a striking beauty like her mother.*

A hush settled over the room, and the diners craned their necks to watch Shilling and Tanner Fischer; after all, they were banking royalty. Tanner wore a simple white dress devoid of bustles and bows. Her thick raven hair cascaded down her back like an onyx waterfall, and she wore a pair of striking diamond earrings that contrasted with her dark skin. Her eyes were bright and intelligent and promising. There was a determination about her movements that reminded Lord Buckingham of the young Shilling.

Charles Buckingham sat on the far side of the dining room, studying mother and daughter. Shilling had not spotted him, but he hoped that she would. He wanted to catch her eye and lick his lips, to remind her that he had touched what was under her bodice.

"Well! Look who's here," Lord Ellington noted enthusiastically to Buckingham.

Charles ignored him. Ellington prodded deeper to get a response.

"By Jove, it's Shilling Hudson," said Lord Ellington, "I wonder what has brought her to Manchester?"

"She's Mrs Hudson Fischer now" said Lord Buckingham quickly, wishing that Ellington would shut up, despite being as awestruck as everybody else in the room.

"Of course, yes. She has a lovely daughter."

"Like a younger version of her mother," replied Lord Buckingham, without attempting to keep the bitterness of rejection from his voice.

"She has become a rather powerful woman in the last years," continued Lord Ellington.

Charles nodded sourly.

"My, my! Is that Baxter Lee sitting at her table?" asked Ellington.

"If she has brought him with her, it must be a business trip. I wonder what Mr Fischer thinks about that?" said Lord Buckingham.

"Do you think she has been invited to the meeting at Dunley Hall?"

"Of course, she has. She does own one of the biggest companies in England, my good man," said Lord Buckingham sarcastically.

"We do not want her as opposition Charles. This is a bit of an upset to our plans," said Ellington.

Charles Buckingham was seething, but Lord Ellington wasn't bright enough to notice it.

"Is Samuel with her?" asked Lord Ellington.

Lord Buckingham face took on a murderous expression and, unconsciously, he rubbed his mangled hand.

"Pity you two couldn't have got along, old chap," laughed Lord Ellington.

"Are you serious? He bloody crippled me for life with his senseless attack," grizzled Charles, who always descended into a dark fury at the mention of Samuel's name.

"You should have done a better job with wooing Shilling when you had the opportunity," Lord Ellington laughed heartily. "Then you'd be his beloved son-in-law, not Benjamin."

Buckingham smirked.

"I'm not finished with Samuel Hudson. I'll still make him pay for what he did to me. You mark my words."

Charles's fat, bulbous eyes gazed across the dining room, settling on Tanner Fischer. Except for the scar, she was identical to her mother. He wondered if Samuel Hudson was as protective of his granddaughter as he was of Shilling.

For a moment, he fantasised about ravishing the young woman—and it would have nothing to do with lust and everything to do with revenge.

*

The bedroom suites were as lavish as the rest of the hotel. Shilling couldn't recall the last time she and Tanner had enjoyed themselves this much. The young woman was exhausted and sank onto the giant bed, and immediately fell asleep.

Shilling slept fitfully, dreaming sporadically, and eventually, woke up drenched in perspiration. If Shilling were a superstitious woman, the dreams would have been viewed as a premonition, but she was logical and practical, and soon she banished the dark thoughts. Finally, she fell into a deep sleep an hour before dawn.

It was Socrates who received the bad news. His habit was to fetch a newspaper and read it while drinking his first cup of tea of the day.

He took the lift to the ground floor. The perfectly polished brass doors opened, and the Hudson's valet stepped into the luxurious hotel lobby. Empty at this time of the morning, he approached the front desk unhindered.

"Good morning, Sir," said the desk clerk in a hushed voice.

"Good morning—" said Socrates cheerfully as he read the man's name badge. "—today's newspaper, please, Mr Meecham!"

The clerk looked at him but didn't move.

"Come now," Socrates laughed, "I know you have been up all night, but surely you can move a little faster. Chop Chop!"

"It's not that, Sir."

The clerk was having difficulty coming to the point. He retrieved an envelope from under the desk and slid it across to Socrates.

"A telegram has just arrived for Mrs Fischer. Can you please deliver it to her personally?"

"Certainly," agreed Socrates. "By the way, are they serving morning tea yet? I am parched."

Socrates noted that the clerk looked somewhat panicked.

"Sir, I'm only saying this because you are one of us," said the young man, implying that he and Socrates were of the same social status—lowly servants.

Socrates raised his eyebrows and stared at the man questioningly.

"Sir, I suggest you deliver the telegram to Mrs Fischer immediately. It's bad news."

"Tell me," barked Socrates.

"Mr Fischer has passed away. He was taken by an accident last night, and the story has made the early morning editions. Perhaps Mrs Fischer should read the telegram before she reads the newspaper."

Socrates ripped the envelope open and read the tape.

```
Regret to inform you stop Mr Benjamin Fischer killed
in mining explosion stop Condolences stop Rudolph
Black stop
```

Socrates was temporarily paralysed as his eyes scanned the message, but gained his wits quickly.

"Send the following telegram to Mr Samuel Hudson in London. Here is his address,"

instructed Socrates and wrote it down on a piece
of paper.

Ben killed at mine stop Escorting Shilling to Newcastle stop
Tanner and Lee arriving London tomorrow stop

The clerk nodded.

"Book Mrs Fischer and I on the next train to
Newcastle. Book Miss Tanner Fischer and Mr
Baxter Lee on the evening train to London."

The clerk nodded again as he scribbled down the details.

Socrates strode towards the lift, gripping Shilling's
telegram in his hand. He called out before the doors closed
on the young face staring back at him.

"Thank you, Meecham. You performed well under the most
difficult of circumstances."

The valet took a deep breath and opened the door to
Shilling's suite.

"Is that you, Socrates?" Shilling called from the
bedroom.

Socrates didn't reply.

"Have you brought the newspaper with you?" she
chirruped cheerily. "We are going to have a very
busy day, and I'd like to catch up with the latest
news on the canal development, en route."

Socrates walked to her bedroom and stood in the doorway. Shilling wore a big smile when she greeted him, although she'd not slept a wink.

"Good morning."

Socrates didn't reply. He looked forlorn, and in her gut, Shilling knew that something was wrong.

"Is it my father?"

"No."

Shilling sighed in relief. Socrates didn't bother to tell her to sit down because he knew that she would refuse.

"What is it?" she asked anxiously.

"It's Benjamin."

"No!"

Socrates nodded and passed her the telegram.

"No!" she exclaimed as she unfurled the message.

"Are they sure that it's him? Why would he be underground?"

"I'm sorry. I have no further details," said Socrates softly.

"No, no, no!" Shilling cried. The news was incomprehensible. She cupped her mouth with her hand to stifle a scream.

"What's all this commotion for? What's happening, Mama?"

Shilling was mute, dumbfounded by the revelation. Tanner rushed to her mother.

"What is it, Mama? You're scaring me."

Shilling was too shocked to be gentle or sensitive.

"Papa has died."

"How?" demand Tanner.

Shilling looked at Tanner in bewilderment.

"I don't know," Tanner struggled to think clearly.

"I do not have the details. There was an explosion. That is all I know."

Tanner didn't know what to do. She wanted to cry, but she couldn't.

"He should've been with us, Mama," yelled Tanner before she fled from the room.

Socrates followed Tanner to the parlour. He watched her clench her jaw and squeeze her fists. He felt for her, but Shilling was his priority.

"When did you find out Socrates?"

"A telegram arrived early this morning."

"She could have prevented this. My mother should've insisted that he come with us."

Socrates realised that nothing he did would console Tanner, but he would take charge of the situation.

"My father is dead."

"And your mother has lost the love of her life," said Socrates. "I need you to be brave until you reach London."

Tanner became sober. She glared at Socrates but nodded her head resentfully.

Baxter Lee knocked on the door to Shilling's suite. He'd arranged to escort Shilling and Tanner to breakfast. He was bewildered when he glanced around the suite, which was in disarray.

"What has happened?" asked Baxter seeing the chaos.

"Benjamin Fischer died in an explosion last night. We received the news this morning, and it's in all the newspapers."

Baxter opened his mouth to say something but had no words. He put his hands in his pockets and paced up and down the parlour in shock."

"Why was he underground?"

"We do not know," answered Socrates.

"How is Shilling?"

"Terrible."

Socrates returned to Shilling's room.

"I want to fetch Benjamin, and I want to take him home," said Shilling.

"Of course. We are booked on the three o'clock train to Durham," answered Socrates.

"Does my father know?"

"I've sent him a telegram. He should receive it shortly. I've booked Baxter and Tanner on the evening train to London."

"Thank you," said Shilling.

"Do you want to speak to Baxter?"

She nodded.

Baxter pushed past Socrates and strode across the room to Shilling.

"I'm sorry, Shilling," Baxter said, looking at the sad, beautiful creature in front of him.

Shilling couldn't speak, and she swallowed hard to choke back the emotion. Then she broke down and cried.

Baxter pulled her into his arms and held her while she sobbed uncontrollably. There was nothing that he could do or say to comfort her.

"Please keep Tanner safe, and take her to Miss Annabelle."

"Of course," replied Baxter. His mind skipped to the night that he betrayed her. Had she mourned him like this? He was filled with deep pity for her, and he was filled with regret that he'd hurt her.

Shilling turned back to Socrates.

"Have there been any messages from my father yet?"

"No, Shilling, he will meet us in Newcastle," answered Socrates.

"How do you know that?"

"Your father will never forsake you at a time like this."

Socrates and Tanner each packed a small bag, eager to reach the station as soon as possible. Socrates watched Shilling with her daughter.

"I want to go with you, Mama."

"I don't know what awaits me," answered Shilling.

"My father is dead. That is what awaits you."

Shilling looked at Socrates, her eyes begging for his intervention.

Socrates looked at his watch. They were running out of time.

"Your mother is going to fetch your father and bring him to you, Tanner. You need to trust her."

Shilling tried to say goodbye to Tanner, but the young woman ignored her. Socrates could see that she desperately wanted a response from her daughter.

"Go on, Shilling," Socrates told her softly, "go ahead, I'll take care of this."

When Shilling left, he went to Tanner's side.

"Tanner, your mother loves you very much. She's a courageous woman to fetch your father. She does not know what awaits her at the mine, and she wants to spare you pain. She wants to protect you, and allow you to remember your father as he was."

Tanner looked at him, and then looked at the floor.

"You need to promise that you will go back to Miss Annabelle without a fuss. I love you, Tanner. I've known you since seconds after your birth. I would never hurt you. If I believed that your mother was being unreasonable or unfair, I would tell her."

Tanner would not look him in the eye or answer him. She felt ashamed and defiant at the same time.

Socrates didn't have time to negotiate with Tanner. It was imperative that he and Shilling reach the station on time. He only turned around once, but Tanner's back was to him, and she was staring out of the window.

As soon as Tanner heard the suite door close, all the false bravado left her, and she began to sob. It was a heart-wrenching sound, and Baxter could hear her from the parlour. The door to her room was open, but he still knocked softly. He saw her tear-stained face, and all the pain she was trying to hide.

"I'm so sorry, Tanner. Your father was a good man," said Baxter.

She sniffed and nodded.

"We are leaving for London on the late train, and I'm taking you to Miss Annabelle, who will care for you," he smiled kindly.

Tanner burst into tears again. Baxter couldn't stand to see the girl so sad. He went to her and put his arms around her.

"It's an unfortunate day, but you are safe, Tanner," he said, gently. "I love your Mama very much, and I promised her that I would look after you."

He felt her body convulsing in his arms, and he held her fast until she calmed down.

"Come on, sweetheart," he smiled at her, "we have a train to catch. We can't be late."

It was an agonisingly slow journey from Manchester to Newcastle. As she travelled east, the towns became more industrialised and shabby. She could see the large black cloud over Durham from miles away. As the train rolled toward the smoke, Shilling felt that the great black cloud was swallowing her, the cloud of doom.

Mr Crump met Socrates and Shilling at the station.

"Samuel Hudson will be here late tonight," Mr Crump told them.

Shilling remained quiet. She didn't trust herself to speak.

"What happened to Mr Fischer?" asked Socrates. He knew that it was the first question that Shilling would ask.

"Let us go to the undertaker's office and discuss it over a cup of tea."

Socrates scowled.

"I'm not waiting until we reach the undertaker, and I want to know now. It's your mine. I want to know what he was doing and how he died."

Mr Crump was an influential man and didn't appreciate taking command from a mere servant.

"Tell us immediately," said Shilling.

Mr Crump knew that he was dealing with one of the most powerful women in the country. He took a few moments to assimilate his thoughts, and then began to tell the story.

"When Mr Fischer arrived, he was adamant about meeting our employees. Mr Fischer had a firm policy regarding safety underground as well as the miner's living conditions. He would not give us the loan if we didn't comply with his standards. We went underground during a shift change. Unbeknownst to us, Mr Fischer's Davy lamp was leaking gas. Against all regulations, a miner lit a match, and the gas exploded. Mr Fischer and three miners were killed in the fire."

Socrates refused Shilling access to Benjamin Fischer's body until he would see the corpse. Benjamin's face was severely burnt, and his skin looked like melted wax. Socrates did his utmost to remain calm, but the sight was so unsettling that he became ill. He couldn't allow Shilling near her husband's body.

"I confirm that it's Benjamin," said Socrates fighting back the tears. "Please do not view him, Shilling. You do not have to," Socrates tried to persuade her, wanting to spare her the pain of seeing Benjamin's mutilated body.

"I'll see him," she answered, "He is my husband."

Socrates knew that voice. Nothing would stop her.

Shilling entered the cool mortuary. The smell of formaldehyde permeated the air. Shilling approached Benjamin's body and looked down at his damaged face. Benjamin was covered with a white sheet.

"Leave me alone," ordered Shilling.

Socrates, and the undertaker obeyed.

Shilling lifted the sheet slowly, almost with reverence. She studied Benjamin's mutilated body from the top of his head to the soles of his feet. When she was finished, she lifted the sheet and slowly covered him, ensuring that the sheet had no wrinkles and hung perfectly.

She accepted that Benjamin was dead. She felt no horror for what she'd witnessed. He was no less beautiful or perfect than when he was alive. He was embedded in her soul, where he was whole. Shilling accepted the finality of his passing, yet she was overwhelmed by a longing for him. She wanted him to get up, smile, and hold her. A terrible loneliness engulfed her, a loneliness that she would suffer for many more years to come.

Socrates collected Samuel at the train station. The weather was fit for tragedy; it was dark, cold and raining. Socrates hailed a cab and climbed into it with Samuel. They rode in silence. What could be said?

Socrates opened the door of the hotel suite where he and Shilling were staying. Nobody had lit the lamps, and the room was cold. Samuel saw Shilling's silhouette at the window. She seemed small and thin, crushed by the weight of her sorrow.

"Shilling," said Samuel.

Slowly, Shilling turned around.

"Oh, Papa," she cried.

Samuel went to his child. Shilling threw herself into his arms as she'd done as a little girl. Samuel couldn't bear the sound of her heart breaking. He kissed the top of her head and wiped her wet hair off her face.

"Oh, my child, I'm so sorry."

Samuel knew that nothing he said would alleviate Shilling's pain. He'd once been in this position himself, and death would have been merciful.

"Oh, Papa," cried Shilling, "it hurts so much, please take the pain away."

"I know it does," he tightened his arms around her. "I'm here. I'm here for as long as you need me."

Tears streaked Samuel's face as he held his precious Shilling. How he wished it had been him and not Benjamin. He'd no answers for her, and he didn't have the power to protect her from sorrow. All he could do was hold her until she was strong enough to stand alone.

5

THE ASYLUM HOSPITAL

Jimmy Sterling returned to the row. He felt sick to his stomach and stank of sewage. He ignored Emmy lying on his bed; she was sleeping after the doctor had drugged her. It'd be many weeks before she was healed as she couldn't move or walk for the pain. Jimmy Sterling collapsed onto Tilda's bed without bothering to take off his soiled clothes. His mind was hazy, and he was exhausted. Jimmy put his hands behind his head and stared up at the ceiling. Within a few moments, he closed his eyes and fell asleep.

But it wasn't a peaceful sleep. Jimmy began to dream. He could see the toxic river, and the hole where he threw the monster. He saw something start to move under the mud, like a mole burrowing under the soil. Perfect hands emerged from the earth, pulling a deformed body behind it. It slithered to the water and swam its way across the river. The monster made its way to the rows and pulled itself up the stairs. Subconsciously, Jimmy knew that this thing that he'd fathered was intelligent, and it reached up to the doorknob and turned it. It approached his bed and quick as a whip put its perfect fingers around Jimmy's neck and began to squeeze. The disfigured face stared down at him. Jimmy struggled. His arms flailed. He writhed and gasped for breath, managing to hit it onto the floor. He watched the aberration climb onto Emmy's bed. Her legs were open, and she was groaning with pleasure when the horrific thing slithered up between her thighs and entered her womb. It was safe with its mother.

Every night for the rest of his life, Jimmy Sterling would have the same dream. He reached for the bottle of cheap home-brewed liquor he kept under his bed and drank most of the bitter potent liquid from the bottle.

Emmy wasn't the same as before. She didn't speak, and her eyes were dead. Tilda studied her big sister, who had always protected and mothered her. It was a week since the terrible day that Emmy gave birth to the baby. Tilda didn't know what they did with the child, but she knew that it was dead. Emmy, unable to get up, soiled herself in the bed, and blood covered her clothes. Mary was a godsend, but she couldn't keep up with the laundry. The weather was terrible Emmy's clothes would not dry. Mary made an appeal to the community for old rags and newspapers to put beneath the girl. Still, it was a losing battle.

"I canna help the lass, doctor," whispered Mary.

"These things happen all the time, Mary, but this is the worst case I've ever seen," said Dr Proctor.

"What is ur meaning then, doctor?" asked Mary.

"This is called Catalectoil Insanity, and she needs to be put into an asylum, Mary," said the doctor thoughtfully. "She cannot care for herself, and the likelihood that she will recover is slim."

Mary was shocked, the idea of putting the girl into an asylum filled her with dread, and it was as good as putting her in prison for the rest of her life.

"Mary, she will be better at Country Asylum Hospital, they have modern facilities for somebody like her, and they're experimenting with new methods of curing the insane."

Mary shook her head, and tears welled in her eyes.

"Where is Mr Sterling?" asked the doctor.

"He only comes in at night, and then he is drunk. I'm terrified for Tilda being alone with him. I've six children of me own, and cannot fit another soul in our two rooms."

"I'll contact the authorities, Mary, which is all we can do."

The winter morning was dark, but the streets were filled with people on their way to work. Men, women and children jostled against each other as they formed a human river flowing to the factories. Tilda was amongst them, on the way to the cotton factory. There was nobody to look after her anymore. Mary had been kind enough to give Emmy, and her a bowl of oats porridge twice a day. Still, Tilda knew that she had to contribute something to Mary's household.

Tilda stepped into the factory yard, and the considerable building loomed above her. It was four stories high, with many chimneys extending high into the sky. The mill was an enormous silhouette on the Salford skyline. Tilda watched the cotton fluff drift on the air, illuminated by the lights. But this time, it wasn't fairies; it was just fluff. She made her way to the great steel doors. She waited for an hour before she saw Sheila.

"My, my, lass," greeted Sheila, "what are ye doing down 'ere?"

"I've come to see Mr Holmes."

"Are you looking for a job?" asked Sheila.

"Yes, I want Emmy's job."

"Wait till me teatime, and will take ye to Tommy Holmes, but stay out of the way, mind you, we do not want no trouble. A lot of lasses want to do that job."

Tilda's heart sank, she did know where she would begin looking for work, if Mr Holmes sent her away.

At noon, Sheila fetched her. She passed Mary on the way to the second floor.

"By Gods, Sheila, where did you find the lass?"

"She's been waiting at the door since six o'clock this morning. She has come to see Tommy Holmes."

"What were you thinking, Sheila, to make the lass stand out there in the cold?"

Sheila was trying to make up for her indiscretion against Emmy but had chosen an inefficient manner to seek forgiveness.

"Here, Tilda, come with me. 'Tis alright, Sheila, I'll take her up."

Sheila looked put out, but Mary didn't care. She was still angry with her.

Tilda took in everything as she walked along. There were rows upon rows of looms, each one operated by a spinner. Tiny treacherous fibres drifted in the air, and soon her nose and throat were parched. The heat was oppressive, and she longed to take off her coat. She watched piecers scurrying up and down the loom, joining threads that were unravelled, children her age crawling under the looms, their heads inches away from the steel spinning wheels, with her head held high with pride. That is the work that Emmy does. It was the youngsters' job to gather the cotton that fell onto the ground and put it back into the baskets. Wastage was a sin in the mill. The raw material that fell below the looms was eventually transformed into yards and yards of thread.

Mary spotted Tommy, who was on his tea break.

"Here, Tommy," said Mary, "This is Tilda, Emmy's sister."

"Ye look like ye sister," smiled Tommy.

Tilda looked at him with big eyes.

"Ye looking for her job?" asked Tommy.

"Yes, Sir," answered Tilda.

"Yer still too small to be a piecer, but ye can collect."

Tilda nodded.

"Be here tomorrow, lass, six o'clock. And do not be late."

Tilda smiled.

"I'll see te her Tommy," Mary thanked him.

"No, problem Mary, I'll do what I can te help yer."

"How is Emmy?"

"Not good, Tommy, not good at all. The doctor is sending her to County Asylum."

"God, and the saints," Tommy swore.

"There is nothing we can do anymore. The lass will not eat or talk. She canna get up, she dunna want te get up, it's a bad situation, Tommy."

Tommy shook his head. "Jimmy Sterling should be in prison."

"The girl can only do that if she accuses him of rape, the courts are not too bothered about it being his daughter. She has no fight left in her."

"Bring wee Tilda in tomorrow, Mary, and we will get her started."

"She can read and do numbers, Tommy. The girl did well at school."

"T'morrow then Mary, me teatime is finished."

That evening two men arrived to fetch Emmy. Mary gently explained to the girl that she was going to a hospital where they would help her. In her heart of hearts, Mary knew that she was telling a lie. Nobody ever got better in the Country Asylum. The men seemed kind, but they always behaved that way in front of the patient's family.

"You do not have to tie her down," Mary said to one of the men.

"No, Ma'am, she is peaceful. That will not be necessary."

"Will you look after her, please? She's but a girl."

"Yes, Ma'am."

"We'll visit her. If she speaks to you, tell her we will visit her on Sunday."

The man smiled and nodded sadly. He couldn't bring himself to tell Mary that children like Emmy seldom spoke again.

Kevin lifted Emmy off the bed and carried her down the stinking staircase. Emmy seemed to be in a dream world, unaware of what was happening. Tilda watched Emmy and started to cry, but there was no reaction from her sister.

"I love you, Emmy, it'll pan out, I promise ye, and you will not be in Country Asylum forever."

Emmy didn't reply. She stood peacefully in the street, staring at nothing.

Tilda watched Emmy climb into the ambulance, and the kind man helped her onto a seat. As Mary watched the carriage leave, she began to weep. People had gathered in the street, and others looked down from the windows above. The mood was sombre. Nobody spoke. The same families that had heard Emmy scream through childbirth watched the ambulance slowly turn the corner as it took the girl away. The sight was so tragic that it could have been a hearse, and the people returned to their tiny homes, devastated by what they'd witnessed.

Two streets away, the ambulance passed Jimmy Sterling. He recognised Kevin Bamborough, whom he knew worked at the County Asylum, and he wondered what poor wretch was about to spend the rest of their life in the madhouse.

Country Asylum hospital made no impression upon Emmy. The girl looked ahead of her. She showed no sign of emotion, her eyes were dead, and it was as if her soul had left her body.

"She was no trouble Matron, no trouble at all."

"Thank you, Mr Bamborough. I'll take the girl from here."

"Matron, may I pop in and see the lass from time to time?"

"Not too often, Mr Bamborough, we do not want her becoming attached to you. Thank you, Mr Bamborough. You may leave now."

Mr Bamborough had never heard anything so stupid in his life.

The man turned to go but heard the Matron give the nurses instructions to shave Emmy's head and find her new clothes.

"We can't afford an outbreak of lice, nurse. Make sure you do a good job."

Mr Bamborough sighed. He was a young man, but he would not do this work very much longer. It broke his heart.

The nurse took Emmy to a hospital ward with thirty women in it. The young girl crossed the threshold, little knowing that the doors would be slammed shut behind her and padlocked for the night. She was taken to a bed, it was clean, but the ward was stark and draughty. Some of the patients were already in bed, and others walked about and talked to each other. They all stopped what they were doing when they saw Emmy.

"This here is young Emmy. Now I want no nonsense from you tonight. Do you hear me?" shouted the nurse. "Make her feel at home."

There was an ominous cackle from the back of the ward.

"That's enough from you, Doris," yelled the Matron, "you will be shackled if ye dare to step out of line with this young 'un."

Some women nodded. Others stared at Emmy. Some saw her as a human, and others saw her as prey.

The great doors clanged shut behind Emmy, and she was left standing at the foot of her bed. Nobody helped her put on her nightclothes, and she was at the mercy of the women around her. Women began pointing at Emmy and whispering behind their hands and shrieked hysterical laughter. The rest ignored Emmy. They were either too afraid to intervene or didn't care. The upper-class women had made a little corner of their own. They ignored what happened to the lower classes, which they considered to be savages. There were immediately two guards at the door shouting for order, but the patients began to torment Emmy the instant the nurse left. Emmy didn't respond. Although she was in a stupor, and her mind was dead, her body was still alive.

Doris Dalby and Janet James got off their beds and began to stalk Emmy. They crept up behind her. Janet prodded Emmy, who turned around and smiled at Doris, oblivious of their horrid intentions. Emmy had only known kind women, and she'd never experienced female cruelty before.

"My lass, ye are a friendly one," Janet cackled at the top of her voice.

"Aw, me lass," crooned Doris, "we ladies have to comfort each other. There are no men to do it. Yes, Yes, come, lass, we will make you feel at home."

The suggestion was lost upon Emmy, who stood dumb, as the two vultures circled her.

Doris began stroking Emmy's arm, "let me help
you into yer bedclothes. Let me undress ye lass,
dunna be afraid now, there you go then, one
button at a time."

Janet stepped closer and sank to the floor and began to
remove Emmy's boots. The rest of the women were
watching, but nobody was attempting to protect Emmy
from the molestation. Doris and Janet undressed Emmy
until she was standing naked in the middle of the room.

"Let her be, you hags," screamed someone from
the back of the ward.

"We'll do ye too if yer doesn't shut ye cakehole,"
shouted Doris in a vicious tone.

The woman stopped protesting immediately.

Emmy stood wide-eyed, looking around her. She'd no
cognition. She didn't grasp what Doris and Janet planned to
with her in front of all the patients. Some of the profoundly
depraved began to shout and gesticulate, panting and
goading Doris to become more intimate with the girl.

Doris ran her hands down Emmy's shoulders and touched
her breasts.

"She ain't a fighter," cackled Janet as she ran her
hand up the girl's leg toward her privates.

But Doris was wrong. Somewhere in Emmy's dormant
mind, she sensed the danger. Deep in her brain, her
subconscious mind recalled a painful experience. She didn't
have the intellect to grasp the threat, but she would the

instinct. Somebody had touched her here before. Emmy began to breathe faster and faster.

"Oh, yes, lass, does that feel good?"

Sensing the threat, every nerve in Emmy's body came alive, adrenalin surged through her body, and her heart beat wildly, pumping oxygen to her broken brain as it prepared to attack. Both women were kneeling in front of her, preparing for the ultimate violation.

Emmy's sinewy arms strained, her hands contorted into claws. She swung her upper body to one side, and with more force than anyone would anticipate from such a frail body, she swiped at Doris viciously. One of her nails caught Doris' eye, mangling the iris. Emmy scratched the woman's face with the strength of a lion. Doris' eye was a bloody mess, and she clamped her hand to her face, covering her eye shouting.

"I can't see, I can't see," Everybody ignored her, delighted that she was getting what was overdue to her.

The hospital ward was deathly quiet.

Janet was still on her knees, staring up at Emmy in confusion. Emmy looked down with big innocent eyes belying her rage. Janet was frozen, still clenching Emmy's inner thigh. Emmy swung her body around, and with a powerful backhand movement, she used all her momentum to swipe her clawed hands across Janet's face. Like a pendulum, the claw swung back and turned her wrist. Her nails dug into Janet's face, ploughing up strips of her skin. Blood began to drip onto the floor. Emmy stood naked in the middle of the room with their skin and blood under her nails. Her mind sensed that there was no more danger. Emmy sighed, her heart began to beat normally, and she returned to the fugue state, where she was safe from the horrors of the world. Emmy smiled as she stood naked in the middle of the room, unaware of the damage she'd inflicted upon the two evil women.

Kevin Bamborough struggled to unlock the doors to the ward. He saw young Emmy standing in the middle of the room, which was ominously quiet, considering that all of the patients were lunatics.

"Who did this to her?" cried, Kevin grabbing a sheet and covering her up.

The Matron charged in behind him. She took one look at the girl and knew that all hell had broken loose. She looked at Doris and Janet; they had gouges down their faces, and Doris' eye would be blinded for life.

"Who did this?" yelled the Matron.

It began with a low hum, and the patients pointed at Doris and Janet. The buzz exploded into a raging chant 'They did, they did.'

"Get them to a cell and chain them by their necks," ordered the Matron.

"I'm blind. I'm blind," cried Doris, but nobody paid her attention.

Doris and Janet had tormented the other women for years, and this was justice. It was a rare night when even the most severely ill patients showed solidarity based on a moral foundation.

6

RAGE AGAINST DEATH

Benjamin Fischer was buried on the Fischer Estate north of London. An ancient family cemetery stood on a hill that overlooked the meadows and forests below. The tombstones of Benjamin's ancestors surrounded his grave. He wasn't alone.

Samuel stood between Shilling and Tanner and watched the coffin descend into the rich black earth.

Shilling knew that Benjamin would not return, yet she also knew that he would live on in her soul, and he was forever the love of her life. Shilling couldn't imagine him in the past tense. She didn't need to control her emotions. After days of grieving, she was eventually numb. Samuel openly wept for his son-in-law, and Miss Annabelle tried to comfort him, but to no avail.

Tanner turned from the grave and began walking down the hill. Socrates followed her, afraid that the girl would feel isolated in her sorrow. Eventually, he caught up with her.

"Stop, Tanner, stop," he called.

"I just want to walk Socrates. I want to walk and never stop. I want to breathe fresh air and escape all the death and sadness of the last weeks."

Socrates smiled and nodded. "You walk for as long as you need to Tanner, I'm right behind you."

The young woman walked ahead of him, hair streaming behind her in the wind. Eventually, she stopped and turned to Socrates.

"I'm ready to go back, Socrates. I think I'm brave enough to face everyone."

"You may run away any time you wish Tanner, just tell me where you are going."

Tanner laughed for the first time in weeks. She hooked her hand under Socrates' elbow, and they walked back to the mansion arm in arm.

Samuel couldn't accept Benjamin's death.

"Why?" was all that Samuel had asked. "Why Benjamin?"

"Sam," said Annabelle gently, "we cannot rage against death. It's inevitable."

"Shilling has not shown any emotion in days. I'm afraid she is going to have a breakdown. Tanner is difficult, and she does not understand her mother's reaction. I'm going to intervene."

"Do you think that is wise?" asked Annabelle.

"By God, Annabelle, I love Tanner," declared Samuel, "still, I'll not allow her to torment her mother. Tanner will be going to university in the summer, where her days will be full. I've given it a lot of thought, and Tanner has only known privilege. Instead, of sending her to Oxford, I'm sending her to Victoria University."

"What? Victoria University in Manchester?"

"Yes. Tanner must gain independence. It's the richest poor city in England. She needs to experience the world from a different perspective."

"She wants to be a journalist," argued Annabelle.

"There is no better place to start. She'll develop an objective view of the world. She analyses everything subjectively. She needs to think critically. It'll make the difference between a good journalist, and a great journalist."

"Why, Sam? She's so young," Annabelle remembered having a similar conversation about Shilling when Samuel insisted she run Hudson Forge.

"I'm not of noble stock, Annabelle, and neither is Shilling. Tanner must appreciate the working class before she embarks on her career. Politics on the privileged side of the fence is different to that of the poor side," Annabelle said no more. He never made poor decisions.

He pulled Annabelle closer to him, and he felt her comforting body against his. Annabelle was a calm place of refuge for him. When she held him, his overwrought emotions began to subside. He felt at peace for the first time in weeks.

Annabelle lifted her face and looked into his eyes. He kissed her gently on her forehead and took a deep breath.

"Stop," she smiled, "Yes, I know, you cannot live without me."

"How did you know I was going to say that?"

"You always do."

As the weeks passed, Tanner became more complicated, and it all came to a head at the dinner table.

"Mama, I want to go to Birmingham with you next week," demanded Tanner petulantly.

"You have lessons, Tanner, and the trip will only take three days. You'll have to stay at home."

Tanner lost her temper. Her green eyes flashed and narrowed like a cat's. She stood up so violently that she knocked over her chair. It clattered onto the floor behind her.

"You didn't allow me to come to Newcastle. Instead, you made Baxter Lee bring me back to London. You didn't want me with you. And now I'm not allowed to be in Birmingham," she yelled at Shilling.

Everyone at the table looked at her aghast.

"Furthermore, you should've been with Papa in Newcastle. You're an engineer, and the accident would never have happened if you were there. Instead, you had to be selfish and follow your own schedule, as you always do."

Samuel had enough, and his temper flared. Shilling was astounded by the attack. Annabelle and Socrates looked at each other, and then they looked at Samuel. Tanner ignored the chair that she'd knocked over and walked around it toward the large mahogany dining room doors.

"Stop!" roared Samuel.

The instruction was unexpected, and Tanner jumped in fright.

"Pick up the chair," Samuel instructed her.

Tanner looked at Socrates, expecting him to help her, but he didn't budge.

"I told you to pick it up," Samuel ordered.

Tanner stooped and stood the chair on its legs. Her face was scarlet with fury and humiliation. Samuel had never spoken to her like this before. Miss Annabelle watched Samuel nervously, but Shilling ignored the situation, she was exhausted, and she didn't have the emotional reserves to discipline her daughter. Shilling didn't care what Tanner said. She didn't care for the day of the week or whether she lived or died.

"Finish your dinner," Samuel instructed his granddaughter, "and meet me in my study after I've excused you from this table."

Tanner was too afraid to protest. She'd very little food on her plate, but it took thirty minutes to finish her meal.

Samuel slammed the study door behind him. His shirttail hung out of his trousers, and his sleeves were rolled up to his elbows.

"You'll never behave that way in my house," shouted Samuel.

Tanner stared into his eyes without flinching. Her green eyes displayed defiance, the same defiance that he'd seen so many times in Shilling's eyes when she was that age.

"So, much like Shilling," Samuel thought to himself.

"Do you know that I'm a very wealthy young woman? I do not need my mother or you," Tanner said coolly.

"Do you have access to this great fortune?" Samuel retaliated, quick as a whip.

"Not yet," she answered sheepishly. "I'll get it when I'm twenty-one."

"You're very far from twenty-one Tanner."

Tanner was correct, and she would be inheriting a fortune. She and Shilling were possibly wealthier than the royal family.

"Do you know our family history?" Samuel asked her.

Tanner shook her head.

"I was born on a farm, and we were poor people. My father was a drunk who beat my mother. Your mother was born on a filthy street in Wapping, and she never knew her birth mother, who was from Ireland. How dare you think that you are better than everybody else? Yes, you will be wealthy with no life experience."

"I plan on being a journalist, and I'll gain a lot of life experience."

"Very well. Your mother and I've agreed that you need to attend university. We are sending you to Victoria University in Manchester."

"Why? You told me that I would attend the University of London or Oxford. Is it as prestigious as Oxford?"

"Not at all."

Tanner glared at him defiantly.

"I'm Annabelle Alexandria Fischer, and my Grandfather Fischer will never allow this."

"Grandfather Fischer agrees with me," said Samuel.

Tanner's jaw dropped. "Why?"

"Because Grandfather Fischer's ancestors were once poorer than you can ever imagine."

"My mother has betrayed me. So have you and Grandpa Fischer."

"You're eighteen, Tanner, and you are way too young to tell adults what to do."

Tanner realised that she wasn't in control of the conversation and wasn't old enough to control her world. Inwardly she baulked at the idea of being told what to do. Her father's death had plummeted her into a grief that overwhelmed her. The only way to vent her sorrow was to attack the people around her.

Samuel dismissed Tanner. She went up to her mother's old bedroom and flung herself onto the bed. Her mind was in a frenzy, and she began to sob. She was in a lot of trouble with her grandfather. She heard a gentle knock on the door, and it opened. Socrates looked over at the heartbroken young woman on the bed. She was so much like her mother.

"I'm going to send for some cocoa," said Socrates.

"Grandpa is so angry with me."

"I promise you that he has already forgotten all about it," said Socrates.

"He is sending me away. They're all sending me away."

"No, Tanner, you need a new experience. It's all going to be an adventure."

"Socrates, can I ask you a question, but you must tell me the truth?"

"Yes?"

"Was my Mama in love with Baxter Lee?"

Socrates was surprised, and he'd not anticipated the question. What had she heard about Baxter and Shilling? Socrates chose to ignore the question. The affair had happened long before Tanner was born, and it was none of her business.

Socrates sighed.

"I'm going to fetch your cocoa from the kitchen."

"Baxter Lee said that he loves Mama."

"They have worked together for many years, and I'm sure that he is fond of her. You should be asking your mother these questions. She'll give you an honest answer."

The morning was freezing. The Thames cooled the land, yet the smoke and fog that usually covered London had lifted, and the sky was ice blue. Shilling stood in the courtyard and watched as Socrates managed the loading of Tanner's trunks and suitcases.

"I'm going to buy a motor car," Samuel growled at Tanner. "This cab is way too small for all your luggage. Do you think we will be able to fit it all in your room?"

"Of course, we will," laughed Tanner.

"Socrates has one suitcase, and you have all the rest. What have you packed in all those chests?"

Tanner looked at her grandfather adoringly, neither one would remain angry with the other for very long. Samuel looked at Tanner, regretting that he'd been so hard on her. He longed to reverse his decision, but he couldn't. Shilling was his priority.

Shilling hugged Tanner tightly.

"You'll come back to London at midterm," said Shilling. "Do not be afraid."

"I'm not afraid, Mama," said Tanner defiantly.

Shilling could feel Tanner trying to wriggle out of the embrace.

"I love you, Tanner," said Shilling and burst into tears.

Miss Annabelle stepped forward and put her arm around Shilling. The tenderness of Annabelle's gesture touched Shilling's heart, and she collapsed into Annabelle's arms and wept.

"Tanner will be fine," said Annabelle, *but you may not be.*

Annabelle was correct. Shilling was broken. As the carriage left the courtyard, Shilling collapsed onto her knees and began to sob. Tears streamed down her face and soaked her bodice. Her body shook as she cried, and sorrow overcame her. Annabelle sank to the ground next to her. She pulled Shilling into her arms and cradled her head, and she stroked her hair and wiped the tears from her face. She looked down at Shilling, her child, the child she'd raised; she was overcome with compassion for Shilling.

"Oh, Miss Annabelle," sobbed Shilling, "I should never have allowed him to go alone. Tanner is right. It's my fault."

Annabelle knew that she would not be able to reason with Shilling. She grabbed Shilling by the shoulders and shook her.

"You listen to me, Shilling. You'll never speak those words again, do you hear me? What happened has happened, and you know that nothing would've stopped him from dying? It was his time."

It was the first time that Shilling had ever seen Annabelle fierce.

"You can mourn your husband, but you are not going to feel sorry for yourself. Get up."

Shilling stood up. Her dress was soiled, her eyes were swollen, and the scar down the side of her face was a bright red welt.

Annabelle walked to Shilling's room. Without speaking, Annabelle undressed and washed Shilling. She brushed Shilling's raven hair and put her into a fresh nightdress. Annabelle peeled back the sheets and put Shilling to bed. Annabelle sat in a chair next to the bed and held vigil over her child.

The train stopped at the central station in Manchester. Tanner may have tormented her mother about sending her to Manchester, but secretly she was delighted to be away from home. Tanner was brave and resilient. The dean had reassured Samuel that Victoria University provided all the subjects that his granddaughter enjoyed. He watched Socrates shouting instructions to the porters. Tanner's trunks were loaded onto a wagon that followed the carriage to the university.

"If your granddaughter is as spirited as you say, Mr Hudson, she has come to the right University," said the dean.

"I hope so, Sir," said Samuel charmingly.

"We tolerate a little more than other institutions because we teach the arts. And goodness knows, all artists are dramatic; they take themselves way too seriously. Most writers are quite temperamental."

Samuel put his head back and gave a deep laugh.

"I'm glad to hear this, and yes, Sir, I think you will have your hands full."

"If I remember correctly, your letter said that she wants to be a journalist."

"Yes, she has been writing since she could hold a pencil."

The dean smiled.

"Do not underestimate the power of female authors Mr Hudson. The Bronte sisters have been fundamental in enlightening the world to the power of women."

"I hope so, Sir, I've supported my daughter in getting a degree in engineering, and I insist that my granddaughter have a degree."

"My, my, Mr Hudson, you are remarkably liberal. You probably agree with women having the right to vote."

"Indeed, I do, my daughter is one of the richest women in the country, and she cannot vote for her representative of choice. It's unacceptable."

The dean couldn't believe what he was hearing. He'd been warned that Samuel Hudson had extreme views, but this was a surprise. The man was unique.

"Goodbye, Grandpa," smiled Tanner, "goodbye, Socrates."

"Goodbye, my darling," said Samuel, his eyes filling with tears.

Samuel watched the dean escort Tanner into the school. Socrates put his hand on Samuel's shoulder and squeezed it gently.

"Come on, Sam," he said to his boss, "let's go have a drink at the hotel, and pretend that we are young men again."

Samuel put his head back and laughed.

"Tanner will do well."

"I know," said Samuel, "she is like her mother."

"And her grandfather."

7

THE KINDNESS OF STRANGERS

Tilda spent most of her day on her hands and knees under the loom. She had to be aware of every movement she made, and if she lifted her head, it could get caught in the twine. If she put her hand out to stop herself from falling, it'd get stuck in the machinery that drove the loom. If she lost her balance, she could fall into the machine mechanism. The dangers of working in the cotton mill were endless. Though she'd a kind master in Tommy, she was still expected to complete her work quota for the day or stay late. The twelve-hour shift was long and gruelling, and the job of crawling about picking up the cotton under the gin was never-ending. Tilda wished that she was two years older, then she could be a piecer which looked a lot easier than being on her knees all day.

When her shift ended at six o'clock in the evening, she was so tired that she could barely walk home. Mrs Dunberry called her when she saw her pass the bakery, and Tilda left with fresh bread and butter. When Tilda broke off the thick crust, she always thought of Emmy, which made her heart sore. Tilda had developed an annoying cough that Mary tried to treat with a homemade concoction, but it did no good. Tilda would go into her room and collapse on her bed. The young girl, still a child, would fall asleep before she could remove her clothes.

Jimmy Sterling would sneak in very late at night if he came home at all. Mary kept a keen eye on Tilda's situation, and she quizzed Tilda regularly over Jimmy. As far as Mary could tell, Jimmy had kept his hands to himself.

Tilda missed her sister, and she looked forward to going to Country Asylum Hospital to see her. Sunday arrived, dull and sombre. The wind blew through the narrow streets, picking up refuse and cartwheeling it down to the river. The detritus would flow down the river until it reached the canals to accumulate and block the locks.

The howling wind made Tilda feel lonely, but she and Mary leaned into it as they made their way to Emmy. The hospital, at Prestwich Woods, was six miles from the rows. The visit used up most of Mary's Sunday, but she'd little choice. She had to see if Emmy was safe. Country Asylum was lauded as one of the most modern hospitals of its time, but Mary was expecting the worst.

Mary reached out and took Tilda's hand as they walked through the asylum gates. The path leading to the hospital was pretty and lined with trees. As they got closer to the redbrick building, they saw patients roaming the gardens. Most of them seemed normal, and they showed no signs of insanity. Some had strange gaits, as if their body was in a spasm while some patients were oblivious. Still, the place felt eerie, and Mary felt chills run up her spine as she made her way to the portal.

Inside the building it was different. Mary heard shouts and some hysterical laughter. She assumed that the most severely tormented were housed in the bowels of the facility. The man who greeted them was the same person who had collected Emmy in the ambulance. Kevin Bamborough greeted Mary and Tilda with a bright smile.

"Good afternoon. Aha! I remember you," he smiled at Tilda. "Yes, your sister is Emmy."

Tilda nodded shyly.

"You must be keen to see her."

Tilda nodded again, suspicious of the man's kindness.

"Yes, we are," said Mary.

"Come along then, let me take you to her ward."

The hospital was clean. Mary was right- as they proceeded along the corridors, the mental conditions of the patients deteriorated. The sound of laughter became shriller, there were shrieks of terror, and twice Mr Bamborough had to fight off leering women who wanted to touch Tilda. He led Tilda and Mary to a ward that was surprisingly calm. Any horrors, and atrocities that took place in the institution were kept well hidden from the visitors. Emmy's ward had thirty beds crammed into it. They were pushed up against each other so that there was enough space for all of them.

"It's overcrowded," said Mr Bamborough, "but we do our best."

Mary looked about her, taking in the scenario.

"The women in this ward display no outward signs of lunacy. There is class discrepancy here, and many of these are from the upper classes."

"Why are they here?" asked Mary.

"Most of them have been admitted here by their husbands."

"How can that be?"

"Sadly, it's a man's world," said Mr Bamborough, "should a society lady displease her husband, she may be admitted here under the auspices of lunacy."

"Aww bloody hell," Mary smiled for the first time, "every woman in Salford will be here."

"There is Emmy," said Mr Bamborough and pointed toward her.

Emmy was sitting in a comfortable chair at the window. The wind was gusting, whipping the trees from side to side. Emmy sat in a daze, seemingly hypnotised by the movement outside. Tilda ran toward her and fell onto her knees in front of her sister.

"Hello, Emmy, it's me."

Emmy didn't acknowledge her sister.

"Emmy, Emmy, it's me, Tilda."

Mary and Mr Bamborough looked on from a distance.

Eventually, Emmy spoke. "Who are you?"

For a second, Tilda got annoyed. "It's me, Tilda. I'm your sister."

Emmy just smiled, but those were the last words she said for the rest of the visit.

Mary was so distressed by what she just witnessed that she cried for the duration of the visit.

"Now, now, Mary, do not cry. The girl has had a severe shock, and there is still hope that she will come out of her stupor."

"I cannot stand to see her this way."

"I know," answered Mr Bamborough. "I thank the Almighty that you have visited. We pray that with enough love, Emmy may be able to return home one day. Some families leave their loved ones here and never return for them. The paupers live here until they die or run away."

Tilda was deeply disturbed by Emmy's behaviour. Still, she was stoic, and her young mind told her that she would look after Emmy, just as Emmy had watched over her.

Help arrived in the most unorthodox manner.

Kevin Bamborough was visiting with Yakov and Rachel Weiner. They sat around the table in the cheerful little kitchen. Kevin had known the Weiners since he was a boy, and he loved the old Jewish couple.

"Can I pour you some kosher wine, Kevin? We received it as a gift from a client. It's delicious."

"Thank you, Yakov."

"When last did you see young Emmy Sterling?" asked Rachel. The older woman had a heart of gold, well hidden beneath her prickly façade.

"So, you heard about her going to the asylum then?" asked Kevin.

"Terrible, terrible. It's the saddest news."

Yakov nodded in agreement with his wife.

"Where is the child she had?" asked Rachel.

Kevin shook his head. "It died after birth, Rachel."

"And the boy? Where is the lad who was the father?" Rachel continued on her quest for information.

"No more questions, Rachel," ordered Yakov.

"I do not live on that row, Rachel, and I canna say what happened there."

"Is the girl safe?" asked Rachel.

"Yes," Kevin said, "but I don't know for how long."

"What do you mean Kevin?" said the fiery Rachel.

"There was an incident on her first night at the hospital."

Rachel's hand flew to her mouth.

"I can't watch her all the time, and there are all types in that Lunatic Asylum. Somebody will hurt her if they get the opportunity."

"Say it, Kevin, you are afraid that the girl will get raped in the asylum. What a disgrace."

Kevin avoided eye contact. He was embarrassed.

"That's enough, Rachel. I know that you are angry. Still, you are making young Kevin embarrassed."

"It's all over the Tanakh, Yakov. How can he be embarrassed? Women have been violated for thousands of years."

Yakov nodded. It was the truth.

"Yes, it's true," shrugged Kevin, "but not by other women."

"What day can I go and visit her?" demanded Rachel.

"She's allowed visitors on Saturday."

Rachel frowned in annoyance and looked at Yakov.

Yakov shook his head at her.

"Do not shake your head, Yakov Weiner. I'm going to fetch Emmy. She and Tilda are coming to live with us."

Yakov looked at her incredulously. It must have been quite shocking for Yakov that his wife was burdening him by taking in two young girls. But evidently, that wasn't his concern.

"No," said Yakov sternly, "I do not mind taking in the girls, but I'll not allow you to break Shabbat."

Kevin looked from Yakov to Rachel, amused that the man was more concerned about breaking the Sabbath than starting a new family.

Rachel couldn't disrespect her husband, and she kept quiet.

"What other days are there available to visit?" asked Yakov.

"Only Saturday, next Sunday, the custodians of the facility are guests of honour, and no other visitors will be allowed there," replied Kevin.

"That is a pity," said Yakov.

Kevin finished the delicious latkes with apple sauce.

"Your cooking is delicious as usual, Rachel," he complimented her.

Rachel grunted a thank you.

Yakov escorted Kevin to the door, "We'll think of something, Kevin, we will," promised Yakov. He closed the door behind Kevin and returned to the table.

Before he could say a word, Rachel began to speak angrily.

"I'm fetching Emmy on Saturday, and I do not care what you say, Yakov Weiner."

Yakov gave her a stern look.

"I'm the head of this family Rachel, how will you explain your disobedience to Hashem? How will I explain your insubordination?"

Rachel stared out of the window, washing the dishes furiously as she did so.

"Yakov Weiner, you are coming with me to fetch Emmy from the asylum?"

"No, no, no, Rachel. I'll have no part of it."

"Besides moving a table Yakov, the only mitzvah we are allowed to do on Shabbat is save a life. I'm going to save Emmy and Tilda. Hashem has put those young women in our path for a reason. We cannot forsake them because Hashem does not forsake us."

Yakov stared at his wife. Sometimes she enraged him, but she was right. It was the one mitzvah that they could perform on Shabbat. He didn't argue with her. She knew the Torah as well as he did.

Yakov spent two gruelling days negotiating Emmy's release from Lancashire County Asylum. He was sent from one government department to the next one, and finally, the state unburdened itself of the responsibility of caring for Emmy- it'd save them money.

Try as he might, Yakov learnt nothing about Emmy's descent into mental illness, and nobody was prepared to share the sordid story with him. At six 'o'clock one evening, Rachel was outside the cotton mill, waiting for Tilda.

Rachel walked toward Mary when she saw her.

"I've come for Tilda," said Rachel.

Tilda looked at Rachel quizzically.

"Emmy is at my house, and she is safe. You and your sister will live with Yakov and me from now on."

Tilda smiled from ear to ear.

"But I've to work tomorrow, "answered Tilda.

"No, more working for you, child," declared Rachel. "We'll look after you, and you will go to school like all children should."

"Oh, Rachel. Thank ye me pet," cried Mary.

When Tilda saw Emmy, she ran across the kitchen and threw her arms around her big sister. Yakov and Rachel watched tearfully as Tilda hung on to Emmy.

"She has no hair, Rachel," said Tilda.

"Do not worry about that. It'll grow again. We'll cover Emmy's head with a shtetl for now."

"What is a shtetl?" said Tilda?

"It's a scarf. All Jewish Women cover their heads, and so she will fit in well and will not be embarrassed."

"Can I also wear a shtetl?" Tilda asked Rachel.

"Of course, of course. You'll both look beautiful."

Tilda nodded her agreement. Although Rachel was fierce, Tilda liked her.

Yakov kept his distance from the two girls, respecting the importance of modesty. Rachel showed them to their tiny room under the eaves of the little apartment above the shop. The wooden staircase was rickety. There was a mezuzah on the doorpost, and it was set at an angle. Rachel touched it as she passed under the lintel. The room was small, and they could hardly stand up straight. Instead, of being bare and sparse, it held a big bed pushed up against the wall. It was large enough for Tilda and Emmy to sleep in. The room was spotlessly clean and smelled fresh. A bright patchwork quilt covered the bed. Rachel made it by hand during the long winter evenings. There were two comfortable chairs, and a cupboard; the room was cramped, but instead of being oppressive, it felt like a nest.

"Tomorrow, we burn those clothes," said Rachel.

"We have no others," said Tilda, a worried look on her face.

"I've arranged new clothes for you. Now here are some bedclothes for you, Tilda."

Rachel moved toward Emmy, unsure how the girl would react when she tried to change her clothes. Emmy showed no signs of distress. She cooperated with Rachel, she felt safe, and Tilda was with her.

That night, Tilda cuddled close to her sister.

"This is wonderful," whispered Tilda, "you never have to be afraid again. I'll take care of you."

Tilda thought for a second.

"Rachel and Yakov will keep you safe as well."

Emmy gave her a dreamy smile, but this time she looked into Tilda's eyes.

"I missed you so much Emmy, you are never leaving me again, do you understand?"

Tilda hugged Emmy closer, and the two sisters went to sleep in a clean bed for the first time in their lives.

It was the first night in years that young Tilda had fallen asleep peacefully. The fear of Jimmy Sterling molesting her was no longer foremost in her mind. Rachel said she would never have to go back to the mill. Tilda wondered what was in store for her, and she was very excited.

Rachel went downstairs. Yakov was studying the Torah as he did every night. He stood up when he saw Rachel and walked toward her, his arms outstretched.

"I love you, Rachel. You're a good woman," he told her, his long beard tickling her cheek.

"Mmph!" muttered Rachel.

Yakov smiled at her.

"The first time I saw you at the Shul in Krakow, I knew that I would marry you."

"You were too busy at the Yeshiva, and you hardly looked at me," contradicted Rachel.

"You distracted me all the time. Eventually, Rabbi Lazarus took me aside and told me that it would take years to complete my studies if I didn't marry you soon. You were a beautiful distraction."

"Nonsense Yakov, you had your eye on Sarah Liebenbach."

Yakov laughed.

"Then I saw how fierce you were, and I decided that if life is as difficult as we are told, I would need somebody like you at my side."

Rachel's face softened, Yakov had told her the story so many times before, and every time he did, she fell in love with him again.

"I'll look after those children as if they're my own," said Yakov.

"I know you will. You're a kind man, but what will Yitzhak and Debra say?"

"Our children will accept them, and the young women will become a part of our family."

"Yes, I believe that our children will be kind to them," agreed Rachel.

"You have taught them well, Rachel. It's a Mitzvot to care for others."

"But, they're not Jewish Yakov. What will Rabbi Katz say?"

"God isn't exclusive to Jews, Rachel. We'll do the best we can, and rely on Hashem to lead us."

Rachel pushed her face against her husband's chest. This man had loved and protected her. Yakov deserved all the respect she showed him.

8

BEAUTIFUL KATE

Shilling moved back to Samuel's house in Mayfair. She craved the familiarity of the people who had raised her. It was a year since Benjamin Fischer had died, but she mourned as though it was yesterday. The pain had eased, but the memories were haunting. Being married into a family as powerful as the Fischers' came with its challenges. Benjamin had provided well for Shilling and Tanner, but the complexity of the large estate was exhausting. Shilling's father-in-law was appointed the executor of the will, and it suited her to have as little influence as possible. Shilling was a very wealthy woman in her own right, and she never needed her husband to take care of her financially. She didn't care if it took a hundred years to solve the legal obstacles attached to Fischer Estates. She simply wanted to bury her head in Hudson Engineering and never look up again. She wrote to Tanner, but the replies she received were brief, revealing very little of Tanner's experiences at Victoria University. She lamented to her father, who brushed it off as Tanner gaining independence. Samuel dared not divulge that once a week, he received long informative prose from Tanner.

"Why not take a sabbatical and go to the south of France?" Samuel asked Shilling.

"Papa, I'm deeply involved with this new bascule bridge they're building across the Thames."

"The bloody thing has been up and working for a few years now."

"If something breaks, I need to be here," answered Shilling, agitation in her voice.

"You do not have to be here all the time."

"It's my patent Papa, I've designed the engines that lift the drawbridge."

"I know it's your patent, but for heaven's sake, can you please behave like a normal person for once? You need to get away from this dreary city and go somewhere warm. Even you, the mighty Shilling Hudson, needs to rest."

Shilling frowned, "I do not want to hurt you, Papa. I'll take leave as soon as I can. Please stop worrying about me."

"Go to the Isle of Wight. It's closer. If there is an emergency, you can be home in a flash."

"Yes, Papa. I think that is a better idea," Shilling smiled at her father.

"There are magnificent horse farms there. You can ride across the cliffs and breathe fresh air."

"Mmm."

"Good, so you will go?" Samuel walked over to his daughter and put his arms around her.

"Papa, stop it!"

Samuel kissed the top of her head. He was about to raise his voice, argue, and cajole, but he was finally beginning to learn that it didn't help after all these years.

Baxter Lee's carriage drove into the courtyard of Samuel's house in Mayfair, London. Baxter had lived there once upon a time, and try as he might, he was always overcome with nostalgia when he drove through the gates. His gaze always travelled to the rooms above the coach house, and he remembered the night that he had told Shilling that he was a married man. He'd made the age-old mistake of falling in love with his pupil. He'd tutored Shilling for many years, and on the evening that she received her degree in engineering, he'd left her. She was still warm from their lovemaking when he broke the news coldly and without emotion, which wasn't how he had felt in his heart. He left by way of the courtyard gates, and when he reached the end of the dark avenue, he leant his head against a pillar and wept.

Socrates met him at the back door.

"Yes?" said Socrates.

"May I please see Shilling?" asked Baxter Lee.

"Please wait in the library," instructed the loyal valet.

"Thank you."

Shilling walked into the library, where Baxter was waiting for her. Baxter, hands in pockets and was pacing up and down. He turned around to face the door when he heard the door open. For once, Shilling wasn't wearing black mourning garments. She was dressed in a simple white dress. Her hair was hanging softly around her face, and she seemed more at peace than she'd been in a long time.

"Baxter," she smiled at him.

"Shilling," he nodded.

"Socrates said that you were looking for me?"

"Tea?"

"Something stronger, please."

Shilling poured two drinks and watched him from the corner of her eye. He seemed uncomfortable, and Shilling didn't know why that was. They'd worked together for a long time, and bygones were bygones.

Baxter got to the point.

"Kate wants to see you."

It was Shilling's turn to be surprised.

"Where is she?"

"At the sanatorium in Birmingham."

"I was planning to move back there. My house is standing empty, and I'll be closer to the forge," said Shilling.

Baxter nodded and sipped his drink.

"You do not understand, Shilling. Kate is dying," said Baxter.

"Consumption," he said, matter of fact, to hide his emotions.

"What? No!" said Shilling in disbelief. "Baxter, I can arrange the best treatment for her. I've the resources."

"We have done everything. Kate has spent a great deal of time in Madrid, where it's dry. There was a marked improvement while she was there, but as soon as she arrived back in Dorchester, the fog rolled in, and she regressed."

"Anywhere, Baxter, tell me where. South Africa? Morocco? Spain?"

"There is nothing they can do for her."

"When is the best time to see her?" asked Shilling.

"As soon as possible, she does not have a lot of time left."

Shilling lowered herself into a chair and closed her eyes. 'Why would Kate want to see her now? It was many years since her indiscretion with Baxter. She'd never interfered in their marriage, and it would have been easy to strike up an affair with Baxter again.

"Why now?"

"I truly do not know Shilling. I know that Kate isn't a malicious person. God knows, she has every right to be."

"Did you confess to your affair with me?"

"Never, I believed that it would destroy her."

Shilling drank her tea slowly. She set the empty teacup down on a small table.

"Yes, Baxter," she smiled, "I'll visit Kate."

Socrates escorted Shilling to Birmingham. The idea of living there was exciting. For the first time since Benjamin's death, she was beginning to feel independent again. The old Shilling was returning. Kate dying, loomed over Shilling like a dark cloud. Why had Kate called for Shilling in her last days? Although they were kind to each other, Kate and Shilling had never become friends, and Shilling was wise enough to keep her relationship with Baxter strictly business.

Socrates drew the cab up to the doors of the sanatorium. He opened the cab door and stood aside as Shilling climbed out of the cab.

"This may not be easy, Shilling," said Socrates.

"Yes, I know."

"You do not have to do this."

"This woman deserves to die in peace, however difficult it is for me to face her."

Socrates noted that Shilling's determination was returning. She was beginning to heal.

They'd designed the sanatorium to trap as much natural light and fresh air as possible. The hospital was painted white inside; the floors shone like mirrors, and the nurses were spotless. A nurse escorted Shilling to Kate's ward. The windows stretched from floor to ceiling, and the garden view created an illusion that Kate was lying between the plants. In the centre of the room was a cot, surrounded by the most beautiful vases of flowers. The bed linen was clean, and there was a fire in the corner, creating a warm cosy atmosphere. There was a wheelchair next to the cot and some comfortable chairs. Shilling noticed a newspaper on a table, indicating that Baxter had been there earlier.

"Mr Lee spends most nights here," said the young nurse. "He doesn't move from that chair."

She pointed to a leather chair with a rough blanket draped over it.

Shilling could imagine Baxter watching over Kate all night like a guardian angel.

"I'll leave you in peace, Mrs Fischer. If you need me, just pull the cord next to the bed."

Kate Lee must have sensed someone watching her because her eyes fluttered, then opened. Her hair covered the pillow, and someone had gone to great lengths to ensure that it was clean and brushed. Her eyes sparkled, but her skin was grey. It seemed that Kate's spirit was happy to continue its journey through this world, but her body had given up. She smiled at Shilling. It was weak but sincere.

"Sit," Kate lifted her forefinger slightly and
pointed to a chair.

Kate was beautiful and fragile, yet so close to death.

Shilling sat down.

"Thank you," whispered Kate.

Shilling moved her chair closer to the bed and leaned her arms on the mattress, determined to hear every word that Kate was going to say. Shilling watched her struggling for breath and instinctively took Kate's hand in hers.

"I forgave you a long time ago."

Shilling got tears in her eyes.

Kate took a deep breath.

"You were so young, and he is so easy to fall in
love with," she rasped.

Shilling looked into Kate's eyes. She was at a loss for words.

"He still loves you, Shilling."

Shilling smiled.

"He loved you more than me, Kate. Baxter went
home to you and James."

Kate nodded. "Thank you, for allowing him to come back to us."

Shilling was overcome by Kate's dignity.

"Promise to look after him," a lonely tear rolled down Kate's cheek.

Shilling was overwhelmed by Kate's kindness, grace and generosity. To want the best for Baxter after he betrayed her was the ultimate sign of love.

"I promise," answered Shilling.

Shilling took a handkerchief out of her purse, and she gently wiped the tears from Kate's face, then she wiped away her own. She'd made a promise, and nobody was better at keeping a promise than Shilling Hudson Fischer.

Socrates met Shilling at the sanatorium's doors. He looked at her red-rimmed eyes and was instantly annoyed.

"You should never have come here. You're not responsible for the past." he blustered.

"Stop Socrates. I'm not sorry I came here. Kate Lee is one of the noblest people that I've ever met. If I can have an ounce of Kate's kindness, I'll die a peaceful death."

Socrates looked at her and smiled. He knew that Kate had won her absolute respect. He also knew that Shilling would never tell him what she and Kate discussed.

On the same day that Tanner arrived in Birmingham for the summer holiday, Kate Lee died in her husband's arms. Baxter was devastated. Later he would tell Shilling that Kate was beautiful and pain-free; she no longer struggled for every ounce of air that kept her alive.

Shilling insisted that Tanner attend the funeral with her.

"Why Mama, I didn't know her."

"Out of respect for Mr Lee," answered Shilling.

"What will I say?" asked Tanner.

"Nothing Tanner, you do not have to say anything," said Shilling? "Baxter and James just have to know that we are there for them."

Socrates escorted the two women to the church, and then into the small cemetery. Baxter Lee was well known and well-liked in Birmingham, and the church was packed. A long train of mourners followed the coffin into the cemetery. The procession was dignified and sedate. It was a perfect summer day. Butterflies and birds fluttered in the trees, flowers had popped up during the spring, and it was warm. The air held hope. It was a reflection of Kate Lee's personality.

Tanner watched the proceedings closely. She remembered the details of her father's funeral, and when she saw the depth of Baxter's sorrow, she felt sorry for him. Shilling showed no emotion at the graveside, she was composed, but her conversation with Kate haunted her. 'Look after him,' Kate told her, and Shilling had promised Kate that she would.

As the minister prayed, Baxter Lee kept his eyes open and took the opportunity to observe the mourners at Kate's graveside. His eyes scoured the crowd and fell upon Shilling. Her emerald green eyes met his across the grave. Shilling gave him a nod, and he returned the gesture. He'd spent his marriage torn between Kate and Shilling, and at that moment, Baxter wished that he'd never met Shilling. Baxter stood stoically as the coffin descended into the wet earth. His son James put his hand on his father's shoulder and squeezed it lovingly.

Baxter couldn't face any more people. Contrary to social etiquette, he deserted his fellow mourners and went to his bedroom. He collapsed into a chair with a tumbler in one hand, and a bottle of rum in the other. He drank one glass of burning alcohol after the next until he was too drunk to lift the glass to his lips. Baxter collapsed onto the floor, awoke sick and miserable, and then began the ritual again, desperate to escape his memories and sins.

Baxter didn't leave the room for a week. Eventually, James Lee jimmied the door and found his father lying in his own vomit, and it was a miracle that Baxter didn't choke to death.

The same afternoon James rode to Shilling's house.

"Only you have the power to help him," said James, "if you do not, he will drink himself to death."

Shilling and James climbed the graceful staircase to the bedroom that Baxter and Kate had shared. The curtains were drawn, and the room was dark. Baxter lay in a deep chair, still dressed in the clothes that he'd worn to Kate's funeral. His shirt was unbuttoned, and his chest was covered in dried vomit. His hair was dishevelled, he was unshaven, and he stank as every pore on his body tried to expel the poison he'd been drinking for a week.

His red eyes and gaunt face stared up at her.

"I need to bathe him, James," said Shilling. "Please put some water in the bath."

"You? You're going to wash him?" asked James in shock. "I just want you to talk to him, that is all. You do not have to clean him. I can do that."

"I've known your father for many years. We understand each other," Shilling said kindly. She removed her jacket and rolled up her sleeves. "Let us get him to the bathroom."

James and Shilling undressed Baxter and managed to get him into the clean water. He lay in the bath limp and exhausted.

"I'll manage now," said Shilling, "I'll call you to take him out. Ask your cook to prepare a light meal, not too rich. And he needs a lot of water to drink."

She lathered Baxter's body with soap and used a sponge to wash him from head to toe. She was entirely at ease with him. After all, once upon a time, he'd been her lover.

"Are you saving me?" Baxter mumbled.

"No."

"Then why are you here?"

"You're a mess. Do you really want your son to wash you after a drunken binge?"

"You do not understand."

"Oh, I do."

"You're stronger than me Shilling, you have always been stronger."

"As far as I remember, you were pretty damned strong. The night you told me about your family took a lot of courage."

"Oh, my darling, I was—, uh, so—broken. The only way I could leave you was to be callous, or I could never have left," he stammered, unable to defend himself.

"Stop. Stop it. I'm tired of pain and regret," she said quietly.

Baxter lifted his hand and traced the scar on her beautiful face.

"You have indulged your guilt and sorrow for a week, Baxter, now it's time to get up and live."

"How?"

"Like you did after you left me, one day at a time."

"How do you know?" He whispered.

"Kate told me that you never stopped loving me."

"She did?"

"Yes, she knew about us."

"Kate told me she forgave me for everything, but I never realised she meant the affair. I never told her Shilling. I promise that I never told her," cried Baxter.

Baxter was shaky, but he managed to get out of the bath without help.

"Is that why she wanted to see you? Why was I so stupid?"

"Kate was an astute wife Baxter, she loved you, and she forgave you."

Tears started to run down Baxter's face, and Shilling took pity on him, putting her arms around him. His body trembled as he cried silently.

Shilling dressed him in clean pyjamas and made him climb into bed.

"What did she tell you?" Baxter rasped.

"That she loved you and wanted you to be happy."

James arrived and put his father's food and water on the nightstand.

"Will you visit me again?" he asked, but didn't plead.

"No," Shilling answered determinedly, "I'll see you at work on Monday morning."

It had been a long day. Mother and daughter ate dinner together, and then Shilling went to her bedroom and collapsed onto her bed, staring up at the canopy above her head. She heard a quick knock, and Tanner let herself into the room. Tanner climbed into Shilling's bed like she'd done as a little girl, and Shilling joined her. It was comforting to have Tanner next to her.

"Mama, how is Mr Lee?"

"His heart is broken," said Shilling.

"Did he love his wife?" asked Tanner.

The question surprised Shilling. "Yes, he did," she answered.

"Did you love him?"

Shilling had a split second to decide her reply. 'The truth will set you free, Shilling', she told herself.

"Yes, I did."

"Did you love him more than Papa?"

"Oh, my sweetheart," she whispered. "Is this what has troubled you for all this time?"

"Yes, it has, Mama. After Papa died, Mr Lee told me he loved you."

"When?"

"On the train from Manchester."

"Oh, Tanner, your father was the love of my life. I was so in love with him. There is nobody else who can ever take his place."

"Did you have an affair with Baxter Lee while you were married to Papa?"

"Where have you learned about affairs, Tanner?" surprised by Tanner's worldliness.

"I've grown up, Mama."

Shilling realised that in her years of grief, she failed to see her daughter become a woman.

"No, Tanner. I married Papa many years later."

Tanner smiled.

"Is that why Socrates and Grandpa are always fierce with Mr Lee?"

"Yes, I was very young, and it was a very complicated time of my life," laughed Shilling.

"Mama, tell me about when you met Papa."

"Well," began Shilling, "it was very romantic."

Tanner laughed as Shilling told her the story.

"He was a very handsome man. At first, I was terrified of him, but later I learned that he was just a big old pussycat."

"Mama, you are never scared," Tanner laughed loudly.

"Did he love me?" Tanner asked in a low voice.

Shilling felt like crying, it had been such an emotional day, and she couldn't hold back her tears.

"He was so proud of you, Tanner. He couldn't take his eyes off your little face. He used to hold you and refuse to let you go. He and Grandpa were in continuous competition to hold you."

"Really?" smiled Tanner, drying her tears with her sleeve.

"Why are you asking me all these questions, my darling? You know the answers."

"I never want to forget him, Mama. I want to talk about him and hear these stories until I'm an old woman," answered Tanner.

Tanner put her arm over her mother and fell asleep. Shilling looked at the young woman next to her. It had taken so long for Tanner to speak her mind. Shilling's instincts told her that Tanner had weathered a violent storm. Shilling knew that the truth was a safe harbour, and having answers to the questions that haunted her, Tanner would be able to continue her life without being haunted by the past.

Shilling put her face in her pillow and began to weep silently. She cried for Benjamin and Kate, who died so young. Shilling wept when she recalled how Samuel had saved her and how Miss Annabelle nurtured her. She cried for Socrates, who was always at her side when she needed him. And then she cried for Baxter. They were not tears of despair or regret, but gratitude for all the grace they'd shown when she needed it the most.

Socrates woke Shilling and Tanner with a tray of steaming tea and hot scones. He added homemade strawberry jam, and an extra-large portion of clotted cream. He smiled from ear to ear, delighted when he saw the two of them together.

"I'm not going to spoil you every morning."

He pretended to be fierce while he whipped open the curtains. Bright yellow sunshine streamed into the bedroom.

Socrates left them alone. It had taken a long time for Shilling and Tanner's wounds to heal, and he wanted mother and daughter to spend as much time together as possible.

The breakfast was delicious, and when they finished it, they snuggled a little longer, but Tanner had one last question.

"Mama, do you think that you will love Mr Lee again?"

Shilling went quiet.

"Mama?" prodded Tanner, then realised her mother would not answer the question.

Shilling had never stopped loving Baxter. He was her first lover, and it had been a passionate affair. They would've made a powerful couple, but that was all a long time ago. She didn't want to dig up ghosts from the past or nurture dreams that would never come true.

9

RACHEL'S FURY

Emmy and Tilda settled into a comfortable routine of homework, housework and school. Yakov accepted that Emmy would never fit into regular society because she withdrew when she encountered people. Rachel took Emmy under her wing, and soon Emmy was happily attending the synagogue every Friday night. Several young men noticed her, yet Emmy hid behind Rachel every time someone approached her. Rachel was astute, and the more she observed Emmy's behaviour, the more she pondered the likelihood that somebody had tormented the girl. Tilda regularly told stories of how Emmy had looked after her when she was a little girl, which convinced Rachel that Emmy was born with a sound mind.

It was a Thursday, and everything was going wrong. Rachel was working frantically to make food packages for the poor. She wouldn't have time to do it on Friday, as she would be preparing for Shabbat. Out of desperation, she asked Emmy to sweep Yakov's workshop, which Rachel usually did herself.

Rachel could never have guessed that this simple chore would change Emmy's life forever. Emmy took the broom and slowly descended the rickety wooden steps to look for the workshop. It was the first time Emmy ventured down into the shop, and the instant she stepped into the room, she was mesmerised by the clocks and watches that ticked away at a steady pace. She looked around her, fascinated by how different each of them was. The clocks had different sounding chimes, and sing-song sounds were emanating from them. Although they'd unique features, they beat to the same rhythm and displayed the exact same time. Each one was beautiful in its uniqueness, which inspired her first intellectual question in years.

"How do they work?" she asked, her voice crystal clear.

Yakov couldn't believe his ears.

"Come with me," he said, and Emmy trotted behind him into the small workshop.

Yakov's workshop had Emmy agog. Cogs, gears, and springs were scattered on the large workbench where Yakov sat. Those belonging to the clocks were larger than those belonging to the watches. Yet, if the timepiece was a lady's wristwatch, the mechanical mechanism was minute, so small in fact that it required Yakov to use a magnifying glass.

Emmy forgot that she was there to clean. She sat down on a stool and watched Yakov working. Yakov said nothing, and neither did Emmy, but his work held her attention, and she concentrated on what he was doing.

From that day forward, Emmy went to the workshop every morning, sat on the same stool next to the workbench and observed Yakov at work. One morning, Yakov dared to give Emmy an instruction.

"Emmy, please pass me that gear," Yakov said in a quiet voice and passed her a small tweezer.

Emmy picked up the delicate part and gave it to him and watched as he assembled the clock.

Within a few weeks, Emmy knew the name of all the clock parts, and a basic knowledge of how the mechanism worked. The first clock that Yakov gave her to repair was a cuckoo clock. Emmy got the surprise of her life when the little bird popped out on the hour. Seeing the little ornamental creature chirp was all the reward that Emmy needed, and soon Yakov allowed her to repair the more robust mechanisms. Emmy spent hours alone in the workshop undisturbed, and she was happy. Yakov was sensitive to her shy manner and took great precautions to respect her and protect her from prying eyes.

As time went by, Yakov gave Emmy more and more responsibility, and within a year, she entered into an apprenticeship under the tutelage of Yakov. Emmy became engrossed in her tasks and had the patience to solve the most complex problems. She was a perfectionist and spent hours cleaning and polishing each item she fixed. This was Emmy's way of caring. It was her way of loving something that would never hurt her. Emmy may have been emotionally damaged, but she was intellectually sound. Slowly, but surely, Emmy began to speak. Her conversation was limited, yet, when Yakov asked her a question pertaining to work, she would answer him. There was no small talk, no humour, no emotion. However, there was primary communication, and for the moment, that was good enough for Yakov.

Jimmy Sterling was experiencing the worst years of his miserable life. He was a fully committed drunk, and the few sober hours that he could spare were spent plotting how to get his next drink. Some women in Salford brewed beer from elderwood or herbs, but it was mild with little effect. Eventually, he found an old man on the outskirts of Salford who brewed strong spirits out of fruit peels which he dug out of the bins at the posh hotels. There was no certainty of what the still would produce, and sometimes the alcohol was so strong that it took only one or two tots to floor a grown man. Jimmy Sterling lived for this potent alcohol. All that he wanted to do was escape the horrid dream that haunted him since he saw the child.

It had been years since he'd seen his daughters, and truth be told, he didn't care whether they lived or died. Jimmy knew that Tilda and Emmy were living with the Jewish watchmaker and his wife. In the years when Jimmy had his wits about him, old Yakov had fixed his watch, but now he made sure to avoid that street at all costs.

Jimmy Sterling was drunk, destitute and desperate when he came up with a brilliant idea. He'd lived on the streets for some time, but his need for grog outweighed his need for warmth. He was desperate for a drink when he heard that Emmy had qualified as a watchmaker and was working for the old Jew.

It was winter, and the streets were already dark by mid-afternoon. The gloom was exacerbated by the smoke that hung over Salford, giving the impression that it was late evening. The streetlights glowed weakly, solid proof that the dark can overcome the light. Jimmy stood in the shadows and watched the small shop, mustering the courage to go inside. He'd not seen the old Jew for years, the man had been kind to him, but he wasn't sure how old Yakov would accept him now. He certainly didn't want to meet Yakov today, so Jimmy waited until Yakov left the shop, and then he crossed the road.

The plaque above the door read 'Weiner Watchmakers'. Yakov swept the pavement and polished the sign every day, demonstrating his pride in the little shop. Jimmy pushed the door open and heard the bell tinkling as he shut it behind him. The small shop was bright and warm, and the watch faces reflected starlight against the walls. It was almost magical. Emmy heard the doorbell and looked up. It took some time for her to gain sufficient confidence to greet customers. The customers had become fond of the shy new worker, and accepted her for what she was.

Emmy went into the little shop to see who had arrived. When she got to the counter, she stopped dead in her tracks. A man stood at the counter. He was poorly dressed and stank, but something about him was familiar, and Emmy couldn't place him as yet. Emmy's instincts told her that she was in danger. The moment Jimmy began to speak, the girl knew it was her father. Gazing at a random spot on the wall above the man's head, her eyes glazed, and she smiled.

"Hello, Emmy."

She didn't move.

"'Tis yer old Da, lass," Jimmy said softly. He noted that she'd become a beautiful woman, and he became aroused.

Emmy continued to smile, and Jimmy misconstrued it as Emmy being friendly. A thought entered his depraved head.

"What if he found a room for them? He would take a new address. Emmy would look after him. After all, he'd physical and financial needs."

"I need some tom," whispered Jimmy in his most smooth, manipulative voice. "I've fallen on hard times, I've. You dunna want yer old Da to suffer now do yer?"

Emmy paid no attention to what he was saying, and Jimmy frowned.

"Do ye have a few pennies for yer ol' Da?" asked Jimmy, a bit more assertive now.

Still no response.

Jimmy was losing his temper. His alcohol starved brain was torturing him, and he needed a drink badly now.

Jimmy strode around the counter.

"We are flesh and blood. Do ye remember our nights together?"

Emmy recalled them all too well. She remembered begging for him to stop raping her, the humiliation of the child growing inside her, and the embarrassment as neighbours and friends whispered behind her back. Then she remembered the pain, and the memory of her body contorting and ripping apart caused a rage that she couldn't control.

Emmy began to scream. It was the shrill, piercing sound of terror.

This wasn't the reaction that Jimmy had expected, and he turned on his heel and fled the shop. The door slammed behind him, and the bell quivered and tinkled for some time.

Rachel heard the commotion downstairs and thought that Emmy was being robbed. She ran from the kitchen where she was cooking and flew down the wooden stairs. Rachel stopped in horror, and her hands shot to her mouth. Rachel couldn't believe what she was seeing or hearing.

Emmy was hysterical, and she cowered in the corner of the workroom shaking in fear, her hands covering her head, and she was howling like a terrified animal.

"No, Papa, no. Please stop. Please."

Rachel flew across the room, grabbed Emmy and pulled her into her arms. As Yakov arrived back in the shop, he heard the noise and rushed into the workshop.

"What has happened?"

"I don't know! I don't know!" shouted Rachel.

When Emmy saw Yakov, she began to scream.

"Go outside, Yakov," said Rachel, "let me get Emmy upstairs."

Rachel dragged the hysterical girl upstairs to her room, shoved her into her bed and climbed in alongside.

"You're safe, Emmy. You're safe."

For all the years of progress, Emmy regressed within an hour, and nobody knew what had caused it. Emmy refused to communicate. She simply disappeared into the recesses of her mind.

Eventually, after a significant amount of prayer and much thought, Yakov gave Rachel an instruction.

"Rachel, go and see Mary. We have never spoken to her about Emmy's past."

For once, Rachel didn't argue with Yakov, and the following Sunday, she walked toward the rows of houses close to the cotton mill. The environment was bleak and oppressive. The closer she got to the river, the worse the living conditions became, until she was standing in front of a miserable tenement.

Rachel knocked on Mary's door.

"Rachel, me angel, what are yer doing at me door then, flower?"

Rachel smiled. Mary always made her laugh.

"Make some tea, will you? I made us dumplings last night."

"Aw, thanks ye kindly," said Mary, delighted to have something different to eat to the broth and bread she could hardly afford.

"How are the girls doing then?" asked Mary.

Rachel nodded, "Emmy isn't good," she answered, matter-of-factly.

"Now, Rachel, why are ye here, me lass? Ye have come quite a distance to see me. Pardon me if I seem rude."

"Yes, Mary," grunted Rachel.

Mary laughed at her gruffness.

"Young Emmy had a bad turn yesterday. She was doing so well, but I found her in the workshop she was in a terrible state. What has caused this disease in her Mary? What is this thing that haunts Emmy? We have young men at the Yeshiva who think she will make a fine wife. But Emmy will only speak to Yakov, Tilda and me, nobody else."

Mary looked at Rachel, and she knew that she would need to tell the truth, however difficult that would be.

"It's a terrible story Rachel, I dunna have the strength to repeat it."

"Last night Emmy was hysterical. She kept shouting for her papa to stop. Why these words, Mary?"

Mary didn't answer her at first.

"Why? Tell me. Now!" ordered Rachel, hitting the table so hard that the tea mugs bounced.

"Do you remember how Jimmy Sterling ran around the rows telling everyone how a young lad had got Emmy in the family way?"

Rachel frowned and nodded.

"It was Jimmy. He got her pregnant. She lost her mind during childbirth. I've never seen anybody go through so much such torture, and agony."

Mary remembered Emmy on the bed giving birth. The memory was vivid and disturbing.

"The doctor said that she was so badly damaged, she would never have children. The pain destroyed her mind," cried Mary.

Rachel had no words. All she could do was listen in disbelief.

"The child was a monster," Mary stuttered.

"I cannot talk about it anymore. That's all yer getting out of me."

Rachel didn't utter a word simply because she didn't know what to say.

"Please, Rachel, do not put her in the workhouse, rather bring her back to me. This will bring a terrible shame upon your family."

"Shame? Shame? This is no shame on my family," hissed Rachel furiously.

Mary was startled by Rachel's response.

"Jews do not desert each other when there are problems."

Rachel's temper flared.

"Why didn't they arrest Jimmy Sterling?" she demanded from Mary.

"Emmy was too sick to go to the courts, and she could never tell her story to the judge."

Rachel looked at Mary aghast.

"This is supposed to be a civilised country, and Queen Victoria is said to be a woman of great morality. How can your laws allow this to happen?"

Mary felt sick to her stomach.

"This is how we live. Fathers do this to their daughters all the time. If the girl does not complain, the law sees it as consent."

Rachel loved Mary, but the comment enraged her more.

"No, I'll not return her to this filthy row to be tormented by Jimmy Sterling again. Emmy will never survive the workhouse or the poorhouse, and she will surely murder anybody who touches her in the asylum," stated Rachel.

"We do not put people like Emmy on the street, Mary. What has happened is called incest in our culture. Where is this man? Where is he? Let me see him."

Rachel was filled with righteous fury, and she was ready to cry havoc.

"The Torah says a man who does this to his daughter will be taken to the gates of the city and stoned to death."

Rachel didn't know how to respond to Mary.

"Mary, you are a good woman for offering to look after Emmy, but Emmy is one of us now. We'll look after her. This abuse isn't tolerated in our community, whether the person is Jewish or a goy."

Mary had never met a woman as decisive as Rachel, determined to uphold a moral code, and she didn't need a court to tell her who was guilty. She had her own book of God's law, the Torah.

"Not to worry, Mary, not to worry. Eat the dumplings. Enjoy them with your tea. I'm a difficult old woman, I know, but I love you very much, my friend."

The two women embraced when they said goodbye, both wishing that it could have been a more pleasant visit.

Rachel made it as far as the corner before she began to cry. She looked about her and took in the crowded living quarters, the stench of the streets, and the ragged souls around her. Although her street was cleaner, she also lived in an impoverished area of the city. Rachel wished that she could leave the miserable cold and find a home in a place where the government cared for people, not property. But it was a moot idea. She and Yakov had nowhere to go. She prayed for strength. Hashem would never lead her here without a purpose, and Rachel was convinced that Emmy and Tilda were that purpose.

Rachel found Yakov alone in his workshop, and she fell into his arms.

"Rachel, Rachel, what has happened?" he asked.

"It's difficult to tell you, Yakov. It's too terrible to repeat."

"Come, come, my love. Calm down," Yakov poured her a cup of strong, sweet tea.

"Tell me everything."

"Terrible, terrible things have happened to Emmy. They're so awful that I cannot even tell Rebbetzin. I can never get the words over my lips."

Yakov knew Rachel to be a strong woman, and if she was this upset, the story must have been horrific.

"I need to understand the girl, Rachel. Help me."

Rachel got halfway through the story when Yakov told her to stop.

"No more Rachel, no more, please. I'm not a fighting man, but I would like to kill Jimmy Sterling."

10

A NEW PERSPECTIVE

Manchester held a grim fascination for Tanner. She'd left behind the sheltered life that she was accustomed to and been catapulted into a world that few people of her status would ever experience.

More than ninety-nine per cent of the students at the university were men. Although they were polite, they treated her with disdain. Their opinion was that women should be domesticated and breeding.

Her lodgings were paltry, nothing like the luxury that she was accustomed to. Her room was a dismal combination of greys and browns, the cot was narrow, and the mattress was hard. The blankets and sheets had seen many years and were threadbare.

"Can I provide better living quarters for you, Miss Fischer?" The dean asked her when she arrived ten months ago.

"I'm having sufficient difficulty being accepted here, Sir. I'll live like the other students do. I'm not uncomfortable," Tanner insisted.

When Socrates told Samuel he smiled, it was what her mother would've done at that age.

Tanner walked the streets of Salford and Angel Meadows, observing the working class. She wore the local's dull uniform of grey and brown, and she relished the anonymity.

The locals spoke in a vernacular that Tanner hardly understood. She slowly developed an ear for the common language, and the curse words used by men, women and children alike. This overwhelming mass of struggling humanity was the real England. These people had their own culture, politics, and language. It was as if Tanner was living in a different country.

It was the first time that she would be exposed to politics. Tanner became aware of the inequality of British society. She pored over the newspapers, eager to understand the working class, middle class and upper class, and for the first time, she read the word underclass.

Her professors introduced her to utilitarianism, communism, capitalism, socialism, liberalism, sexism, racism, sectarianism, theology and law. The more that Tanner read, the more she wanted to. She spent hours in the library.

The dean saw Professor Newton sitting in the common room, marking papers.

Professor Newton smiled as the dean approached him.

"Hello, professor," the dean greeted him.

"Good morning."

"I'm glad to see you. I want to discuss Miss Fischer."

"Yes? How can I help?"

"Is her grandfather expecting too much of her?"

"Not at all. Tanner Fischer is working harder than any man in her class," the professor muttered to the dean.

"I'm surprised. I understood her to be very spoilt," replied the dean.

"Yes, yes. I also thought that, yet the girl has surprised me. She's polite, and she is proving herself most capable."

"Her mother is also well educated and highly intelligent. She's a great believer in social reformation. But, Shilling Hudson isn't very popular."

"I didn't know if I must admire this family or run a mile," laughed Professor Newton.

"If you met Samuel Hudson, you would understand why they're so driven," the dean replied.

"Is he an ogre?"

"Not at all. He is a charming man. Self-made, of course, answers to nobody, unperturbed by society and so on."

"Do you think he can be troublesome?" asked the professor.

"Perhaps; he is supportive of his granddaughter, and I believe he has faith that she will become a famous writer one day."

The professor raised his eyebrows.

"Yes, she is going to pursue journalism. It'll be interesting to see who will employ her," said the professor.

"Why have they sent her here? Why not the University of London, or somewhere more reputable?"

"Yes, that is an interesting question considering that she has an impressive pedigree."

"She shows great talent Professor, are you prepared to hone it to perfection?"

The professor smiled.

"It'll be a pleasure to have a student who is as committed as she is."

The dean smiled.

"I'm glad to hear that. I'm sure that we can use this opportunity to our benefit. It'll be a pleasure if her grandparents chose to offer the university donor support. I hope that you are ensuring that she has excellent results," winked the dean.

"Are you suggesting that I show leniency toward her?"

The dean put his head to one side and gave a small smile.

"No, Sir, that is out of the question. I'll not ruin my reputation, and Miss Fischer is quite capable of achieving distinctions without my assistance."

"I'm glad to hear that," the dean said sarcastically, "I would not want to dismiss you on the grounds of poor performance."

The irony wasn't wasted upon Professor Newton.

Tanner sat in a coffee shop reading the daily newspaper. The place was full of students and academics discussing social ills and politics. As her eyes perused the pages, she noticed a small advert, saying that Leonora Mackay would present a speech at the Salford Quays on Saturday. She'd heard of Leonora Mackay, and her colleagues mentioned that Leonora McKay was a powerful orator. Tanner Fischer was a liberal woman, and she admired that Leonora McKay was brave enough to go into the heart of Salford to protest against the government's lackadaisical attitude and negligence of the poor. Tanner made a note in her diary. She would not miss the speech for the world. Tanner was careful not to mention her intentions to the other students. If word reached the dean, he would suspect her of being subversive.

Tanner slipped from the hostel and into the street. It was raining and blowing a gale, her cheeks stung from the cold. By the time she reached the corner, her coat was drenched, and she was ankle-deep in filthy water. Despite the discomfort, Tanner was excited, as only the young and naïve can be on their first illicit adventure. Soon enough, she was absorbed into a steady stream of people squashed together, all on their way to the docks. Tanner glanced at the people around her, men, women and children. They wore hats, flat caps and bonnets. Their scarves and ragged coats were a fruitless attempt to stave off the cold. Irrespective of their poverty, they were a happy lot, made more so by the pints they consumed. There was a sense of camaraderie among them, and for once, Tanner felt that she belonged to something greater than herself.

When they reached the quay, Tanner saw a small podium standing in the middle of a sea of people. As usual, her keen instincts took in the scene. The local urchins pretended to climb up ladders and staircases to get a better view of the proceedings, but in reality, they were identifying drunkards they could pickpocket when the show was over. Bobbies stood in a long line with an air of authority, waiting for the first threat of trouble. The crowd was quiet, eager to hear what the woman would say. There was word on the street that she was organising a strike. There was a stir near the podium, and Tanner saw an entourage pushing their way through the people. Tanner craned her neck to get a better view, but she was too short to see anything through the dense crowd.

Leonora Mackay had no striking features. She was of medium height with brown hair, and she was dressed simply. After climbing onto the podium, raising the cold steel megaphone to her lips, she began to speak. Her voice sounded educated, and she was bold. Leonora showed empathy while she lectured on the necessity for better living conditions, working conditions and public service. The crowd was captivated by her, and there was just the occasional "yeah, yeah" of agreement. Everything was peaceful until she mentioned capitalists and industrialists. It took only one drunk to ruin the atmosphere. For some unknown reason, Jimmy Sterling picked up a stone and threw it at Leonora Mackay. The projectile hit her in the face, and blood streamed from her nose. The police descended upon Jimmy, truncheons in hand. He made a vain attempt to fight the Peelers off when two of his friends stepped in to help him. Within seconds a fight broke loose, and within minutes it developed into a riot. Police officers appeared from everywhere, but it was too late. Thugs began to vandalise properties and loot stores while foul-mouthed urchins cheered them from the high ground. Leonora Mackay stood on the podium, fearing for her life. Her dress was full of blood, and she was terrified, trapped in the eye of a hurricane of hatred. There was nothing that she could do to stop the carnage.

Tanner and many others turned and fled. The crowd was panicked, and she felt the mass of people stampeding from behind. Tanner saw Professor Newton ahead of her and grabbed at his coat, trying to steady herself, but unable to reach it, tumbled to the ground and landed in the dirty water. All she could see were hobnailed boots stomping around her head. People were no longer stepping over her, they were stamping, and she knew that she would surely be crushed. Tanner put her hands over her head to protect herself, but she was being kicked around like a rag doll.

A large boot missed her head by inches, and she knew that it could have crushed her skull. Against all odds, the boot took a step backwards. Tanner looked up and saw the grey sky, and within seconds, strong arms reached down and picked her up.

Tanner was hysterical as the man crushed her to his chest. She remained pinned in that position until he reached the top of the hill, lugging her upwards like a sack of potatoes. Once at the brow, he looked down at the girl in his arms. When she met his eyes, on seeing her beauty, his heart missed a beat. She blushed, shocked by what had happened, and at the sight before her. The man was handsome and intense.

"Is anything broken?" asked the stranger, taking her face in his large hands and inspecting it for wounds.

"I do not think so."

He took her hands and looked at the palms.

"You have scraped your hands. I dare not look at your knees," he laughed.

Tanner blushed again.

"Where do you live?"

"I'm a student at Victoria University."

"I'll walk with you," said the man.

"I'll be fine. Thank you."

"I'm going that way."

Tanner reached her hostel.

"Thank you, very much. You saved my life."

He nodded. "What's your name?"

"Tanner Fischer," she replied.

"I'm Sean Carlyle."

They didn't speak again until they reached the campus.

"I'm glad I met you," he smiled.

"I must go," said Tanner, embarrassed by what
had happened.

After turning around to run up the stairs, she surprised
herself by turning to wave before disappearing behind the
door.

Professor Newton saw Tanner sitting at the far end of the
library. He was almost sure that he saw Tanner at the
Salford Quays, and he was in two minds whether to
approach her about it. He sauntered toward her casually.
Tanner was too engrossed in her reading to notice anyone
around her.

'Leonora Mackay Speech Incites Violence' was the headline emblazoned across the daily newspaper. Had Tanner not been there, she would've believed the lie. She was incensed that a publication entrusted to report the truth was misrepresenting the facts.

"Good morning, Miss Fischer," said Professor Newton nonchalantly.

"Good morning, professor," answered Tanner, distracted.

"Ah, you are reading about the debacle down at the dockyards."

Tanner nodded.

"It ended very badly," said Professor Newton.

Her intense green eyes flashed.

"This isn't what happened," she said, pointing to the article.

"How so?"

"Leonora Mackay didn't incite violence. A drunk started throwing stones."

"Who told you that?" asked the professor.

"I was there. I know what I saw."

"You were there? Why on earth would you take yourself off to such an event?"

"Everybody has a voice Professor, and I like to hear what other people wish to say."

"For what it's worth, I agree with you. I was there as well."

But Tanner knew that anyway.

"What would be the next step in correcting this misinterpretation of events?" she asked him.

"Well," he paused, "you start by writing and publishing the truth."

"How would I do that?"

It was the question that Professor Newton was waiting for.

"First, if we are going to be friends, call me Harry."

Tanner smiled at him.

"You'll need to write an article and get it published here in Manchester."

"How will I get it published?"

"First write the article, then we will find a publisher," he smiled down at her.

"Thank you, Harry."

Even Tanner believed that she'd written a masterpiece. Harry Newton read the article slowly, then sat back and looked at the lovely girl. Instinctively, he knew that this was the article that would launch her career.

Professor Harry Newton read Tanner's article twice.

"How long did it take you to write this?" he asked.

"A few hours," replied Tanner.

"A piece of work like this, I would imagine you were up all night perfecting it."

"The introduction was tricky. Reporting the facts is easy."

"Which newspaper are you taking this to? I imagine that your family has contacts who can help you."

"I'll do this by myself," she sounded annoyed.

"I apologise, Tanner."

She nodded.

"I'm taking it to the Manchester Herald."

"What?" gasped Harry, "it's the most liberal rag in the city."

"I realise that, Harry. I've decided that the comfortable conservatives need to hear the facts from the only newspaper brave enough to print them."

Harry's eyes scanned the article again.

"I cannot fault this writing, Tanner."

"Thank you, Harry. I'll hand-deliver the article myself."

"When will that be?"

"This afternoon."

Tanner ran up the steps, eager to get out of the rain. She pushed open the front door to the Manchester Herald and tumbled into a crowded foyer.

"I would like to speak to the editor," said Tanner.

"Only the sub is available." said the thin little man, peering over his delicate gold-framed spectacles.

"He will do," Tanner replied, matter-of-factly.

The thin man had met people like her before. He could see that she was uninclined to leave without a fight, so he decided to spare himself the aggravation of arguing with her.

"Follow me," he ordered.

She fell in behind him, and he led her to a door which led onto a mezzanine. From the mezzanine, she could see over the massive press.

Next to the rail was an office with glass windows around it.

"He will be here in a minute," said the man.

"Sit there and wait," he ordered in an unfriendly manner.

"Thank you," she smiled at him.

Fifteen minutes later, a man appeared, reading and walking simultaneously. It amazed Tanner that he didn't fall over the rail. The tall, blonde good-looking man was Sean Carlyle. He looked her up and down, and then smiled.

"Fancy that!" he smiled.

"You have found me."

"On no," she muttered, embarrassed.

He laughed. "Do not be embarrassed. Why are you here?"

"Well, I've an article I want you to read."

"Sit down, would you like tea?" asked Sean as he pushed things around his desk and tried to make space.

Tanner took the typewritten article out of her bag and put it down in front of him.

"What is it?"

"The truth."

"Your truth or the facts?"

"What?"

"We all have a subjective view of the truth. What's your name again?"

"Tanner Fischer."

"Oh, of course, yes."

Tanner nodded.

"Why are you so well dressed today?"

"What?" asked Tanner, confused by the sudden change of subject.

"You look far better than you did on Saturday."

"Yes, that wasn't my finest moment."

"Right then, here is the tea," he smiled and walked toward the tray.

Tanner couldn't bear the suspense any longer.

"Stop! I'll pour the tea, you read the article," Tanner ordered.

Sean seemed oblivious to her assertiveness, and Tanner picked up the teapot and began pouring it into the mismatched cups and saucers.

"Have you ever been published before?"

"No? Is it important that I have?"

"No, not at all," he replied, with a broad grin on his face.

She looked at him quizzically.

"How old are you?"

"Twenty-two?"

"You can start Monday week."

"I didn't come here looking for work."

"I know, but you are good, and you will learn more about journalism here than you will learn in five years at Victoria."

"Are you sure that you are making the correct decision?"

"I think I'm capable of making the decision, and I fell over you for a reason, Tanner Fischer."

"Is it because of who I am, my family?"

"You seem to think very little of yourself, do you not?"

"This is all happening rather fast, Mr Carlyle."

"Yes, in this business, you have to make quick decisions."

"I'd like you to meet the owner of the newspaper, Mr Keith Downs. Wait here," he ordered.

Sean disappeared for a few minutes and came back with a short man of almost seventy. Keith Downs had sparkling blue eyes, a ready smile. He behaved like a gentleman, as opposed to Sean, who gave the impression of being a likeable rogue. Mr Downs shook Tanner's hand.

"I'm getting too old for this job," smiled Mr Downs.

"I've a weak heart, and my wife has told me that I should retire."

Tanner nodded.

"I'm not ready to die yet," he laughed.

"I've no experience. Where will I begin? I don't know if I'll be good enough," said Tanner.

"Of course, you are. There is nothing that I do that you cannot master."

His eyes sparkled.

"Why me?"

"Sean says that with the right mentorship, you will be a brilliant asset to our newspaper."

Tanner paced the office. She decided to be brave.

"Alright," she smiled at last, "I'll see you next Monday."

11

THE ARTICLE

Socrates put the Manchester Herald on Samuel's desk.

"There is an interesting article on the front page, Sir."

"Where did you find the Manchester Herald?" asked Samuel, looking at the date on it.

"It was hand-delivered this morning."

"Who sent it?" asked Samuel, looking over his spectacles.

"Tanner."

Samuel raised an eyebrow.

"Tanner? Oh, dear God! I hope she has not got herself into trouble and found herself in the newspaper."

Samuel unfolded the newspaper and stared at page one. A headline blazed across the front page.

"Injustice Served on Leonora Mackay." The article went on to describe the events at the Salford quay.

"About bloody time that someone spoke up for Leonora McKay. This is a surprisingly liberal article. It'll rattle some conservative feathers."

"Yes, Sir," smiled Socrates. "The Manchester Herald seems to have appointed a new journalist."

Samuel went back to the headline and read the reporter's name. Bold as brass, it read: Tanner Fischer.

Samuel laughed loudly.

"That's our girl, Socrates, that's our girl. I knew that she would do us proud."

Socrates couldn't contain his delight and laughed with Samuel.

"Indeed, Sir, but you may have to steel yourself. It's accompanied by a letter," Socrates said as he handed the note over.

Samuel was filled with trepidation. What if she was in trouble with the law?

Samuel opened the letter like there was a snake inside, ready to bite him. He read it and smiled.

Dear Grandpa.

I've decided to leave Victoria University. I believe that I've learned everything I can. I'm now employed at the Manchester Herald. I'm being mentored by Mr Sean Carlyle and Mr Keith Downs.

I love you. Please do not be furious with me.

Tanner.

Samuel didn't hide his delight.

"Pour us a drink, Socrates."

"You do not drink, Sir."

"Today, we celebrate."

Samuel couldn't suppress his pride.

"Yes, Sir."

"She's just like Shilling," laughed Samuel.

"Yes," laughed Socrates, "and her grandfather."

Samuel took a mouthful of the liquid and cast the glass aside.

"Why do I do this? It tastes so bloody horrid."

"Please fetch Miss Anabelle, Socrates. I must tell her the good news."

Shilling also received a letter, accompanied by the article from Tanner. Shilling was packing for a trip to Germany. She smiled when she read it, determined to take Samuel's advice, and allow her Tanner to plot her course to happiness. She was impressed that Tanner dared to confront the opinion that Leonora Mackay was a subversive element. Shilling sent a telegram: 'Congratulations, I love you.'

Shilling had walked the streets of London, witnessing the squalor of the rows. The Hudson family was widely criticised for their political opinions. Shilling was confident that Tanner had walked the streets of Manchester and seen the horrors first-hand. Leonora Mackay was a controversial figure who promoted the only sensible economic and political solution to raise the poor from their misery. For this, she was deemed a rabble-rouser.

"I've taken your advice, Papa," Shilling announced at the dinner table.

She was taking advantage of the fact that Miss Anabelle was there. It'd soften the blow and pour oil on troubled waters.

Samuel sat at the head of the dining-room table. He wore his regular uniform; no tie, shirt sleeves rolled up to his elbows and his shirt hanging over his pants. Miss Anabelle looked serene in a white dress, and Shilling wore a simple black skirt, and a white blouse.

"Aha!" laughed Samuel.

"At last."

"Papa, I'm going to Germany to meet Mr Benz. I predict that he is going to manufacture the first Motor Wagens for resale."

"Yes, Socrates, and I want one of those when they become available," said Samuel.

Socrates smiled and nodded.

"The bloody public is in a furore over these Motor Wagens. Some say that the speed will cause internal bleeding. Others say that it's from the devil himself."

Samuel shook his head.

"It's the same thing they said about the steam locomotive, Papa. It's a storm in a teacup."

"When are you leaving?"

"In two days."

"Did you consider taking Tanner with you? She can write an article on it."

"I did Papa, but she is engrossed in her work. She turned down the invitation."

"How can you go alone?"

"Papa, I'm a grown woman, but no, I'm not going by myself. Baxter Lee is escorting me."

Samuel threw down his knife and fork, and they clattered onto the plate, making a tremendous noise.

Socrates looked at Miss Anabelle.

"I knew it was too good to be true. I knew it!" exclaimed Samuel at the top of his voice.

"We have had this discussion, Samuel. I'll leave your table if you refuse to calm down," said Miss Anabelle fiercely and stood up.

Socrates and Shilling were aghast. They seldom saw Anabelle being so assertive. She was always the gentle, level-headed soul in the house.

"This is the last time that you criticise Shilling on her choices. This has gone on far too long. Every time that you have an outburst, you promise never to do it again."

Samuel wilted under his wife's ferocious stare, and he was ashamed of himself. For Anabelle to correct him publicly meant that she was truly furious. Samuel stood up and looked at Anabelle, he didn't like ultimatums in his business life or private life.

Shilling and Socrates looked at each other, anticipating, waiting for Samuel's temper to get the better of him.

Instead, he got up and went to Anabelle.

"I'm sorry, Annabelle. I'll never do anything to make you leave our table or our home," he told her, loud enough for everyone in the room to hear. Then he reached out and took Anabelle in his arms.

"—or our bed," he whispered in her ear.

"I'm sorry, Shilling, you have the right to live your own life, Baxter is no longer a married man, and you are no longer a girl."

Then he turned to Shilling and Socrates.

"I apologise for the way I've treated Anabelle, and I'm ashamed of my behaviour in front of you."

Samuel looked at Socrates.

"Socrates, I believe that the time has come to forgive Baxter Lee. You and I'll end our vendetta against him today."

"Yes, Sir."

Shilling studied her father, and she got tears in her eyes. He was ashamed of himself, and his apology was humble and sincere.

Shilling smiled at him and nodded through the tears.

"Thank you, Papa."

Miss Anabelle walked to his side and looked up at him.

"I love you, my darling," she said with adoration in her eyes.

Samuel kissed her on her mouth.

"I love you. Anabelle." Samuel put his arms around her and didn't let go.

Shilling and Socrates knew to leave. It was a private moment between Samuel and Anabelle.

12

ANOTHER CHANCE

Shilling and Baxter took the ferry to Calais, and in Paris, they boarded a train for Germany. They had known each other long enough to be comfortable in each other's company. Mostly, they remained in their separate compartments and only met for meals.

Baxter was reluctant to spend time with Shilling. He was still in love with her, and the more he watched her, the more it hurt him. Baxter was surprised when Shilling asked him to accompany her to Mannheim. He watched her over dinner, noting her green eyes still flashed the same intense colour as the pendant at her throat, the striking scar down the side of her face still reflecting her bravery.

Baxter observed that Shilling had changed physically. She no longer had the soft curves of youth, her features were more defined, and her body was taut. It seemed like the loss she suffered when Benjamin Fischer died had chiselled the heartbreak onto her face. She was still stunning, but nowadays, utterly disconsolate.

It had taken many years for Shilling to become comfortable in Baxter's presence. She'd spent many tortured days and nights longing for him. She remembered the pain of denying him at the hotel in Manchester. She mourned losing Baxter almost as much as she mourned Benjamin, but she dared not tell anybody. Baxter was still a very handsome man, but he was serious. Gone was the playful young man she'd known. Years of guilt had taken their toll on him. She looked at his mouth that had kissed her, his hands that had explored her body and his chest that crushed against hers. He was her first lover, and she still had a deep yearning for him.

"How many days will we be with Mr Benz?" asked Baxter.

"He has put two days aside for us. He is a busy man."

"I believe that Mannheim is a stunning city."

"Yes, clean compared to London and Manchester, or so I hear."

"Yet, you have booked us into a hotel for two weeks."

Shilling nodded.

"Yes, to tell the truth, my father is right. I need a break from grubby old England."

Mr Benz was a gentleman. Shilling had not known what to expect, but he was polite and forthright. Beneath the stoic German façade lay a warm, welcoming personality. Shilling had written to him and explained that she wasn't looking to manufacture a Motor Wegen but was interested in supplying components. Mr Benz assured her that there were enough artisans in Germany to do that, but he would be happy to demonstrate how his patent worked. The Benz family were intrepid explorers of all things mechanical, and Mr Benz gave her a guided tour of the factory and introduced her to the owners.

Shilling absorbed every engineering detail, and she was impressed by the skill of the German artisans. The factories were immaculate, and they took pride in what they did. By the end of the second day, she and Baxter agreed that they'd seen everything that they could. Shilling was relieved that the work was over, and she could begin her vacation.

Shilling booked them into a typical small German inn. There was nothing lavish about it, but it was cosy, as the name 'Schnoekelhof' suggested. The inn stood in the same cobbled street as the cathedral, and there was a constant stream of young people walking through the university town. They added energy and vitality to the city, there was laughter, and when one passed a coffee shop, there was the sound of vigorous debating.

Broad black beams held up the hotel, and the roof was thatched. The ceilings were low, and Baxter had to stoop in certain places. The staircase was narrow, and there was no lift, so Shilling had to carry her luggage to the second floor. There was only a bed in her room, and the ceiling sloped under the eaves. A small leaded window looked onto a courtyard, and someone had planted flowers along the edge of the cobbles. There was a communal bathtub that everybody shared. Shilling couldn't have felt more at home. There was a simplicity about the room which cleared her mind, and for once, she began to think of things non-work-related.

There was no room service, so if guests were hungry or thirsty, they'd go to the dining room for refreshments. Beer was stacked on the shelves behind the black wooden bar, and everybody in the small pub had a large glass in front of them. Shilling soon realised that this wasn't the place to order a cup of tea.

It was spring, and the wildflowers were beginning to blossom all along the picturesque rhine valley. Long barges navigated the sparklingly clean river, as small boys fished on the banks.

"Do you like it?" asked Baxter.

Shilling nodded and smiled broadly. Baxter had not seen that much joy in her smile for a long time.

"I like the hotel as well," she laughed.

"What is so appealing about it?" asked Baxter.

"I'm anonymous."

Shilling and Baxter spent their days walking through the old city, visiting museums and churches. Shilling enjoyed walking along the Rhine. She looked up at the hills and saw the turrets and towers of the splendid castles, built for kings of times gone by. The water was calming, and Germany was unusually warm for early spring.

As they walked, Baxter dared to take her hand. She didn't pull it away but allowed it to rest in his. They walked through the town and stopped at a small coffee house, where they ate pastries and drank coffee. They hardly spoke to each other, and each was absorbed in their own thoughts.

It was the first time a man had touched Shilling since Benjamin died. It was a delight to connect with another human, but she was filled with guilt. She could hardly remember Benjamin's face anymore, or Kate's, yet still they haunted her.

They left the coffee shop and walked down the cobbled street where the great cathedral stood. Stops were made at bookstore, a chocolatier, and then, an antique shop. Finally, they returned to the small inn. The twilight reflected soft pink light, and the lane was devoid of raucous youths.

Shilling and Baxter climbed the two flights of rickety stairs, and they lingered outside her hotel room door.

"May I come in?" Baxter asked her.

Shilling took a deep breath.

"I don't know if it'll be the same as it was before."

"I hope it's not," he answered. "This time, I'll not leave."

Shilling unlocked the door and stepped inside. Baxter followed. Once the heavy wooden door was closed behind him, he stepped toward her and looked into her eyes.

"Oh, God, I've missed you," he whispered.

Shilling showed no emotion and remained silent. She removed his coat, then his jacket and finally his tie. She unbuttoned his shirt slowly. He was still beautiful. He took her in his arms and kissed her softly, then he began to undress Shilling. She stood naked in front of him, her hair cascading down her back. He couldn't read her green eyes. Baxter knew that he was home, but he would never be free. This woman would be a part of his soul until he died.

They made love slowly and quietly. Afterwards, they lay in one another's arms. Both were sad for what had been, and afraid of what was to come.

13

TERROR FROM THE PAST

Emmy refused to go downstairs into the watchmaker's shop. She didn't speak, and she'd regressed into her world. Rachel, Yakov and Tilda didn't change how they treated her. They hoped that Emmy would recover if she was exposed to the familiar. Emmy began to fix clocks again, this time at the kitchen table. She would sit there for hours and do her work, refusing to leave the cramped flat. Where previously she'd accompanied Rachel and Yakov to the synagogue on a Friday night, she now screamed blue murder if they tried to take her anywhere near the staircase. Lately, Tilda looked after Emmy when Rachel and Yakov needed to go anywhere.

Emmy seemed to delight in teaching Tilda how to understand the workings of the delicate timepieces, and very soon, Tilda found herself as engrossed in the work as Emmy was. Emmy began to recover and communicate, but nothing could convince or lure her down the steps into the shop.

"Rachel, our children, have their own lives. They're successful. They do not want to live here

and run the shop. If we die, Hashem forbid, let us
will it to Emmy and Tilda."

Rachel didn't have to think twice. She agreed immediately.
They wrote out a will together and put it into the kitchen
drawer.

"Tilda has a good head on her shoulders, and she
has done well at school," said Rachel.

"Yes," agreed Yakov. "I'll teach her how to keep
the ledgers and do the bookkeeping."

With the matter settled, Rachel went back to her daily tasks,
and Yakov went to tell Tilda the good news.

Jimmy Sterling stepped onto a pavement covered with soot.
After The Manchester Herald published Tanner's article,
Jimmy was arrested for assaulting Leonora Mackay. It was
a coup for Tanner. It was her first experience of the power
of the press—Jimmy was sentenced to six months in gaol.

"You're lucky yer didn't kill the woman Jimmy,
next time ye will not get off so easy. Get out of
here, and remember that we are watching you,"
said Constable Richards.

Jimmy didn't dare to say what he was thinking. His opinions
contained far too many expletives.

Once again, Jimmy ambled around Salford and Angel
Meadows, feeling sorry for himself, leeching off old friends
and begging. He believed that life had done him wrong,
people had done him wrong, and his misery was due to
everyone else and no fault of his own. His successful

daughters had deserted him in his hour of need. He visited his old haunts with a sense of entitlement, hoping to celebrate like a hero. Nobody was interested in Jimmy Sterling, and nobody offered him a pint in celebration of his freedom. Jimmy was a pariah in the community which was quite an achievement in a society fraught with criminals. Jimmy was sober for the first time in years, and the horrors of the past haunted him. He'd all but lost his mind, and the warped senses that he still retained convinced him to return to Yakov's shop. He remembered that it was Friday and realised that Yakov and Rachel would leave for the synagogue before sundown.

This time, he went into the little shop. He would not say a word but would stuff something into Emmy's mouth, take as much loot as he could fit in his pockets and run. Jimmy watched Rachel and Yakov leave for the synagogue. He gave sufficient time to ensure that they were well away, and then he went to the shop door and opened it. Nothing had changed. The same bright light spilt onto the dark pavement. The aroma of wax furniture polish filled the air. This time, a young woman stood behind the counter, polishing a gold fob watch for a customer and having a friendly chat. She looked magnificent, with a fair complexion and gentle blue eyes.

"It was a minor problem, Mr Clarke, no damage done, just a small jewel out of place."

"Thank you, Tilda," smiled Mr Clarke, thinking that Yakov had made the right decision when he chose to employ Emmy and Tilda.

Weighing up the situation, Jimmy couldn't believe that the beautiful girl was his own daughter. Tilda looked at the dishevelled man behind Mr Clarke and smiled. Yakov taught her to treat all customers with courtesy, and many times the worst looking people surprised her by purchasing something. 'You can never tell a book by its cover,' Yakov would tell them.

"May I show you something, Sir?" she asked in a professional voice.

"Hmm, yes, I guess so, sweetie."

Tilda was on her guard. There was something familiar about the words, and the lilt in his voice. She couldn't place it, but it sent shivers down her spine.

Jimmy turned his back to her and randomly chose a cabinet to search.

"This one—" he pointed to a modern gold wristwatch.

Tilda stepped past him, opened the cabinet and picked it up to show him.

As he took it from her, he brushed his dirty hands and blackened fingernails against hers.

She pulled from him.

"Now, now, no need for that now, is there?"

"Who are you?"

"Would not you like to know, you little snoot?"

She took a step back. Tilda was at a loss. The face was haggard and leathery from being exposed to the elements.

Then he laughed and spoke in a soothing tone.

"Hello, Tilda, me little one."

Tilda was dumb with horror as her unconscious mind identified the owner of the voice.

Jimmy touched Tilda's shoulder, but she shrugged it off and moved back until she felt a cabinet behind her; she was trapped. He stepped forward and squeezed her bosom. Jimmy was close, whispering horrible things in her ear, telling her what he wanted to do to her. Tilda still remembered what he'd done to Emmy, and she was terrified. She screamed, hoping that Mr Sutton next door would hear her desperate cry for help. Tilda twisted out of his grasp and turned to flee. She stopped dead. She remembered that Emmy was in the kitchen. Tilda didn't dare lure him upstairs; Emmy's fragile mind would never survive a second attack.

Jimmy took advantage of the pause and grabbed Tilda from behind and pushed her to the floor. He put his mud-encrusted boot on her head and began to unbutton his pants.

"How dare you run away from me?" he growled.
"I'm yer Da, and I'll show you who the boss is. I'll
show ye what to expect from a real man."

Jimmy loved watching Tilda squirm underneath his boot, and he pushed it down with such force that Tilda thought that he would break her neck. Her skirt lifted, and he could see her legs. He wanted her to suffer just a little more, beg him to stop. He was so engrossed in his depraved thoughts that he didn't hear someone coming down the stairs.

Emmy heard Tilda scream, and it mobilised her to action. Her fear for her sister was greater than her fear for herself, and she slowly descended the stairs. She caught sight of Tilda on the floor, the man's filthy boot on her pale skin, and her dress almost around her waist. Embeth Sterling recognised the attacker immediately. Da!

"Ah!" exclaimed Jimmy in a sick voice. "Two daughters in one day. How lucky can a father be?"

Emmy edged towards the counter and picked up a large wooden clock. Jimmy was taken off guard by her slow movements. Jimmy was convinced that Emmy was going to bribe him to leave. He would take the clock when he was finished with Tilda.

Emmy lifted the clock towards him as if she were handing him a gift. But, instead of her giving it to him, she lifted it above her head as a confused Jimmy looked on.

"What are you doing, Embeth?"

With unbelievable force, Emmy brought the clock down upon his head. Jimmy groaned and fell to his knees. Blood was dripping from a large gash on his head. He was still conscious, but his battered brain was confused. Then Emmy lifted the clock again and brought the heavy wooden case down upon Jimmy's head for a second time, then a third, then a fourth, until Jimmy Sterling's skull was shattered. An unrecognisable man lay awash in blood.

Unaware of the dark turn of events, chatting and chuckling together, Yakov and Rachel opened the shop door. Their happiness turned to horror when they saw the gore splattered all over their premises. Tilda was paralysed with fear, sobbing in a corner, and Emmy was sitting in the workshop piecing together the blood-drenched clock. Emmy looked serene as she fixed the broken instrument, with the utmost care and tenderness.

Within minutes there was pandemonium. The neighbours heard Tilda's screams and came to help. The bobby who was patrolling the street ran to the crowd. It was his duty to keep peace on his beat. People pushed their noses up against the glass to get a good look at the corpse so that they would be the first to tell the 'real' story.

Rachel and Yakov were devastated that Emmy was arrested and put into the local gaol cells.

"She would never harm anybody unless they threatened her," argued Yakov.

"That is for the judge to decide," answered the investigator.

Looking around him, he thought that Yakov had lost his mind. It was one of the most gruesome murder scenes he'd witnessed.

Three days later, Emmy appeared before the judge. She was a model prisoner, and the policemen couldn't conceive that this meek soul could have caused so much damage. The police knew all about Jimmy Sterling. They'd always known that one day he would suffer someone's wrath, but they didn't expect the person to be his daughter.

Yakov and Rachel were beside themselves with worry. News travelled quickly, and people began to walk past the small shop, pointing through the windows, hoping to get a glimpse of the scene where the grisly murder had taken place. Eventually, Yakov had to pull down the blinds to have privacy.

"An eye for an eye, Yakov," said the Rabbi.

"It's murder."

"You know what they say, Yakov," said the Rabbi, "even a broken clock is right twice a day."

Yakov laughed wryly.

"From what you have told me, the man was a monster. I'm surprised he didn't hang a long time ago. Some courts would've sentenced him to death under the circumstances."

"But Rabbi, most of those countries are in the Middle East."

"That does not make them wrong, Yakov."

"I fear for Emmy, Rabbi. She's of sound mind—just different. How can she ever testify in her defence and convince the judge of her innocence if she refuses to speak?"

"I don't know the answer, Yakov, but there are many witnesses to how he treated Emmy."

"Yes, there are, but we need to keep Emmy out of an asylum. The girl isn't mad, Rabbi. With love and kindness, she can have a good life."

"Well, then that is what we will pray for. That Emmy can show that she is sane."

"Then we are praying for a miracle," answered Yakov dismally.

"If you are losing faith, Yakov, go back to the Tanakh. It's full of miracles."

14

THE DECISION

"Call Tanner," Sean Carlyle instructed his secretary. "And, tell her it's urgent."

Sean's long-suffering assistant gave a tired nod and made his way to the room where the journalists sat.

"Tanner!" he called.

She spun around.

"The boss is looking for you."

Tanner knocked on the door and let herself into the cramped glass cubicle the editor, Sean Carlyle, called an office.

"You called for me," she smiled.

Every time Sean looked at her face, he admired her dazzling eyes and broad smile.

"There is an interesting case in Salford. A young woman beat her father to death with a clock."

Tanner looked at him wide-eyed.

"You're coming with me."

"Why me?"

"I need a woman to write the article."

"Why?" Tanner smiled.

"I need a liberal approach. We have woman readers as well."

"And if the other journalists complain?"

"Tell them to come and see me."

Sean smiled and watched her walk away. It wasn't only her smile and eyes he admired. She'd delightful curves, a head of wild raven hair, and a sharp mind.

Sean didn't hear Keith Downs come into the office.

"Ah!" exclaimed Mr Downs, "I've caught you in the act of daydreaming about the lovely Miss Fischer."

Sean smirked. "Was it that obvious?"

"I notice that Tanner is smiling from ear to ear. What have you done? Did you give her a promotion or an increase?" prodded Keith.

"Neither," Sean laughed. "She's helping me with the Embeth Sterling case. You know, the girl who beat her father to death with the clock."

"Do you think she is up to it?" asked Keith.

"Of course, she is."

"The details are shocking, Sean, and she is young and inexperienced. How will she cope with it? You must consider this before you throw her to the lions."

"That is why I've chosen her. I want an unbiased report. I want the horror of any injustice to resonate throughout the article. I do not want this article construed as a regular working-class spat. There is a truth lurking behind this terrible story, and we need to expose it."

"Yes, I can understand that."

"Tanner Fischer has surprised me. I was convinced she could do the job when I employed her, and I followed my instincts. She's outshining the other reporters, and they're all a bit glum. She has a passion that we seldom see in this business, Keith. I think that we have chosen a winner."

"Yes, we have a lazy bunch of bloody reporters here. Tell them to get their arses out of the office and onto the streets, Sean. We need something to publish for the morning."

Sean Carlyle grabbed his coat and hat off the peg and rushed toward the door. He flew down the steps and sidestepped his secretary who was desperate to speak to him. Sean walked into the newsroom and looked around for Tanner.

"Tanner," he shouted above the din. "Come on, get on with it. We need to get to court early if we want a seat in the press gallery."

The other reporters looked at him, annoyed by what they considered favouritism.

"What are you all looking at?" shouted Sean.

There were a few sniggers.

"Well, chief, she is a good looking girl like, and she is getting special treatment," Sean couldn't fault Danny Hodges for being honest.

"Yeah, and she comes from a rich family," shouted Davy Hawkins.

"And she can outwork you all," laughed Sean.

The reporters expected Sean to defend himself. They didn't expect him to laugh at them. Besides, what he said about Tanner was true.

A large group gathered around the law courts in Ducie Street. Sean grabbed Tanner's hand and pulled her through the dense mob. For a moment, Sean felt as if he was in the middle of a bloodthirsty medieval horde, because they were surrounded by people of all classes pushing and shoving to get to the front to better view the murderess.

Sean had seen it all before, and he predicted that the mass would scream for her execution the moment she stepped out of the police wagon. Toothless, ragged, uneducated people surrounded him. Watching the scene in the courtroom was the only entertainment they could get for free.

A hush fell over the crowd when Emmy climbed from the wagon. The onlookers expected to see an unkempt, drunken woman being hauled into court. The accused usually made a scene, screaming and shouting, fuelling the hysteria, yet this time, it was different; Emmy wasn't your typical criminal.

Emmy's hair was clean and brushed. She'd wide innocent eyes and was young, way younger than the public anticipated. She was a mild disappointment, and some of the people on the edges of the crowd began to leave.

There was one seat left in the gallery, so Sean stood behind Tanner. Tanner studied the people below, trying to gauge the mood in the courtroom. Sean recognised some of the spectators, and he pointed out barristers and bailiffs whom he knew.

"They're quite generous with information, as long as you do not publish it."

Rachel and Yakov sat behind Emmy. Rachel was tearful, and she repeatedly wiped her eyes and nose on a handkerchief while Yakov was dignified. Many orthodox Jews were there to support the Weiners, which added insult to injury as not many people liked them.

"Bloody Christ killers should be thrown out of the country," Tanner heard somebody say.

"Any more of that, and I'll remove you from the courtroom," said a policeman.

Tanner couldn't stop staring at Emmy.

"What could have made this girl kill her father? She was brutal in her execution".

"It's our job to expose the truth, Tanner. That is why we are here. That is why we are journalists."

"I feel that she is so young and innocent."

"We are not here to feel; we are here to tell the story. Sometimes there is way more to the story than meets the eye, and we need to dig out those details. If you believe that there is a good motive for her actions, follow your instincts and pursue the investigation. I'll support you every step of the way but be aware, there will be challenges."

The judge didn't waste his time. He announced that as per the police report, Emmy was incapable of speaking. She was considered dangerous and was to be incarcerated at the lunatic asylum until such time that she decided to divulge her story. She would be isolated from the other patients and put in a separate cell until the court decided whether she should live or die. Certain onlookers cheered, but the Jewish community had nothing to celebrate.

"I thought that it would take longer," said Tanner.

"This is a complicated situation, and it'll warrant serious investigation."

"How so?"

"She's a respectable young woman. The court needs time to investigate the circumstances that drove her to this."

Yakov, Rachel and Tilda gave a collective sigh of relief. For now, Emmy was as safe as she could be.

Sean and Tanner found a tea shop. It was snowing, and for a few hours, the white powder would hide the soot covering the streets and buildings. It was almost as if the city was pretending to be clean, by dressing in a new set of clothes. The tea shop was clean and cosy, which was a surprise, and there was the smell of fresh bread, which they would lather with butter and honey. For a moment, life felt normal; until they began to discuss the trial.

"I'm not sure that this is the correct assignment for you," said Sean.

"What? Why?" she exclaimed loudly.

"I do not think that you are ready to write this story."

"You can't stop me now," she retaliated furiously.

Sean shook his head. He felt he'd made a terrible decision by asking Tanner to report on such a disturbing story. He was struggling with his conscience, terrified that Tanner would be subjected to the awful details of the crime.

Sean took her hand across the table.

"You know that I care about you, trust me, Tanner, trust me."

She looked at him with cool, green eyes.

"How can I trust you if you go back on your word?" she demanded.

"I've been thinking about it. I can't expose you to this horrific story. My instincts tell me that terrible things happened to that girl."

She pushed the food and tea away from her.

Tanner's mind drifted away for a moment. "You know that I care for you," he said.

"The other reporters will think that I'm a weak woman."

"You have plenty of time to prove them wrong."

"Why are you doing this to me?"

"I want to protect you."

"You sound like my grandfather, Samuel."

"I like him already," Sean said, trying to lighten the conversation.

Tanner didn't laugh.

Tanner shook her head. "Sean, I can either face the world with you next to me, or I can go and work somewhere else and face it alone."

"What do you know about the streets, Tanner? You come from an upper-class family. What do you know about the working class and how they live?"

"I've walked the streets of Salford and Angel Meadows since I lived here. I've seen enough to know the appalling conditions they live under."

"And do you think that is enough?"

"I've also followed the progress of women like Leonora MacKay, who are trying to change this God-forsaken hole. I understand how unpopular it is to speak on behalf of the poor and starving. Leonora MacKay is the daughter of Karl MacKay, whose political ideology has made him unacceptable to Whitehall."

"Politics is a man's world."

"My mother is Shilling Hudson Fischer, and she affected change by refusing to accept the ancient philosophies of the Parliament. She has taken a stand against the upper class political and social bullies. She was young and passionate, and I'll follow in her footsteps. This will be our family legacy. My mother never kowtowed to the government, and today, she is a powerful industrialist with loyal staff. My grandfather was as poor as a church mouse and worked himself out of the pit he was born in. I'll not be any

different. I'm privileged. I'm under great pressure
to prove my worth, and I will."

Sean listened to her impassioned speech. This girl was proud of her heritage, and her family had worked hard to reach their goals without standing on the shoulders of other men to achieve them. Yet, she would be witnessing a different aspect of life in the court of law.

"What do you know about rape, sodomy and
incest?" he whispered harshly.

Tanner was taken aback by the question, unsure of how best to respond.

"So, this is your way of keeping me pure?" Tanner
retaliated.

"I think so," he said, without smiling.

"Well, do not! This is my job, or should I pursue a
life of writing obituaries?"

"Obituaries can be oodles of fun," he added,
trying to make her laugh but failing.

He took a different tack.

"This job exposes you to the worst of humankind,
Tanner."

"I know."

"I do not think you do. Be that as it may, you will
argue this matter to the bitter end, and annoy me
way more than you already have."

"May I continue with the story?"

"Against my better judgement."

Keith Downs was at his favourite club, reclining comfortably in a chair close to the fire. It was routine for him to have dinner at his club, and then stroll back to the office and spend an hour or so with Sean. Since he employed Sean as editor-in-chief, he could relax. Sean was a commanding character whom the staff respected. He had powerful instincts for when to follow or discard a thread. He was liberal, hounding, and fearless. Keith couldn't have chosen a better editor.

Keith spotted Sean in the doorway and waved to attract his attention.

"Good afternoon," said Keith. "Sit down," he pointed to the chair opposite him. "How was your morning in court?"

"Unsettling," Sean said moodily.

"Yes? How so?"

"The accused is a beautiful young woman, not a toothless wonder as is usually the case."

Keith sighed. "The job still gets to you, doesn't it?"

Sean nodded slowly. "The court has put Embeth Sterling into an asylum until she decides to speak. If not, she will hang for murder."

"Do you really think that she will hang for the crime?" asked Keith.

"I don't know Keith. I don't know."

"How is Tanner?"

"She was fine. I don't know how she will react when she listens to Embeth Sterling's testimony, though."

"You're keeping her on the story? God forbid that Embeth Sterling is sentenced to death. Even seasoned reporters struggle with executions, and if she has to report on the court proceedings, the public will expect her to report on the execution as well."

"Almighty God," sighed Sean, "I've not even thought that far.

"Look after her, Sean," said Keith kindly.

"I will."

"You have feelings for the girl." It was a statement, not a question.

"I think so."

Keith looked at the young man in front of him. Sean had been a reporter for many years before Keith employed him. He knew that Sean had investigated some of the most savage and twisted stories that still haunted him.

"I believe she killed her father because she was afraid of him, but I don't know why. She has to present a motive," said Sean quietly.

Keith nodded. "Well, the press is censored on how they publish the facts."

"I know, but I cannot censor what Tanner hears in court."

"Why are you troubled, Sean?" asked Keith gently.

It took a while before Sean answered.

"I do not want Tanner's first exposure to physical—. l," Sean was too embarrassed to continue. "I do not want her perception of men to be tarnished by what she hears in that courtroom."

"I agree with you, but if we clip her wings, she will leave, and we will lose the best journalist we have had in years. I think that you are falling in love, my boy."

Sean didn't answer him. He got up and ordered a drink at the bar, then walked to the window and watched the scene below him. For the life of him, he couldn't say what he was looking at. His mind was preoccupied with Tanner.

15

DEFIANCE

Samuel sat in the doctor's waiting room surrounded by pregnant women, children, and geriatrics. He was annoyed that he had to waste thirty minutes of his precious time, only to have Dr Griffin to examine a heart, which some people told him he didn't have.

"Grumpiness isn't a disease, Annabelle."

The comment was so funny that Annabelle burst out laughing and rushed into his arms.

"Oh, Samuel, you are so funny," she laughed at him.

Samuel huffed.

"I've never felt better," he insisted.

"You're tired, and I would rather you see a doctor than play with your life. It's off to Harley Street for you."

"Will you give me any peace if I refuse to go?" asked Samuel.

"No, you will have no peace Sam, so I suggest that you listen to me."

Samuel resented being sent off to the doctor, yet Annabelle was right. He didn't have the energy he used to have and often found himself falling asleep in his chair.

"Did you come of your own accord?" asked Dr Griffin.

"Of course, I bloody didn't," replied Samuel.

"Ah, the beautiful Annabelle sent you, did she?"

"Yes," he muttered. "And do not speak about my wife that way."

Dr Griffin laughed loudly. He'd been the family physician for many years.

"You certainly have become a grumpy old codger."

It was Samuel's turn to laugh.

"Sit on the bed, Samuel, take off your shirt."

"It's the dead of winter. Do you want me to catch my death?" asked Samuel, trying every tactic he could think of to avoid the examination.

Dr Griffin looked at Samuel's body.

"You're still in good shape for your age Sam. You put younger men to shame. What is wrong?"

"Annabelle says I'm tired," huffed Samuel?

"Mmm? And is she correct?"

"Well, I doze off in my chair occasionally."

"Yes, well, Annabelle sent me a note."

Samuel rolled his eyes.

"Yes, Socrates delivered it yesterday."

"Everything happens behind my back."

"Annabelle says that you lose your breath when you climb the staircase or do any rigorous activities."

"Sometimes."

"I want you to lie down there, Sam. I'm going to listen to your heart."

"I do not have one," grumbled Samuel.

"That's not what I hear. If it's as good as people tell me, you have quite a few years left."

Dr Griffin not only listened to Samuel's heart but also poked and prodded around his abdomen until Samuel had enough and told him to hurry up. But Dr Griffin wasn't intimidated by Samuel and took his time.

"Sam, do you have chest pain?"

"No."

"I cannot help you if you do not tell me the truth. You're not fair to Annabelle."

"Yes, sometimes," Samuel surrendered.

"The science of heart disease is still very young, Sam, so I cannot make a perfect diagnosis. I believe that you have ischemic heart disease. It's uncomfortable, debilitating, and annoying but may not necessarily kill you."

Samuel nodded.

"How do you fix it?", he asked, practical as ever.

"I'm going to give you some tablets. When you feel pain, please put one under your tongue."

"What is in them?" asked Samuel.

"Nitro-glycerine."

"What?" exclaimed Samuel. "Do you want me to explode."

The doctor put his head back and laughed heartily.

"You'll not explode. Nobody has exploded to date," he laughed. "There has been a lot of research into nitrates as a solution to heart disease."

"Are you sure?"

"As sure as you are that the train wheels you forge will not crack."

Annabelle was waiting for Samuel in the library. She rushed into the foyer as soon as she heard footsteps in the hall.

"What did Dr Griffin say?" asked Annabelle without greeting Samuel.

Samuel pulled his jacket off, ripped off his tie, undid his collar and rolled his sleeves up.

Samuel took her in his arms and looked into her eyes, smiling.

"I'll live to fight another day."

"Is that true, Socrates?" she asked.

Socrates shrugged.

"I'm sure that Socrates has a full report in his pocket, Annabelle."

Annabelle looked at Socrates.

"Well? Out with it, Socrates! It's obvious that Dr Griffin does not trust me with information about myself."

He looked sheepish, then laughed and handed Annabelle an envelope.

She opened it immediately, and Samuel saw her body relax.

"This is good news Sam. Socrates and I'll administer your medication when necessary."

"Now, I can't be trusted to take my medication," grumbled Samuel.

Socrates knew that this was a bitter pill for Samuel to swallow. He'd lived a robust and vital life. Now he had to rely on a third party, in the form of medication, to help him remain that way. Samuel was a natural-born rebel, and Socrates knew that the only person who could persuade him to comply was Annabelle.

"Do I've an option to refuse?" he looked at Annabelle.

"No!" she was emphatic.

He reached out to her, took her in his arms and gently kissed her head and stroked her hair.

"Good," he smiled down at her, "I want to stay with you for as long as I can."

Socrates heard the telephone ring in the hallway- two long rings and one short one. There was the risk that the switch operators at the post office would listen in on the conversations, but Samuel didn't care. The new-fangled invention changed his life. No sooner had Samuel read about the telephone when he sent Socrates on a reconnaissance mission to source one. It was the most innovative communication tool of the century. Once it was installed, Samuel spent a lot of time communicating with Shilling and Tanner, who lived hundreds of miles from London.

"By far, the most sophisticated and useful invention of the 19th century," mused Samuel. "Why did Shilling, and I not think of it? We could have been using it twenty years ago."

Socrates answered the telephone. He held one piece of the device to his mouth, and the other part to his ear.

"Socrates, can you hear me?"

He heard Tanner's voice.

"Well, hello, Miss Fisher!" exclaimed Socrates.

"How are you Socrates? I miss you so much."

"I'm glad to hear that."

"May I please speak to Grandpa?"

"Yes, I'll call him."

There was a short pause, then Tanner heard Samuel's voice.

"Tanner, my darling," Samuel greeted his granddaughter.

Tanner was all business.

"Grandpa, it's the annual Charity Ball at the French Embassy, the one that Grandpa Fischer forces me to attend every year."

"Yes?"

"Grandpa, have you been invited?"

"Yes."

"May I bring an escort?" Tanner asked shyly.

She knew that she didn't need permission, but it'd soften the blow of her arriving at the Mayfair house with a stranger.

"Of course, who is he?"

"Sean Carlyle, the editor of the Manchester Herald."

"The French Ambassador may not enjoy having the press at his party," Samuel said firmly.

"I know, Grandpa, but I'll not be attending as the press. Mr Carlyle and I have a meeting in London, and I thought that he could accompany me."

Samuel laughed.

"Yes, Mr Carlyle is welcome," said Samuel, imagining a man in his sixties, wearing a peaked cap, apron, and spectacles on his nose.

"Is it acceptable to take a guest to such a formal occasion if you are not married or engaged to him?"

"Who is there to stop you, Tanner? You're an independent woman. You earn an honest living. As I told your mother when she was your age, you do not have to answer to anyone but yourself."

Samuel didn't have time to say goodbye. The line went dead. He sat quietly at his desk and stared across the gardens.

"Socrates!" he shouted.

"Yes, Sir," he heard Socrates call from outside the door, "on my way."

"Close the door, please."

Socrates closed the door.

"This must be important."

"It is. I want you to go to Birmingham and see what is happening between Shilling and Baxter Lee."

Socrates frowned. "No, Samuel, I'll not."

"What?" cried Samuel, "I need to know what is happening in the business. You're the only person who can assist me."

"I'm sure that Shilling updates you regularly. She has run the business expertly for many years."

Samuel looked sheepish.

"Alright, alright!" he exclaimed, "I want you to see what is happening between her and Baxter. Book yourself on the early morning train."

"No!"

Samuel clenched his jaw and gave Socrates a hard stare.

"How dare you say, no?"

Socrates was fearless.

"I refuse to spy on Shilling, Sam. You promised her that you would stop. I'm not being drawn into this obsession you have. I've more important things to do," he said, slipping from employee to friend.

Samuel tapped his desk with a pencil.

"Is that your final word on the matter, Socrates?"

"It is."

"Are you be prepared to escort Tanner back to Manchester after this circus at the French Embassy? Her old boss may not be able to protect her, and Manchester Station is in a terrible part of the city."

"No, Sam, I'm not allowing you to do the same to Tanner as you did to Shilling," said Socrates fiercely.

"About Birmingham—."

"No, Samuel, do not ask me again."

Samuel dropped his head.

"You're bored, Sam. You have an active mind. You need something to keep you busy."

"You're right, Socrates," Samuel finally admitted as he slouched back in his chair.

"I'm considering going to the country house near Birmingham for a while. Do you think Shilling will allow me near the business?"

"She'll be delighted, Sam. You two love working together."

Sam smiled. Socrates had come up with the best idea so far.

"I'll telephone her immediately," smiled Samuel. "Amazing bloody invention," he muttered as he turned the handle to reach the exchange.

16

THE EMBASSY BALL

Sean's office was stifling. The massive printing press below generated hot air that rose and got trapped under the roof.

Tanner sat at Sean's desk, tapping her pencil against her notebook. She was struggling to erase the image of Embeth Sterling in the dock.

"What are you thinking about?" asked Sean.

"We are roughly the same age," answered Tanner.

"Who are we?"

"Embeth Sterling and I."

"You find that disconcerting?"

"Of course," answered Tanner, "I'm rich, and she is poor. She was raised in poverty until Yakov and Rachel Weiner took her in. It's unfair that I—."

"Stop!" said Sean fiercely.

She sat upright and frowned at him.

"This murder would've happened whether you were rich or poor."

"I can't help think that if we were all born equal, these things would not happen."

"People are people Tanner, rich or poor, and they sometimes do bad things."

"It's way more frequent in the slums, Sean. You must admit that."

"Yes, it seems so, but remember that you have almost two hundred thousand people living in a very small area. That is where the problem starts."

"How can we help?"

"The press is powerful Tanner, why do you think I do this job? We are responsible for raising awareness, reporting honestly and eventually, gaining the attention of somebody powerful who can change things."

"Like my mother, who ended child labour in her factories?"

"Yes, we change the world one person at a time. Owens University was started by a man who left money in his will to build it. The locals became more humane when a private donor began to formulate change. If we never published articles telling of the inhumanity, no one would've known better."

"What about Embeth? What if the court has no mercy on her?"

"I don't know," he answered, troubled.

Tanner fought back the tears, and she realised that Sean was correct. She was struggling to keep her emotions neutral but wasn't succeeding.

"You have only worked here for three years, Tanner. It'll get better."

Sean stopped short of reminding her that she would demand he leave her on the assignment.

They sat in silence for a long time, each one lost in their own thoughts. Eventually, Sean changed the subject.

"By the way, I've received an invitation to a charity ball at the French Embassy in London. Is this your doing?"

Tanner blushed.

"I do not do balls and other grandiose occasions," he said, stubbornly.

"I've no choice, and this is the only annual occasion that the Fischers make me attend."

"Why am I on the guest list?"

"This is a wealthy newspaper, and you can afford to contribute to the greater good."

"Really?"

She expected Sean to reject her request; instead, he surprised her.

"Of course, I'll come," he smiled roguishly. "Will I meet Samuel?"

"Of course, you will stay in his home."

Sean raised his eyebrows.

"Yes, he knows that you are coming."

"One surprise after the next," he commented. "When do we leave for London?"

"Friday morning."

"I'll send Mr Jenson to purchase the tickets."

"I already have them."

"You're certain of yourself, aren't you, Miss Fischer?" he laughed.

Tanner chuckled too.

 "Thank you for agreeing."

She put her head down and continued to work. Sean stared at her with a smile on his lips. He liked her. No other woman would have been permitted to arrange his life. Sean was long overdue for a holiday, and a few days in London would do him good.

Tanner and Sean boarded the train at the Manchester Central Station. The wind howled, and their thick coats did little to keep out the cold. Tanner was hopeful that the weather would be warmer in London. The train pulled out of the station, leaving the black haze of the city behind them. When they reached the countryside, it was already dark, and all they made out were the lights of small villages twinkling romantically. They both sat staring out of the window, preoccupied with their own thoughts.

By dinner time, Tanner was fast asleep, and Sean wasn't hungry. He put his elbows on his knees and leaned forward to look at her. A strand of black hair hung over her pale cheek, and her blanket had fallen to the ground. He stood up, gently pushed the hair out of her face, and covered her again. She didn't move. Sean dropped onto his haunches next to her bunk. He wanted to touch her, but he would wake her up. Eventually, he moved back to his bunk and fell asleep as well.

There was no snow in London, but it was still icy. The station was a riot of people of all nationalities. The empire invited many countries into their fold. Cabs lined up outside, and porters pushed large baggage carts to and from the platform. Sean took Tanner by the arm, and they walked in the direction of the great doors.

Tanner spotted Socrates immediately. He was parked as close to the station as anyone could get. Socrates was smiling from ear to ear.

"Tanner," he cried when he saw her, "here!"

Sean and Tanner walked toward the cheerful man, who was more family than a servant to Tanner.

"Your grandfather was up at the crack of dawn, and he is so excited to see you. Your Mama, equally so. And Miss Annabelle has a selection of dresses to choose from for the ball."

Tanner laughed. It was beautiful to be home after such a long time.

Socrates noted Sean's quizzical face.

"Please introduce your guest, Tanner."

"This is Sean Carlyle, the editor of the Manchester Herald where I work."

Socrates and Sean shook hands.

"And this is Socrates, my very own guardian angel."

The Mayfair house was geared for Tanner's arrival, and the staff rushed into the courtyard to welcome her. The little girl who had run around the house was now a beautiful woman. Samuel and Shilling followed close behind them. Baxter Lee and Annabelle joined them, and soon there was a massive commotion in the courtyard.

"The neighbours will think the house is on fire," shouted Samuel. "Socrates, get Cook to put tea out for the household, tell Lizzy to get the library ready, we will all meet there."

It was the first time that Sean Carlyle heard of a millionaire having tea with his staff, and this one act of kindness endeared Samuel to him immediately.

"We have a guest, Sam," whispered Annabelle.

Sam swung around to greet Sean Carlyle, the editor of the Manchester Herald. He was taken aback for a moment. Sean didn't look like the old man with spectacles, and a white apron that he'd imagined. The man was tall, good looking with a ready smile that reached his eyes. He seemed confident without being arrogant. Sean saw the shock on Samuel's face as they shook hands.

"Did you expect someone, hmm, different?"

Samuel smirked.

"I did. You have caught me out."

Samuel and Sean were immediately comfortable with each other, and Shilling would not let Tanner out of her sight since she arrived.

"I want to know everything," begged Shilling with glee. "Everything!"

"Oh, Mama, there is so much to tell. I don't know where to begin."

"Are you living your dream Tanner, is your work fulfilling?"

"It is, Mama. But, it's difficult to watch the suffering."

Shilling nodded. She was glad that her formerly precocious daughter could now feel empathy.

It was a joyful day, and they were going to celebrate Tanner's arrival and shut out the world once the foundry work was dealt with. Socrates made every attempt to lighten the mood and even went as far as to be pleasant with Baxter Lee.

As with all celebrations, Samuel's household staff were simply themselves. The library atmosphere was casual, but the festivities drew to an end when Cook insisted that it was time to prepare for dinner.

Eventually, it was only Samuel and Sean left in the library. Sean was sipping his drink, and Samuel was on his third cup of tea. They were enjoying a comfortable silence after the chaotic hours behind them. Without making small talk, Samuel dived into a topic that concerned him.

"Are you in love with Tanner?" he asked Sean.

"It's none of your business."

Samuel put his head back and gave the loud contagious laugh.

Sean stared Samuel in the eye, daring him to ask another question. When Samuel did speak, it wasn't what Sean was expecting to hear.

"I'm glad that Tanner has chosen a strong man."

Sean was quiet. Years of being a reporter had taught him to listen and not interrupt.

"I need to know that she is in safe hands."

"Why are you telling me this?"

"I'm not going to live forever, Sean, and I want to die in peace."

The conversation didn't shock Sean, but it surprised him that Samuel was so quick to trust him. Samuel was astute. He watched how Sean looked at Tanner; Sean's eyes had not left her.

The French Embassy was lit up for the whole of London to see. The streets were full of carriages, and the drivers stood about in small groups warming their hands over small fires and smoking. Besides the debutante ball, this occasion was one of the most critical social gatherings of the year. If you were not invited, it could only mean two things- you had no money, or you had insulted the French ambassador.

Like many French men, the ambassador was easily annoyed by the English. It took months to approve the guest list every year. When he was first in post, the ambassador invited everyone until he realised that most of the aristocracy was flat broke, and they were only there to indulge in Russian Caviar and French Champagne. The canny ambassador changed the tradition by charging an exorbitant entrance fee, some of which went to charity, and the rest paid for the extravagant food. It was amazing how many people were suddenly on holiday, ill, or dead.

Shilling could still command a room, and there was a stir when she arrived at the embassy with Baxter Lee at her side. Shilling wore a cream dress. It was designed in a severe, modern style that accentuated her perfect body. She wore an emerald at her throat, and a magnificent diamond and emerald bracelet adorned her wrist. The concierge announced her arrival, but there was no need to. The woman with the scar down her face was a legend. She was Shilling Hudson Fischer.

Samuel and Annabelle followed Shilling. Samuel was elegant in a black dress suit, looking as handsome and distinguished as ever. Annabelle was dressed in a powder pale green lace dress, embellished with beads on the skirt. It offset her magnificent aquamarine and diamond engagement ring.

Samuel looked at her and smiled.

"You're beautiful."

Samuel kissed her cheek in full view of the press. He knew that the kiss would head up the articles in the social column. He knew that kissing your wife at a function like this was almost as bad as kissing somebody else's wife.

When Tanner arrived, even the music stopped. The Duke of York was clearly annoyed. It had not happened when he arrived. Clearly, he wasn't popular enough to warrant an orchestra holding its breath for him. It was seldom that the elite saw anyone from the House of Fischer in public, and Tanner was greeted as if she was royalty. Only the wisest men in attendance knew that she was more important than royalty. Her grandfather, Lord Fischer, was head of the banking dynasty, Fischer and Sons, who financed almost every enterprise in Britain.

Tanner was dressed in an emerald green dress. The dress was modest without being dull, and Shilling had given her a pair of beautiful diamond earrings, which lay against her skin like stars and twinkled every time she moved. Her long black hair hung down her back in big curls, and a small delicate tiara kept her hair off her face. The dress exposed Tanner's shoulders, and it was the first time that Sean saw more than her ankles. Her skin was flawless, and Sean was tempted to caress her shoulder. Sean had only seen her running around Manchester in her browns, and when she descended the stairs at the Mayfair House, she took his breath away.

Samuel looked at the three women. They were beautiful, intelligent and successful. For a second, he thought of the twin boys who would've carried his name, then he let it go. He was blessed and grateful. He would rather have his values perpetuated through his daughters than his name.

Lord Charles Buckingham looked down from the gallery and studied the guests as they arrived. Charles Buckingham had aged poorly. He was never an attractive young man, but now he was a bloated, florid lump of lard who struggled to move comfortably. He held a drink in one hand and pointed at Samuel Hudson with his crippled other.

"There is Samuel Hudson and his wenches," said Lord Charles Buckingham.

"Stop it," instructed Lord Ellington. "You're becoming a bore. Stop being a bad loser, old chap. You had a jolly good grope at Shilling Hudson, and Samuel protected her reputation. Come, old man. Enough is enough."

Lord Charles took a large swig of his drink.

"Shilling was a wild one. She deserved a good fondle. Rumour has it that Baxter Lee more than tutored her."

Lord Ellington looked at him with distaste.

"Mmm, I see that Tanner Fischer has grown up to be a beautiful woman, like her mother," said Lord Ellington, hoping to lighten the mood.

"Talk of the devil. There is Baxter Lee," Lord Charles pointed. "Seemingly, he is still tutoring her."

Lord Ellington was struggling to remain diplomatic.

"I see that your hiding from Samuel Hudson did no good."

If Charles Buckingham had a knife, he would've shoved it into Lord Ellington's heart. But he didn't have the knife or the strength to fulfil his dreams.

Baxter Lee stood back and watched Shilling talking to the French ambassador. She spoke fluent French and held the attention of all the men in the circle. Baxter knew she would be discussing business or politics. She wasn't given to chit chat. Baxter Lee joined the group. He was one of the most reputable engineers in Europe, and he had no time for politics. He'd seen way too many politicians ruin opportunities that would've served the greater good.

He took Shilling's arm gently. He always felt a stirring when he touched her. Bending down to whisper in her ear, he caught a whiff of her perfume.

"I've come to rescue you."

She looked up into his face and smiled, then gently excused herself from the group.

"Thank you," she laughed, "the conversation was becoming heated.

"Yes?"

"They were discussing Captain Dreyfus."

"That must have sparked some heated debate."

"It did. I believe that Alfred Dreyfus is innocent. There is a plot against him."

"He squeezed her arm gently, I know that the affair upsets you, and I agree."

"Thank you," she smiled.

"Let's try and enjoy the evening and drink as much of the champagne as we can," Baxter said, trying to change the mood.

Samuel felt breathless and tired, so he retired to a quiet annexe where he would not be noticed.

"You do not seem well Samuel, you look pale, and I can see that you have no energy," said Annabelle.

Samuel loosened his tie and undid his top button. His chest felt uncomfortable, but he didn't want to burden. Digging round in his pocket, he removed a tiny pillbox with an ebony lid, discreetly took out a small tablet and popped it under his tongue. Within a few minutes, he felt better. He'd no desire to mingle with the crowds and remained where he was. He took Annabelle's hand gently in his.

"Have I given you good years, my dearest? Have I loved you enough?"

"Stop it, Sam. You're scaring me. Why are you asking me this?"

"Do not be afraid, my darling. I must be certain that I've done my best."

"Oh, Sam, there is no question that you have done more than your best."

"Annabelle, do you regret that we never had our own child?"

"But we did have our child Sam. We had Shilling. We both got a second chance when you found her, hours old. We raised her together from the first day until now. We both loved her, protected her. You sat with me in the nursery every night. She was our baby."

Samuel squeezed her hand. "Yes, I remember those nights. I want to say thank you."

"Oh, Sam, you have said thank you so many times before."

"I know, but I must say it tonight."

Annabelle rubbed her hand gently over his wedding ring.

"I would choose you every time, Sam."

"Can I've a dance with the most beautiful woman here tonight?" asked Samuel with a twinkle in his eye.

"Is that me?"

"Who else?"

Samuel escorted Annabelle to the dance floor, and he took her into his arms. The music was a slow two-step. Samuel was filled with emotion, and he wanted to crush Annabelle to his chest and never let her go. They danced without speaking. She looked up at him and smiled, and he closed his eyes to hide his tears.

Samuel heard Annabelle giggle.

"Sam, Sam," she whispered.

"What is it, darling?"

"You aren't wearing your tie."

Samuel put his head back and gave a joyous laugh, and Annabelle started to giggle as well.

"What will the ambassador say?" laughed Annabelle.

"Oh, frog's legs to him, my angel, it's just you, and I here tonight."

"And the Duke of York?"

"Annabelle, I'm not a wigs and stockings man. And now I'm not a tie man."

Once more, Lord Charles Buckingham couldn't get control of his fury, and the desire for vengeance. He was envious of Samuel's family. The radiance and grace of the women enraged him. As he stared down at the guests below and watched the festivities, he did his best to quietly nurse his negative emotions—yet they still managed to boil.

Sean Carlyle was distracted as he spoke to the editor of The Times. Tanner excused herself from the conversation and made her way up the gilt staircase to talk to an old friend. Sean watched her out of the corner of his eye. A smile formed on his lips and desire flourished in his heart. So, distracted by the thought of her, he didn't hear the last few sentences of what the man said.

Tanner reached the balcony, and Sean watched a man approach her. He didn't consider it strange as many people were politely mingling and making small talk. The man took her elbow and steered her toward the ambassador's private art gallery. Sean presumed they were going to peruse the collection. Sean Carlyle knew nothing of Lord Charles Buckingham, nor did he know the history of the odious man's poisonous relationship with the Hudson family. Tanner was never told the man's sordid history with Shilling, so she too was oblivious to any possible danger.

Once Tanner reached the gallery door, Lord Charles Buckingham smiled charmingly, and approached her.

"Good evening, Miss Fischer," he greeted, warmth in his voice. "You're as beautiful as rumour has it."

"Why, thank you, Sir," she blushed. "And you are—?"

"Lord Buckingham," volunteered the man.

"I'm pleased to meet you," answered Tanner shaking his hand.

"I wonder if you have seen the beautiful pieces that the ambassador has in his gallery. There are two Rembrandts definitely worth seeing."

"Thank you—but perhaps later, Lord Buckingham."

Charles applied lashings of his trademark fake charm, keen to catch his prey.

"Oh, don't be a spoilsport," he teased. "Let me give you a quick tour. You'll not regret it. I promise."

Tanner capitulated.

"As long as it's no longer than ten minutes, Lord Buckingham, I've someone—I mean, I'm meeting a friend in the library."

Lord Buckingham put out his arm, and Tanner was too polite to refuse it. Something about the man made her uncomfortable. Shilling could see Tanner being escorted into the gallery by a man, but alas, only able to see Buckingham's back, she couldn't identify him.

Once inside the small room, Lord Buckingham closed the door softly behind him. Tanner turned around and looked at him, biting her lip with nerves.

"Just a little privacy, my dear. We do not need
unwanted company."

All of Tanner's senses heightened. Instinctively, she knew
that the man had plans to hurt her. Her eyes grew wider,
and she made an attempt to run past him. Grabbing her by
the arm, he threw her against the wall, just below the
Rembrandt she'd been lured with.

It was the first time in years that the old man became
aroused. Shocked and delighted, he decided to take
advantage of the rare opportunity he'd been given to
deflower the innocent Miss Fischer. He was surprisingly
strong for his age, and it was easy for him to manhandle the
slight young woman. His strong hand held his cane, and he
jammed it under Tanner's chin with force. She was trapped,
standing tip-toed against the wall, unable to breathe,
unable to scream. Charles Buckingham began to undo his
trousers with his crippled hand. It was agonisingly slow.

Tanner, an inexperienced young woman, needed a few
seconds to realise what his intentions were. His trousers
unbuttoned, he shoved his crippled hand down into her
bodice, as he'd done to Shilling many years before. The
physical exertion was causing Charles Buckingham to
breathe loudly, and perspiration dripped down his fat pink
face.

"I'd your mother pinned like this—and it would
have been much more fun if your servant
Socrates had not interfered," he grunted. "So, I'll
have you! This is payment to your grandfather for
what he did to my hand. Tonight, he will not be
able to help you."

Tanner's legs became weak. Her air supply was almost cut off completely, and she was starting to weave in and out of consciousness.

Shilling, having watched the man lead Tanner away, was looking out for her return. Her protective instincts overcame her. She excused herself from the circle of people around her and walked toward the staircase with purpose. When she reached the top, she couldn't see Tanner.

Charles Buckingham's lust got the better of him, and he allowed himself to groan with pleasure, terrifying Tanner. Once she collapses, I shall have my way with her. Licking his lips in anticipation, he shoved the cane harder still against her windpipe. Finally, her body gave up. She lost consciousness and fell to the floor.

Now, Shilling was desperate to find Tanner. She began to open every door leading off the balcony, searching for her daughter, shouting Tanner's name as she went from room to room. Shilling was unprepared for the scene that met her in the art gallery. An ugly old man, with a sickening bulge clearly visible through his unbuttoned trousers, was sweating and groaning in pleasure as he stood over the collapsed girl.

At first, Shilling thought that Tanner was dead. She threw herself onto the floor next to her, putting her ear to her daughter's chest, relieved to hear a weak heartbeat. Shilling ran to the balcony and shouted.

"Baxter, Baxter! It's Tanner. Help!"

Baxter and Sean heard Shilling's cry for assistance, then both stormed across the reception room and tore up the staircase.

"What has happened?" shouted Baxter.

Hearing the furore, the guests were starting to gather at the bottom of the staircase.

"Second door to the right," yelled Shilling.

"Shilling, what has happened to Tanner?" called Baxter.

Sean came out of the room carrying Tanner, who was still unconscious.

Charlie Buckingham was caught unawares and forgot to button his trousers. He rushed out of the room. Below him, he saw the inquisitive crowd, and he knew he needed an excuse for being in the room with Tanner.

"I went to help her," he shouted. "A masked man was trying to strangle her. I saved her."

Sean laid Tanner down on the plush carpet and knelt on the ground next to her, willing her to breathe. Tanner's eyelids fluttered. Mercifully, she was coming around.

Samuel saw the commotion above and rushed toward the staircase. He saw a murderous Shilling walking towards Charlie Buckingham, her fists clenched and a steely gaze. Defensively, he stepped back until he was against the balustrade, his trousers fastening still wide open.

"My father told you what would happen if you touched one of our family again," she said quietly.

"Your father is an old man."

"But I'm not an old woman."

Charles Buckingham began to perspire again. He looked over his shoulder and saw the guests looking up at him, slowly realising that he would never survive the social shame that his latest indiscretion would unleash. He would not be welcome at his club. He would not be invited to country houses and hunts. There was a strong possibility that he would be stripped of his title. The few friends that he had would ostracise him. He would not be able to fight the accusations in court because there were too many witnesses. Lord Charles Buckingham turned around and faced the handrail, gripping it tightly. His fat head and shoulders bent over the balustrade as he looked down at the guests. Then, he gave the slightest push with his feet, and his top-heavy torso plummeted to the ground below him, landing at Samuel's feet.

News of the episode reached the carriage drivers, and they began to crowd around the palatial doors to catch a glimpse of the scene. Socrates pushed his way through the drivers. He was bold enough to open the doors and elbow his way through the elite guests. He reached Samuel's side and saw Charlie Buckingham laying in a pool of blood at his master's feet.

Socrates put his hand on Samuel's shoulder.

"It's over, Sam. He will not torment our family anymore."

"I'm going up there."

"No, Sam, leave Shilling to care for her."

"Please take the women home, Socrates," said Samuel, "and ride over anyone who gets in your way."

"Of course, I will."

The ambassador approached Samuel. He was a tiny little Napoleon with black hair, and a hooked nose.

"Get these people out of here," ordered the diplomat.

"Monsieur Hudson, I was warned against inviting your family. You have caused a scandal."

"It's not one of my family lying on your marble floor with their trousers unbuttoned, is it?"

"Lord Buckingham was one of our greatest patrons. Your daughter must have enticed him and changed her mind. No woman can do that to a man in the height of passion. No man can stop himself."

Samuel lost his temper, and he moved as fast as a boxer and punched the ambassador with a powerful right hook, and then a left which brought the ambassador to the ground. The ambassador landed on his French derrière, his mouth bleeding and his eye turning blue.

"I'll have you arrested for assault," screamed the ambassador.

"To hell with you, Mr Ambassador. Nobody hurts my family and gets away with it."

"I'll report this to the press. Your reputation will be ruined."

Sean Carlyle interrupted the tirade.

"I don't think you will be the one to reveal the facts. I'm the editor of the Manchester Herald. The editor of The Times is also in attendance. Every person here heard your slanderous remarks about Tanner Fischer. We will print the story, and it'll be emblazoned across the front page of every newspaper in the country."

"What—? You dare to threaten me in my embassy?"

"Yes, I do!"

The ambassador softened, realising being confrontational was achieving nothing.

"We can discuss this. It must be kept out of the newspapers."

"I've no doubt you will be recalled to France," said Sean.

"My country cannot afford to have a diplomatic row with Britain. We already have this story of Captain Dreyfus causing an international scandal."

"You're prepared to insult my granddaughter's dignity," Samuel told him. "You are a poor excuse for a man."

A steely-eyed Samuel looked at Sean.

"Print the story. I'll deal with the consequences."

The three men left the French Embassy together. Samuel leaned heavily on his cane. His shoulder hurt, and his fists were grazed. He was sure that this would be his last fight. In fact, he should not have fought at all. The shock of what happened lay heavily upon him. He allowed Baxter to help him into the carriage, and the taxi began the journey back to Mayfair.

17

TO THE LETTER OF THE LAW

The office was grand. The Jewish community had pooled their resources, and hired the best solicitor in Manchester to defend Embeth Sterling. Yakov and Rachel crossed the gleaming polished floor to reach the elegant leather chairs in front of Arnie Schultz's enormous mahogany desk. A short man, the large desk dwarfed him.

"Let us go and sit on the settees, or you will never be able to see me," chuckled Schultz as he peered at them.

Yakov viewed him with suspicion.

"In my job, there is very little worth smiling about Mr Weiner. If I was as miserable as my cases, I would be a very melancholic man indeed."

Yakov nodded.

"How can we save our child?" asked Rachel, keen to make some progress.

"Rachel, you have taken step one. You have raised enough money for us to appoint a highly experienced Barrister to defend Embeth in court. Unfortunately, in our society, poor people have little chance of winning in court because they can only afford inept solicitors."

"How do we proceed, Mr Schulz? My wife and I've no experience with the law."

"Call me Arnie."

Yakov nodded.

"We have two frustrations at the moment. Embeth does not talk, so she cannot defend herself, and all the witnesses against Jimmy Sterling are women."

Rachel jumped to her feet.

"That is a poor reason not to defend her," said Rachel loudly.

"Now, now Rachel, do not be angry," Arnie Schulz consoled her. "I've not said I can't defend her."

"Jimmy Sterling is the criminal."

"I believe that it'll serve Embeth if we can find a man to testify against her father. The court isn't seeking justice for Jimmy Sterling. This case is controversial, Embeth has killed a man, and the court wants to understand her motive for doing so."

Yakov felt despair.

"Is this the best that the courts of a supposedly civilised country can do?" snapped Rachel.

"Rachel, we have a month to find another witness to Jimmy Sterling's cruelty. The court must be thorough in inspecting evidence. The law is here to protect the innocent as much as to convict the guilty."

"Well, Emmy is innocent. That monster has ruined her life. I'll find a witness if I've to die doing so."

"Don't say that, Rachel. We'll find somebody. I don't know where and how, but Hashem is great. He will lead us," insisted Yakov.

"We'll not give up," smiled the cheerful little man. Rachel was so irritated that she could have wrung his little neck. She didn't appreciate his nonchalant attitude, and she was looking for somebody with more fire.

"Rachel, the community has told us that he is the best. Give the man an opportunity to do his job."

"His job Yakov? An opportunity? If he makes any mistakes, Emmy is as good as dead."

Yakov took Rachel's hand.

"You must have faith, Rachel. We must trust Mr Schulz—Arnie."

*

The further north Tanner went, the more depressing the weather became. One of the coldest winters that England had experienced, the countryside was snowed under. The picture from the train window was black and white. Hordes of labourers stood back from the track as the train passed, then returned to shovelling snow. They were dressed in layers of tattered clothes. Tanner wondered how much the poor wretches were paid for their endless backbreaking and icy toil.

Tanner sat bundled in her coat and was covered by a blanket that was pulled under her chin. She stared out of the window, seeing nothing, lost in her thoughts. She'd hardly said a word since they left Paddington Station, and the light banter that accompanied their trip to London was nowhere to be heard. Tanner stayed awake throughout the night as the train crossed England, but Sean nodded off. He woke up in the early hours of the morning. With his teeth chattering as he slowly chilled to the marrow, he looked across to Tanner, who too was shivering.

"It's freezing in here," complained Sean, his breath condensing instantly in the cold carriage.

Tanner agreed.

"I can't warm up, and this blanket is useless."

"Let's share the blanket. We can warm each other up," he suggested, now in genuine need of some form of warmth.

"Of course," she smiled.

He noted it was her first smile since London. He climbed in under the blanket, and soon they both began to thaw.

"Tanner, you have looked out of that window for hours. What were you thinking?"

"Nothing."

"You have been thinking an awful lot of 'nothing' through the night," smiled Sean gently.

"I'm fine."

"Tanner, not all men are like Charlie Buckingham. I'll never hurt you."

He smiled and took her hand.

"I know," Tanner looked into his eyes, aware of his touch. "But, I'm long over Charlie Buckingham. I'm thinking about Embeth Sterling."

"That can all wait for the morning," he consoled. "Come, put your head on me. You can sleep a little longer."

Tanner put her face on his shoulder, but she was uncomfortable, so she slid under his arm, and without hesitation, he held her close to him.

Sean lifted his hand and stroked her hair, pulling Tanner firmly against his chest. It was the closest she'd been to him since he rescued her at the quayside in Salford.

She stared up at him and experienced a desire that she never experienced before. Instinctively, Sean was aware of her hidden longing. He bent his head and kissed her, first softly, then becoming more passionate. She loosened a shirt button, then ran her hand over his chest. Sean pulled her onto his lap and ran his hands over her body, then he stopped himself.

"Not here, Tanner. I love you, and I want you—
but not here."

This time, Tanner kissed him with open desire. Sean could have made love to her right there in the rickety cold carriage, but he didn't want to. She deserved better.

When they arrived at the station, they went straight to work. It was hardly past six o'clock, and the building was dark. They sat down at Sean's cluttered desk, and he immediately began reading his mail.

"Would you like coffee?" asked Tanner.

"Yes, please," Sean smiled without looking up.

He was behaving as if nothing had happened between them.

Fifteen minutes later, Tanner returned with two cups of steaming coffee and put one in front of Sean.

"Well, the world didn't come to an end while I
was gone," he smiled.

Tanner laughed.

"Sean," said an earnest Tanner, "I want to visit Yakov and Rachel Weiner."

"Why?"

"I need to tell the world her story."

"Do you want me put in gaol?" asked Sean, looking at Tanner over the rims of his spectacles." "We may not publish anything about Embeth while the court case is in process. You of all people should know that."

"Well," Tanner paused, "I'd a different idea in mind."

Sean raised his eyebrows.

"One that doesn't include a gaol sentence?"

"Sean, we do not know what drove Embeth to kill her father, but you, and I are convinced that he abused her in some way."

"Oh, dear God, Tanner. Do not tell me that you are thinking of printing that. That is slander against that dead blithering idiot, Sterling. Worse, you will be accused of swaying the jury."

"Stop!" exclaimed Tanner, annoyed that he would not allow her to finish.

"I want to write a story about Yakov and Rachel Weiner. I want to write about how Emmy was the first female watchmaker in Manchester. I want people to realise that this girl isn't a mute lunatic, but a respected, intelligent part of society."

"That is a ridiculous idea. It's too close for comfort, Tanner. Any article with Embeth's name in it'll incur the wrath of the justice system. Not only will they lock me up, but they'll close the newspaper. We are treading a thin line."

"What about the freedom to publish, the freedom of speech?"

"There is no such thing as freedom of the press in England. We are governed by antiquated laws. If you want to write what you please, Tanner, go to America."

"I refuse to accept that."

"If you ever became an editor, you would spend more time in court defending yourself than working behind your desk," Sean laughed.

Tanner smirked at Sean. What he said was humorous but still unacceptable. She'd never been good at hearing the word 'no'.

Tanner sipped her coffee and listened to people beginning to arrive for work. Suddenly she'd the answer.

"Sean!" she exclaimed, bouncing in the chair excitedly, "Listen, I know how we can get around it."

"Mmm?" he responded dismissively, not lifting his head up to look at her.

"I'm going to write a story about Tilda."

"What?" said Sean, taking his glasses off and putting them on the desk.

"Tilda, she is also a clockmaker, and she runs the shop."

Sean frowned.

"I do not need to even mention Embeth's name. I'll write the story under the auspices of great achievements. The suffragettes and feminists will love it. Everyone knows that Embeth worked in that shop. Everybody will associate the article with her, without publishing her name."

Sean leaned back in his chair and stared at her. Then he developed a broad smile. He sat back in his chair, tapping his pencil on his notebook.

"Do it!"

"What?"

"I love the idea. We will be chastised, but I doubt that we will be dragged into court. We may not be acting within the spirit of the law—but we are acting within the letter of it."

A proud Tanner burst out in fits of giggles.

"Do it. I'll publish it on Sunday morning when the upper class is admiring themselves in the social columns," Sean stood up and walked around the table. He sat on the edge of his desk, with his hands in his pockets.

"Come here," he said, to Tanner and grabbed her hand as she passed him.

"You're the most brilliant journalist that I've ever employed," he kissed her. "And the most beautiful."

Tanner dashed through the newsroom, and as her stunned male colleagues looked on agog, she grabbed her plain hat and brown coat and headed for the door.

"Where are you going?" Somebody called out.

"Is there a fire?" shouted another.

"Neither," she yelled in triumph.

"Well, what are you going to do that is making you so happy?"

"Hopefully, I'm going to save somebody's life."

In unison, they shook their heads as she left. Some people felt that Tanner was too big for her boots. Others commented that she'd more money than sense. Another bunch sniggered at her relationship with the sub-editor, implying they were more than colleagues. But despite the prejudice, nobody could deny that Tanner was a talented writer. Slowly, but surely, she was on her way to becoming the most accomplished journalist at the Manchester Herald.

'Weiner Watchmaker', read the sign on the door. Tanner knocked firmly and, without waiting for a response, opened the door and stepped inside. The counters shone, and she could smell the wax polish. There wasn't a spec of dirt on the floor, and if one had not known better, you could imagine that you were stepping into a pristine jewellery shop in Vienna.

A beautiful young woman with white-blonde hair and blue eyes introduced herself.

"My name is Tilda," she smiled. "How may I help you?"

"Tanner Fischer," replied the customer as she held out her hand. "I'm a journalist for the Manchester Herald."

Tilda was taken aback, hesitant to say anything that could be quoted in the newspaper.

"What do you want?"

"I would like to write an article about you."

"Me?" Tilda was confused.

"Yes. I believe that your sister is the first female watchmaker in Manchester."

"Oh, yes!" exclaimed Tilda. "That is my sister, Emmy."

"I know," said Tanner.

Tilda frowned.

"Let me fetch the Weiners," Tilda told Tanner. "I do not quite understand what you want from me."

Tanner stared around the little shop. Tilda's sense of pride was written in every detail, from the immaculate counters to the spotless floors.

An old orthodox-looking man came down the stairs and looked at Tanner questioningly. He was wearing a skull cap like Grandpa Fischer's, and the tassels of his ceremonial prayer shawl hung below his shirt.

"Ah, young lady," greeted Yakov, "you are a journalist, yes?"

Tanner nodded.

"My name is Yakov Weiner. Tilda is my ward."

"Tanner Fischer, Sir. May I shake your hand?"

He eyed the girl. She certainly understood Jewish etiquette.

"Of course, you can," Yakov smiled as he politely reached out.

"You're family of Lord Fischer?" asked Yakov.

"His granddaughter."

"Ah, yes, he is a great and generous man."

"Thank you."

"And your mother?"

"My mother is Shilling Hudson Fischer," replied Tanner.

"Oh, my word," smiled the old man. "I was sorry to hear of your father's death all those years ago. Your mother is quite a trailblazer, isn't she? She has certainly changed a lot of things around here for the better. Thanks to the trade school up in Angel Meadows, she has given so many young men a good education and hope for the future."

"Yes, she has indeed," said Tanner proudly.

"Well, now young Tanner, my wife Rachel isn't here, and I would like to have her with me when you speak to us. Come and join us for dinner tomorrow night."

Tanner frowned, "May I bring somebody with me?"

"Of course, my dear, who is it?"

"Sean Carlyle, the sub-editor of the Manchester Herald."

Wide-eyed, Yakov agreed.

*

Rachel and Yakov invited the two journalists into their tiny but immaculate home. On the kitchen table, a snow-white starched cloth lay beneath the best china, set out as if the visitors were royalty. There was a delectable smell coming from the range's glowing oven.

"Come in, come in," ordered Rachel. "Welcome to our house."

Tanner was surprised by Rachel. She had not expected such a vivacious, feisty woman. She'd anticipated meeting an obedient shadow of a person, devoid of any vitality. She was wrong.

"Rachel makes the best brisket in Manchester. If the community knows that she is cooking, they invite themselves to eat with us," laughed Yakov.

"And she has made cheesecake for dessert," smiled Tilda.

"Oh, you just say that to keep me in the kitchen," complained Rachel.

Rachel shuffled everybody around the table and ordered them to their seats. Sean called Yakov aside.

"Is Rachel always this bossy?" he asked tongue in cheek.

Yakov laughed. "You should've met her when she was young. I was too scared to speak to her."

The brisket was indeed the best that Tanner ever tasted, and she'd two servings of cheesecake.

"My Grandpa Samuel would love this," laughed Tanner.

"When he comes to Manchester, you will tell me, and I'll feed him right here at this table."

Sean watched the people around the table. This remarkable couple had taken in two young girls, and against all odds, they created a family. Sean explained to Yakov and Rachel what they wanted to achieve by publishing an article about Tilda.

"I'm not sure Yakov," said Rachel without mincing words.

"We already have people staring through our windows. Tilda has no peace during the day. Everyone is so inquisitive. This will just make it worse."

"Rachel, Embeth cannot speak for herself. We cannot report on the case in progress, but we can write about Tilda. We want to tell the public that these aren't just any two women; they're successful women."

Yakov looked at Rachel, and they both shrugged.

"I'm not sure, Sean," said Yakov.

Rachel looked earnestly at the sub-editor.

"I think you need to ask Tilda. It'll be her name all over the newspaper."

"Will this save my sister?" asked the girl.

"It'll educate the public."

"Will that be enough, Miss Fischer?" croaked the anxious girl.

Tilda stood up and excused herself from the table. Rachel looked at Tanner, hinting she should follow. Tanner made her way up to the girls' small room under the eaves.

"May I?"

Tilda patted a space on the bed next to her and smiled.

"Rachel saved us," confided Tilda. "Emmy, and I slept together in this room, every night since we were little."

Tanner smiled, gazing at the pictures and ornaments dotted around the spartan but spotless room, which gave the place a welcoming, homely ambience.

Tilda and Tanner immediately warmed to each other. After a little more small talk, Tanner was brave enough to broach the subject of Jimmy Sterling's demise.

"Why do you think she did it?"

Tilda blushed scarlet.

"It's a long story, really," explained Tilda. "With our mother passed on, we lived alone with our father."

Wanting to listen in on the conversation, Rachel knocked on the door and came in.

"Miss Fisher, how do we know that you will not put this in the newspaper? It'll make you very famous."

"Firstly, Sean Carlyle has years of experience on how to handle delicate stories with tact. Secondly, he would be sent to gaol if he published anything that might affect the case. My job depends on people trusting me. My editor trusts me, and I need you to trust me. But if I'm going to help you, I need to understand—everything."

"It's a terrible story. You mustn't breathe a word of this to anyone other than Mr Carlyle. Promise me."

Tanner nodded solemnly, her hand cupped over her heart, then listened intently as Emmy's story tumbled out.

Tanner showed no emotion, but she was shocked. She'd been protected all her life, and she couldn't conceive how a man could do this evil thing to his child. Worse, still, she didn't know how she was going to repeat it to Sean without feeling ashamed.

"There is a witness, whom I believe could help with the case. His name is Martin Blackburn."

The five sat around the kitchen table once again. It was the first time since the night that Emmy was arrested that they dared to hope.

"You have brought us hope," said Yakov.

"I want to visit Emmy in the asylum—speak to her myself," said Tanner.

"But the ordeal has made her mute. What are you going to achieve by talking to her?" asked Sean.

It was Sean's turn to be silent.

Rachel smiled for the first time.

> "I think that this is a good idea. Embeth is a lovely girl. Perhaps, in time, she will talk to you, Miss Fischer."

> "Well, we'll never know if we don't try. I think it's best I come with you," Sean suggested.

> "No, I need to go alone. A man's presence will no doubt frighten her."

> "I suppose so," he conceded.

Sean was terrified that something would happen to Tanner, some deranged soul attacking her again. Yet, it was as if the altercation between her and Buckingham had been her baptism of fire. The young woman seemed stronger, braver and more determined than ever to bring justice for Emmy.

*

Sean took Tanner's hand as they navigated the dark alleys that never slept. There was an underlying pulse in the darkness. They heard the sighs and snores of people who were sleeping, wrapped in the filthy rags that kept them from freezing to death. There was the crying of infants who longed to be comforted at their mother's bosom, except that their starving mothers had no milk. They heard the panting of men as they used prostitutes in the shadows. But one had to listen carefully because these sounds were almost drowned by the constant sounds of the monstrous factories that never slept, for the sole purpose of enriching the empire.

"Sean, we need to find a man called Martin Blackburn. I believe that he was aware of Jimmy Sterling's crime against his daughter."

The two of them wound their way through the labyrinth of dirty tenement alleys. Slowly, the streets became wider, and the houses were more liveable, but the dark clouds of smoke and soot hung over them like a bad omen.

The only thing that lightened the darkness was love and hope.

"The moment I picked you up at that riot, I knew that I sealed my fate. I knew that you would never let me go," said Sean stifling a smile. "I've never had a woman throw herself at my feet like you did."

A playful Tanner punched him forcefully on the arm.

"You took advantage of my vulnerability, Mr Carlyle. I should've slapped you."

"But how could I resist you?" he teased. "You were the most beautiful woman I'd ever rescued."

"You'll be telling me I liked the ordeal next."

She put her head back and laughed, the same way that Samuel would have.

Sean pulled her closer and kissed her. This time, it was passionate and promising, and Sean had difficulty letting her go. Nobody around them cared. Their passion was absorbed by the ever-present pulse in the darkness and drowned by the despair of the people in the shadows.

The county asylum hospital could have been misconstrued as a manor house set in beautiful gardens. Men and women strolled about the grounds, keenly watched by nurses and porters. The patients took advantage of a break in the icy weather to get fresh air, which was ironic considering the pollution that blanketed the city.

It was only the semi-sane who were allowed outdoors. The 'normal' patients remained behind locked doors and strong steel bars.

The head nurse looked at Tanner suspiciously.

"Who are you?"

"I'm Embeth Sterling's cousin," she answered, not daring to tell the nurse that she was a journalist.

"She can't talk. You're wasting your time. And she is violent," said the nursing sister.

Tanner nodded, trying to suppress her annoyance.

"Mr Bamborough," called the nurse. "Embeth Sterling has a visitor."

"Be careful," warned the nurse.

"Thank you."

Kevin Bamborough looked to be a kind man.

"I've looked after Emmy since the first time she was hospitalised," he told Tanner. "Rachel and Yakov said to expect you. Thank you for taking an interest in her."

"Do you know them?"

"Yes, very well."

"She was a mere girl when she was sent here."

"The nurse said that she was violent, is that so?" asked Tanner.

Kevin smiled. "Yes, and no."

Tanner looked at him.

"Emmy has a problem with being touched—you know," said an embarrassed Kevin, "—in the wrong places—her private parts. Some women here prey on innocent young women, and they tried to molest her."

During the last months, Tanner was compelled to mature quickly, and she was unflinching when she heard the information, which made it a lot easier for Kevin to disclose the details of Emmy's experience.

"Do you believe that Emmy can have a normal life?" asked Tanner.

"No, not at all. I do not believe that she would allow anyone to come near her. Emmy is like a feral cat. She distances herself from people and is wildly protective of the people she loves. I believe that Jimmy Sterling was trying to molest her beloved Tilda, and that is why Emmy killed him."

"Really?"

"Yes. Can you imagine if Emmy had a child, and somebody threatened it? She would murder them."

"The Weiners told me that she would start to communicate with strangers before she'd the setback."

"Kevin, do you think she will ever speak again?"

"I doubt it, Miss Fischer. It'll take a miracle. I do not carry much hope for it."

Kevin Bamborough led Tanner down a flight of stairs to a dark, gloomy space, more a basement than a dungeon. The area was divided into cells, all lacking any privacy. They passed inmate after inmate. It was like being in a medieval gaol, and for a moment, Tanner imagined the Bastille.

Tanner saw women beating their heads against the bars, their heads bruised and bleeding. Others shoved their arms toward her, trying to touch her while the rest made crude sounds and remarks. She saw a woman with her dress hitched up around her hips, and her hands in her underwear. Kevin averted his gaze, wondering how to explain.

"I should not be here at all, but Emmy trusts me. I might be able to break the ice a little for you."

"Ultimately, that woman back there will be restrained," clarified Kevin. "The severely insane area is one floor below."

Tanner couldn't believe that it was any worse than what she had already witnessed. It was like Dante's seven circles of hell brought to life, with each zone managing to be more terrifying than its predecessor.

"What will ultimately happen to the women on the next floor?" she asked him.

"They'll be moved to another hospital for the hopeless."

"Is Emmy hopeless?"

"No, Miss Fisher. Emmy is undoubtedly damaged, but the Weiners have proved that she can function normally with sufficient love and protection. I believe that with her father dead, she may begin to heal properly. Well, we've finally arrived."

Tanner studied Emmy through the bars. The woman was beautiful. She'd white-blonde hair, large innocent blue eyes, and a serenity that belied her vicious crime. Her hair was brushed and pinned, her dress was spotless, and she sat on the side of her cot, staring at something that nobody else could see.

18

THE DIAMOND

Shilling's home in Birmingham was a haven. It was years since she finally dared to be alone. She either lived in London's Mayfair, with Samuel and Annabelle, or had Socrates with her in Birmingham. She was relieved that Tanner had established her career and was happy. Shilling had not entertained Baxter for some time. They saw each other at Hudson foundry, but not at her home.

Shilling's house wasn't a mansion. She'd gone out of her way to create a home that was warm and intimate. She employed a few servants and never entertained; it was her private space. She spent hours working in the garden, much to the horror of her gardener, who was terrified of her. Eventually, he realised that the beautiful, powerful woman had few airs and graces. They became good friends, and it was customary to hear laughter emanating from the garden as they worked together. The cook couldn't believe that Tanner was satisfied with bread, butter, and jam at afternoon teatime. It was such a humble meal. The only people who visited her were Samuel, Annabelle, Socrates, and Tanner. If she needed to entertain anybody, she would meet them at a fine hotel. She was undemanding of her staff and found solace in front of the fire, reading and studying new engineering techniques.

Shilling was confident that Baxter's son would be as fine an engineer as his father, and she enjoyed his research on new trends and machinery that would advance the company into new production methods. He was a pleasant man, and they'd become good friends when he realised that she was supportive and open-minded. He knew that his father loved Shilling, but it had hurt him when he learned of Baxter's affair. It had taken a long time to forgive his father. He grasped that Shilling was a victim, and he had to come to terms with the fact that he couldn't influence their future; besides, he liked Shilling.

Baxter couldn't fathom Shilling's sudden rejection. He was disappointed, but when he tried to broach the subject, she told him that she didn't want to discuss the relationship. Baxter refused to give up, and finally, he found an unusual ally in Socrates.

One afternoon, he called Socrates into his office and shut the door.

"I know that we have a torrid past," admitted Baxter.

"Yes, we have."

"Let me be honest, Socrates, there will never be another woman in my life. I love Shilling."

Socrates smiled.

"Few people get a second chance."

Baxter lifted his eyebrows, surprised at Socrates's response.

"Do you approve of our relationship?"

"Yes, I do."

"Shilling has cut herself off from me, physically and emotionally. I don't know what I've done to warrant her rejection. I want to marry her."

"Shilling is a complicated woman Baxter, you of all people should know this. My interpretation is that she is afraid to offend her father."

"But she does as she pleases. She has never needed his blessing."

"I know, but you need Samuel's blessing. You need to earn her respect Baxter. Her father is the strongest man she has ever met, and she needs to admire you as much as she admires him."

"What do you suggest I do?"

"Face Samuel, for once and for all."

"How can you tell me to do this Socrates, you are Samuel's servant, friend and confidante?"

"I know, "answered Socrates, "but have known Shilling from the moment she was born, and I love her as if she were my own. Samuel has lived his life. He is a fine man, and he found happiness after a lot of pain. It's Shilling's turn now."

Baxter gave it some thought, then he boarded the first train to London.

Samuel was surprised to see Baxter on a weekday.

"Is there something wrong at the foundry?" asked Samuel.

"Not at all." answered Baxter.

"Let me call Annabelle. We can have tea together, "said Samuel knowing that Annabelle would ease the tension between him and Baxter."

"I would prefer to speak to you alone," said Baxter.

Samuel looked at him quizzically.

"Let us go to my study."

Baxter sat down at Samuel's desk.

"May I pour you something to drink?" Samuel asked politely.

"No, thank you."

"You're not a drinking man?"

"You know that I'm not," said Baxter, irritated by the question.

Samuel sat down opposite him.

"Samuel, I'm going to marry Shilling."

"Are you asking for my blessing?"

"No, I'm not."

It was Samuel's turn to be annoyed.

"Have you asked my daughter?"

"No, Sam, I'm going to tell your daughter."

Samuel raised an eyebrow.

"Nobody tells Shilling what to do."

"I've been on the peripheries of her life for too long. I love her, and she loves me. If she cannot make up her mind, I'll make it up for her."

"When last did you see her?"

"At the French Embassy."

"You're a brave man Baxter, I can only wish you luck."

"Thank you."

"Besides," said Samuel, "who am I to stand in the way of love. I've no doubt that my daughter loves you, and I want her to be happy."

Samuel and Baxter shook hands. When Baxter left, Samuel had a new respect for him.

Baxter returned to Birmingham with confidence. It was sunset when his driver collected him at the station. Baxter instructed him to go directly to Shilling's home. Baxter knocked loudly on the front door. Socrates opened it and saw the determined man in front of him.

"Where is Shilling?" Baxter demanded.

"In her bedroom," said Socrates.

"Can I escort you?"

"No," answered Baxter, "I know the way."

He pushed past Socrates and climbed the stairs with determination.

Baxter didn't knock, but opened Shilling's bedroom door, entered the room, and slammed it shut behind him. Shilling looked up in surprise.

"What has happened?" she demanded.

"I'm not living like this any longer," said Baxter.

"I'm no longer paying for the sins of my past. I've paid enough."

Shilling frowned.

"I don't understand."

"You'll marry me."

"Oh, will I?" she asked, annoyed.

"Yes, you will."

"You'll not instruct me on what to do."

"Yes, I will. This time, I'm taking what I want, and I want you. You were mine from the first day in the study."

Baxter was speaking so loudly, she knew that the entire household could hear them.

"You cannot simply barge into my house and command me into marrying you."

Baxter looked at her, and he felt his temper rising. How many times would she deny him? Her green eyes bored into him, daring him to challenge her. He looked into her defiant eyes, but this time he would fight until the end.

"I was in London," said Baxter.

"I don't care where you were," she replied with venom.

"I'd business to take care of."

"I'm sure you did. Were you at your favourite brothel?"

"And what if I was? What is it to you?" he shouted at her.

She couldn't answer him. It was a valid question. Shilling turned around and looked out over the garden.

"Do you think that you are the only woman that can please me?"

She refused to answer him. The thought of him being with another woman devastated her.

"I told your father that I would marry you, whether he approved or not."

Her eyes went ice cold.

"You want to spite my father by marrying me?"

"No, Shilling, I've waited for Samuel's approval for way too long. I'm my own man, and I do not need his permission to take what I want."

"You took what you wanted when I was eighteen. Now, I don't want you," she shouted, "Go back to London if she pleases you more."

Baxter felt deeply hurt, but he had to finish what he started, or he would never have the courage to face her again.

"You're a liar. You're a terrified liar. You do want me. You always have. You may have married Benjamin, but every night you were thinking of me," he roared.

She slapped him across his face.

"How dare you desecrate my feelings for husband?"

If he were honest, Baxter felt nothing for Benjamin, only passion for Shilling.

"I'm marrying you tomorrow even if I drag you to the registry office."

Shilling couldn't believe what he was saying. For years Baxter tolerated her rejection. He accepted their relationship on her terms and had no expectations of her. Now, Baxter was forcing marriage upon her which she desperately wanted, yet was too afraid to admit to herself.

Benjamin's death left her dead as a stone. She'd chosen to remain that way, but the intensity of her attraction to Baxter was melting her pain.

She went back to staring at the garden, barely hearing his voice wafting out from the parlour window.

"You love me, Shilling! Admit it, damn you!"

When the comment did sink in, she chose not to answer.

"Turn around and look at me," he shouted.

Shilling didn't budge.

Baxter stormed up behind her, grabbed her by the arm, and turned her around to face him. Shilling yanked herself away.

"Tell me," he commanded her.

He took two steps forward, and she toppled onto the bed behind her.

"You're lying to me. You're lying to yourself. I dare you to tell me that it's over," he roared.

Baxter stood over her. He was leaning on his fists, and her face was close to his."

He looked into her emerald green eyes.

"I do. I do love you," Shilling thundered back at him. But our relationship has always been messy, and I don't have time to waste on something that cannot be.

Baxter dug in his pocket.

"Don't you dare move an inch, do you hear me?" he commanded her roughly.

He lifted her hand and shoved an engagement ring onto her finger. The large diamond was surrounded by emeralds. Baxter stood back and looked down at her.

"You'll never remove that ring. Do you hear me? From this day forward, once and for all, you are finally mine."

Baxter turned around and left the room, slamming the door behind him.

Shilling looked down, casually extended the fingers on her left hand, and admired the dazzling Cartier ring.

19

IN SEARCH OF A WITNESS

Tanner sat down at the bottom of Emmy's bed, close enough to talk but not to touch. She'd given much thought to her approach and decided that if she could pique Emmy's interest, she would win the girl over. Yakov made the suggestion that she take a watch, magnifying glass, and tools with her.

Tanner took out her diary and began to write. She made no attempt to speak to Emmy, taking the opportunity to note her experiences thus far. Yet still, Emmy was motionless. Tanner sketched the girl while she waited. Two hours passed, and Emmy had shown no signs of fear or aggression. Tanner started to hum while she was drawing, and she saw the girl's head move. It didn't move more than an inch, but it was all the hope that Tanner needed.

Tanner leaned back against the wall and sat cross-legged. She put her satchel on the bed and took a small gold watch off her wrist. Then she took the tools Yakov had given her from her bag. Yakov had shown Tanner how to open the back of the watch and how to remove the glass. Yakov had loosened the components in the timepiece so that the whole mechanism would spill out when opened. Yakov added a few unnecessary bits and pieces to make the repair more complex. 'You'll need all the time you can get', Yakov had told her.

Tanner clumsily opened the watch, and everything went tumbling onto the bed. She grabbed a small screwdriver and feigned an attempt to fix it. As quick as lightning, Emmy grabbed the screwdriver out of her hand and began collecting all the little pieces. Tanner was euphoric; it was the reaction that she'd hoped for.

Emmy was sitting right next to her, oblivious of her proximity to Tanner. Tanner removed the magnifying glass from her satchel and gave it to Emmy. Tanner was sure that the young woman was aware of the ruse, but Emmy couldn't bear to see the delicate timepiece destroyed. She had to bring it back to life. She longed to hear the tick of its heart before she could find peace.

It was Tanner's turn to be fascinated. Emmy set up a makeshift workbench on the bed, and soon she was wholly absorbed in her work. Emmy worked with a precision that Tanner knew Shilling would appreciate. It was Tanner's turn to be speechless.

"Tweezer," said the girl.

She couldn't believe her ears. Emmy spoke. As Tanner turned to her, she upset the cogs and wheels.

"Sit still," warned Emmy.

Tanner did as she was told and watched Emmy begin again. The repair was a slow, tedious exercise, but Emmy was comfortable giving Tanner orders. Tanner drew parallels between Emmy, and a horse; if she backed off a little, Emmy would approach her.

Tanner stood up and went to the cell door. Emmy looked up, terrified, and covered the watch with her hands, afraid that Tanner was leaving and would take the timepiece with her. Tanner turned around and looked at her.

"I'll not take it away from you," smiled Tanner.

Emmy smiled at her. It was the most beautiful smile that Tanner had ever seen.

"What is your name?" Tanner asked her.

"Emmy," It was a one-word answer, but it was enough. The court was amenable to one-word answers.

"My name is Tanner."

There was no reaction from Emmy.

"What is wrong with my watch?" asked Tanner.

"You broke it."

"Can you fix it?"

Emmy nodded?

"Is it difficult?"

Emmy shook her head.

Tanner spoke to her and gently asked questions unrelated to her case, but Emmy didn't speak.

Whatever Yakov had done to the watch was taking hours for Emmy to repair, but she showed no signs of frustration. Tanner didn't know what to do, she'd run out of ideas, and then she began to ponder Emmy's earlier response at her taking the watch.

"I've to go now," said Tanner and stood up.

"No," Emmy told her firmly. "The watch is still broken."

It was the first complete sentence that Emmy had spoken for months.

"And what about you? How do you feel?"

"Emmy broken—everyone says so."

Tanner couldn't hold back her tears.

"Who broke you?"

Tanner could see the panic on the young woman's face, so she tried a different tack.

"I'll help you, Emmy. I promise."

The young woman looked at her with big eyes.

"Will you make my heart tick again?" she asked Tanner, who nodded and choked with emotion.

"But you must be brave. You must tell the judge who broke you. I'll be with you."

"Can I keep your watch?" asked Emmy.

"Yes, you can keep my watch and fix it."

Tanner left Emmy's cell in tears. As she fled the main gates of the asylum, Sean Carlyle was waiting for her. Tanner's eyes were scratchy and hot, and her face tear-stained.

"Did she hurt you?" Sean asked in a serious tone.

"No, Sean. She was kind and gentle. She told me that she was broken."

"Oh, dear God, Tanner. Did she talk?"

"A little."

"Did she tell you who broke her?"

"No, after today, we can only hope that she tells the judge. But she spoke, so we have a slim chance."

Sean steered Tanner toward a waiting cab. Once they were both safely inside, he put his arms around her, and she told him of her experience meeting Kevin, the inmates and Emmy.

"I'm afraid, Sean, I don't know if she can face the court. She's so delicate. I cannot even hope that she will. All I know is that she isn't the violent monster she is portrayed as."

"You can't be sure of that, Tanner."

"She knows that she is broken. She has introspection, and a unique way of shutting out her fear, but a monster she is not."

"That is a progressive interpretation and highly debatable."

"Before she went to court, the Daily News published a racy headline, 'Killer with the Angel Face.' How is that fair?"

"We have to be objective Tanner, we have to report the truth, not the truth as we see it."

"The Daily News didn't print the truth. Their article was biased and sensational," complained Tanner.

"And we don't want to earn the same reputation. We can expose the truth, but we cannot suppose motive. If you want to help Emmy, find Martin Blackburn."

"I don't know where to begin," she admitted.

"We'll do it together."

"I want to see her solicitor, Mr Schulz."

"What will you achieve by doing that, Tanner? Write the article on Tilda? We cannot publish anything Mr Schulz tells us."

"Please, Sean. I need to tell him what happened today."

"No. Get Kevin Bamborough to go and visit Mr Schulz. If you are seen to be breaking the golden rule of protecting your source, you will never be trusted again."

"I do not care," said Tanner passionately. "I must save her life."

"Make up your mind, are you a journalist or a lawyer? Are you acting as her defence counsel or taking the opportunity to expose this heinous act that pervades English society? We are already straddling the legal fence with the article that we are publishing about Tilda. I'm ordering you as your boss and your editor. If you dare go against my instructions, I'll fire you."

Tanner had to control her temper. The cab stopped outside Sean's apartment.

"You're welcome to come in," he told her.

"No, thank you, "replied Tanner, "not tonight."

Sean watched the cab round the corner. He wasn't going to beg her to come to his apartment. No matter what he felt for her, he wasn't going to put his job or the newspaper in jeopardy. He'd a responsibility to his staff, and his readers.

Tanner wanted to cry. *You're not going to cry over a man,* she lectured herself. Her focus changed to Martin Blackburn. She needed to find him sooner than later.

"Where to, Ma'am?" called the cab driver.

"Angel Meadows."

"That is a dangerous place for a lady at this time of the night."

Tanner ignored him.

He dropped Tanner in a market square on the outskirts of the slum.

"I can walk from here."

The cab driver shook his head. The woman was stupid, and he warned her against it; there was nothing more that he could do.

Tanner looked up and down the busy road, unsure of which way to go. Every pickpocket on the street watched her leave the cab. Tanner was aware of eyes watching her, and she knew that she was the perfect target for petty crime.

The first hotel she saw was owned by the Italian money lenders, renowned for their violence. The hotel had large windows with a well-lit lounge visible from the street, and everybody could see what was happening inside it. The bright hotel served as a keen reminder of the Italians' status in The Meadows. Tanner ascended three steps, and a courteous concierge opened the door. He greeted her in an Italian accent.

Tanner looked around her, wondering whom to approach so that her plan would work. She saw a well-furnished office with a man inside. He was dark-skinned, and his hair was slicked back with some kind of oil. All the parasitic pick-pockets were watching her from the shadows. When Tanner was invisible to the street, she undid the buckles on her satchel. As she passed the office door, she tripped, and the contents of her bag went scattering across the floor. Even though she planned it, she still blushed with embarrassment. Always charming, the Italian man stood up and went to help. He took Tanner's hand and helped her to her feet.

"Signorina, what a terrible accident."

He looked down at her beautiful face and green eyes. This was an exceptional woman indeed.

"I'm so sorry," Tanner apologised, "I've been clumsy."

The gangster motioned with his hand, and a bellboy ran across the foyer and started gathering all Tanner's notes.

"No need to apologise, signorina, please sit down. I'll arrange a cup of tea for you."

The procedure was exactly as Tanner had planned it. Every thug on the street would watch her having tea, and within minutes the entire Angel Meadow would assume that she was protected by the Italians.

But, she underestimated the bellboy's ambition. He could read, and he was determined to win his bosses' trust. The young man returned her satchel, then nonchalantly strolled to the office.

"What is it, Mario?"

"Signor, I read some of the woman's papers. She's a journalist."

The Italian's eyes narrowed.

"Get her in here, Mario, and be charming. We do
not want to frighten her."

The bellboy escorted Tanner into the office and shut the
door behind him.

"Sit down, my dear," The Italian told her.

Tanner smiled and sat down.

The Italian moved around the desk in a flash. He produced
a lethal stiletto blade as if from nothing and put it to her
throat. She felt the razor-sharp point of the knife pierce her
skin, and a drop of blood trickle down her neck.

"You're a journalist. Your fall was no accident.
What are you looking for?"

"It was an accident. I'm looking for someone."

The man grabbed her hair and wrenched her head back.

"Tell me the truth, or I'll slit your throat from ear
to ear and get rid of you in the harbour."

He pushed the knife a little harder, it hurt, and she felt more
blood dribble from her neck. Tanner knew that he would
kill her. She made her decision in a split second, she
couldn't have the Italians after her blood and even worse,
she didn't want to be murdered.

"Yes, I'm a journalist," she admitted.

He jerked her head back harder than before.

"I'm not here to investigate you," she growled. "Stop."

The Italian released his grip. The knife was lowered.

"You better have a good story," he glared at her.

"I'm looking for someone, the pickpockets were following me, and I was scared. I thought that if they see me with you, they would leave me alone."

He was still suspicious of her, "what is your name?"

"I'm Tanner Fischer from the Manchester Herald. I'm looking for someone."

"I'm Johnny Bocelli."

Tanner nodded.

"Who are you looking for?"

"Martin Blackburn."

"Why?"

Tanner repeated Emmy's story. She knew that she would have to be honest, but bet on his silence.

"Jimmy Sterling was a pig," said Johnny in a harsh whisper.

"I'll help you. We know where Martin lives. We have helped Martin from time to time. He always pays his debt on time. One of my men will take you to his house, you will be protected, and you do not have to fear anyone."

"May I leave now?" asked Tanner. She was terrified, her legs shaking so much that she didn't trust them to stand.

"Of course, signorina."

"Do I owe you anything?" she asked.

"Not at all. signorina. And don't be afraid if you need to do an article on me, I'll not hurt you. You do your job, and I'll do mine."

Johnny didn't smile or tell her that he recognised the name Fischer. He knew that the most powerful family in banking had enough power to have him executed if he touched their granddaughter.

Vinny escorted Tanner through the mean streets of Angel Meadows. The narrow streets never slept, and the congestion, filthy air and low clouds made her feel claustrophobic. Vinny took her arm and steered her through the streets. Johnny had given him strict instructions not to lose her. Vinny was ordered to take her to Martin's house, return her to the square, then put her in a cab and hope Tanner never returned.

Tanner could see the fear on Martin's face when he opened the door. Yes, the Italians had helped him from time to time, but Martin was sure that he'd no outstanding debt.

"Evening Martin, somebody to see you," said Vinny.

Martin looked past him and saw Tanner.

"Who is she?" asked Martin.

Vinny shrugged his shoulders and pulled a face.

"Who knows?" he answered sarcastically.

Tanner pushed past Vinny and put out her hand to Martin.

"My name is Tanner Fischer from the Manchester
Herald," she smiled, hoping to alleviate the
tension."

"What do you want with me, Miss?" asked Martin.

"You were friends with Jimmy Sterling, correct?"

"Look now, I don't want to talk about Jimmy
Sterling. He deserved his lot."

"I'm not here as a journalist, but I need your
help," said Tanner.

Martin studied her up and down at length.

"You'd better come inside."

Tanner looked around the small two-roomed flat. For all
the misery in The Meadows, Martin's wife had managed to
make it cosy, clean, and cheerful. Two little faces appeared
from the other room, Martin and Celine's daughters.

"Say good evening," instructed their mother, and
they both greeted Tanner with a smile.

They were poor but clean, and it was clear that their mother took pride in her surroundings.

"Would you like a cup of tea?" asked Celine.

"Yes, please, if it's not too much trouble. I'm freezing."

Celine looked at the two little girls.

"Off to bed, you two. And close that door, no listening in tonight."

Once the children had departed, the adults began their discussion in hushed tones.

"I don't want the girls to hear anything we discuss, especially if it's about that rogue, Jimmy," said Celine with disdain.

There was a pause while Tanner took a sip of her tea.

"What do you want from Martin?" asked Celine.

"As you know, Jimmy Sterling was beaten to death by his daughter Emmy."

Martin nodded slowly.

"Martin, I'm here to beg you to testify on Emmy's behalf."

Martin frowned.

"What would Martin be able to tell the courts that they don't already know? Martin has not seen

Jimmy for years. Martin never trusted him around our girls since all that trouble with Emmy when she was a young thing."

"Yes," agreed Martin, I believed all that talk about his daughter was just Jimmy acting up, but then the baby and Emmy going to the madhouse, I never wanted to see him again. I didn't want to be seen around with him, especially after my two were born. I'm not that kind of man," Martin told Tanner.

"So, Jimmy did discuss his intentions with you?"

"Yeah, he did. But like I said, I didn't take it seriously."

"Martin, will you be prepared to testify on behalf of Emmy?"

"Now, now, Miss. I don't want to get involved in this mess."

"Do you know that Emmy and Tilda are qualified watchmakers and have good lives? The Weiners took them in and have cared for them."

"Yea, I read that in the newspaper," answered Celine.

"Emmy needs help Martin. She has been wronged by her father. If you do not testify, she will likely hang for murder."

Celine nudged Martin.

"I say you do it, Martin. If it were my daughter in a pickle, I would want somebody to speak up for her."

Martin nodded but didn't answer immediately.

"Alright then. I'll do it."

"Where do I go? Who do I speak to?"

Tanner was elated and gave him Mr Schulz's details.

Martin escorted her outside.

"Thank you," Tanner said.

"If we can keep this visit confidential, I'll be grateful," she advised.

"Of course," replied Martin.

When they finished their conversation, as Tanner left, Vinny pulled out ten quid and handed it to Martin, who was hesitant to accept it.

"Take it," said Vinny in a menacing voice, "it's from the boss. He says you will need it to travel to court every day."

Vinny escorted Tanner to the market square without saying a word. As she climbed into the cab, she looked back.

"Thank you," she smiled.

"The boss says don't come back. These are dangerous streets."

It was the early hours of the morning, but Tanner headed straight to Sean's apartment. She ran up the stairs and knocked loudly on his door. Sean opened the door, and before Tanner had time to close it again, he was already walking back to his bedroom.

"Why are you here?" he called out as he walked away.

"We need to talk."

"I'm going back to bed."

"I want to tell you something," she persisted.

"I don't have time for a love quarrel at four o'clock in the morning. There was a crisis in Liverpool late this afternoon. We'd to pull out all the stops to cover it. I only got in an hour ago. Sleep on the couch if you must."

"A love quarrel? My, my, you do think a lot of yourself."

It wasn't the response Sean expected, and he stopped mid-stride. He truly believed that she'd come to make amends. He fought to contain his embarrassment and didn't want to look weak or stupid. Sean realised that she wasn't as predictable as he thought, and now she'd his full attention.

"I found Martin Blackburn."

"What? When?" Sean asked, surprised.

"How?"

"Johnny Bocelli helped me," she answered.

"Where did you meet Johnny Bocelli?"

"At his hotel? He was a perfect gentleman."

"How did you find Martin's house?"

"Vinny, his henchman took me to it."

Sean put a pot on the stove and began to make coffee. Then he changed his mind and poured them each a whiskey. He drank his fast, and then had another.

"You went to Angel Meadows in the middle of the night, asked the biggest gangster in the city for help and you were escorted to Martin's house. Is this correct?"

"Yes, and Johnny gave Martin ten quid to help him get to Mr Schultz, and the courthouse."

Sean lifted his hand to his forehead.

"Almighty God, woman, what was going through your head. I told you that I would help you find Martin. Why didn't you take me with you?"

"Because you would've got us killed."

Sean shook his head again. He couldn't believe what he was hearing.

"Do you expect me to congratulate you for being so stupid?"

"Frankly, I don't need your approval. I just need to provide you with the best story you have ever published."

"Will Bocelli allow you to use his name in your article after the trial?"

"Of course not. He is a source."

"And will you honour your agreement?"

"Of course."

"What else did he say, "asked Sean in shock.

"To never come back," replied Tanner coyly.

"And are you going to honour that command?" asked Sean.

"Of course not," smiled Tanner, "this is the beginning of a long relationship between Johnny and I. I'll get all sorts of scoops. You'll see."

Tanner left his apartment delighted with her achievement, and Sean returned to his cold bed with his tail between his legs. He was furious with Tanner. He'd never experienced such a headstrong journalist. Most reporters were happy to sit in the pubs all afternoon and pick up scraps of gossip and develop them into stories. Tanner was different. She knew that the press had the power to be a catalyst for social change. And how dare she have the nerve to approach Johnny Bocelli. Nobody ever received help from him. In fact, Bocelli hated the press.

"Damn it!" he cursed as he lay in bed.

There was no possibility that he would fall asleep now. It was hours before daylight, but Sean got dressed and walked to work.

20

THE BRIGHTEST
STAR IN THE SKY

"I do not trust your motive for going to
Birmingham," said Annabelle sternly.

"My darling, wouldn't it be lovely to wake up in
the morning and gaze across our lovely gardens,
and appreciate the promise of springtime?"

Annabelle looked at Samuel suspiciously.

"That is way too poetic for you Samuel, you are
up to something."

Samuel put his head back and laughed loudly.

"If we go to the country house, it's a short train
ride to the foundry. I was thinking of working
with Shilling for a few days a week. I've discussed
the idea with her, and she is delighted."

"Aha, how long have you planned this Sam? The doctor said you should be resting."

"Annabelle, the doctor also told me that I'm in better shape than some men half my age, which is very lucky for you, my angel."

Annabelle raised her eyebrows and smiled. Samuel exuded charm when he set his sights on doing something she disagreed with.

"No, more than twice times a week Samuel," said Annabelle, then waited for an objection.

"Of course," he said, earnestly, knowing that he would do everything in his power to break the rules when he got to Birmingham.

"If you don't comply, you can sleep in a hotel."

"Will you come with me?"

Annabelle shook her head and chuckled.

"Unfortunately, I can't resist you."

Samuel laughed again.

"I'm serious, Samuel, only a few days a week."

Reluctant to have his plans scrutinised and his motives questioned, Samuel kissed Annabelle on her cheek and escaped to his study.

Samuel and his household arrived at the small village station close to the country house. The house was as grand as the house in Mayfair, only smaller. The coach turned into a driveway shaded by a canopy of branches. As the cab rounded a slight bend in the road, the canopy gave way to a limestone manor house set in the middle of a beautiful garden. Other grand country houses had manicured lawns and man-made ponds, but Samuel and Annabelle chose to keep their land undisturbed. They'd sit on the veranda, overlooking the river, and appreciating the weeping willows that lined the banks.

On summer evenings, they would watch the game come to drink at the water while the birds settled into their nests for the night. Not too far away from the house was a natural pond that froze in the winter, which was where Shilling taught Tanner to ice-skate in the winter and swim in the summer.

It was also a haven for the staff, who enjoyed the freedom of the outdoors, and the privacy of separate lodgings. For them, it was like living in a hotel, and over the yuletide, Samuel permitted them to take part in local festivities. They had a deep respect and loyalty for their master who had risen from poverty and never forgotten his roots. On Christmas and Boxing Day, they were always given the option of going back to their families in London. Samuel knew what it was like to be alone.

Samuel seldom attended local social events because he couldn't identify with the neighbouring gentry or aristocracy. Whenever someone asked him if he was landed gentry, he would answer, 'No, I'm just a farm boy, call me Sam'. It was this attitude that endeared him to the locals. Samuel and Annabelle were happy to entertain themselves, and their greatest joy was exploring the countryside. They found small villages and slept in quaint hotels, took boats down the river just to identify a particular bird. Even when they were younger, they hired a houseboat to chug along the river, going from village to village. They didn't need to be socialites to enjoy their lives.

There was one event that Annabelle was fond of, the annual Spring show in the village, and for that day, Samuel would escort her and indulge her every whim.

It was at one of these events that Lord Mundy deliberately put himself in Samuel's path.

"Good afternoon Mr Hudson," said Lord Mundy.

Samuel gave him a nod.

"Good afternoon."

"I'm glad to see you in person. You don't seem to be very involved in the community. Lady Mundy has told me that you have turned down all our social requests for your presence at the manor."

Samuel ignored the snide remark.

"Lady Mundy has also said that your people are causing a lot of trouble for us."

"My people?" Samuel frowned.

People were stopping to listen to the conversation under the auspices of studying the bluebells.

"Your servants!"

"They're not my people. I do not own them. They're my employees."

"Well, whatever you want to call them, they're servants. Local opinion is that you are way too liberal."

Annabelle was aware of a small crowd gathering around Samuel, and she strolled across the beautifully trimmed lawn to see what was happening. When she reached Samuel, she took her place at his side and took his arm. Lord Mundy continued to speak without acknowledging Annabelle.

"Please have some manners and greet my wife," Samuel told him.

Lord Mundy was painfully embarrassed but greeted Annabelle none the less.

"We are all in this together, old boy. Servants must not rise above their station, or we will have anarchy. They meet in the markets, and the pubs from time to time where they talk to each other. And of course, they have families on the outside who gossip."

"On the outside? Are you running a gaol?" asked Samuel.

"Of course not, old boy," said Lord Mundy frustrated, "but there are a few simple rules that our class adheres to."

"And what are those rules? Please educate me," Samuel could feel his blood rising. He longed to wallop Lord Mundy, but after the drama at the French Embassy, he realised he was getting too old to fight; his fingers had taken weeks to heal.

"Well, the local gentry all agree that we pay the same labour rates. Holidays, you know, they shouldn't get too many of those, it upsets the in-manor's routine. Oh, and days off, more than one afternoon a month is ridiculous."

"Are you a church man?" asked Samuel, deliberately omitting the man's title.

"Oh, yes, yes. We treat our staff in the most Christian way."

"Well, I'm not a church man and even I know that Sunday is the day of rest."

There was a collective gasp from the small crowd that had gathered around the men.

"How much work do you do in a day?" demanded Samuel.

Lord Mundy went scarlet.

"I thought so," Samuel glared at him.

"If this is your attitude, my good man, you will be very unpopular in these parts," said Lord Mundy.

"I'll take care of my household as I wish, and you will not lecture me in public."

"You allow your staff leave on a Sunday."

"Yes, I do."

"How can you do without a cook on a Sunday, Mr Hudson? Our cook must be on the premises to prepare every meal. Your servants have been a negative influence. Mine are demanding two Sundays off a month."

"That is a reasonable request. I'm a farm boy. I know how to make a cup of tea and butter a slice of bread."

"We are not prepared to eat bread and butter like peasants."

Lord Mundy was furious.

"Well, then you tell your wife to get off her backside and make you dinner when the cook is away."

Annabelle's eyes became huge, and she knew that she had to get Samuel home.

"Sam, we are leaving," said Annabelle firmly.

"Mr Hudson, you are a disgrace to society," exclaimed Mundy.

"Well, be damned if I'm going to change at this age, old boy."

Socrates stood watching the exchange. Of the many things Samuel had done over the years, this was probably his most entertaining demonstration of social rebellion.

The sun had not risen yet, but Samuel and Socrates were already at the foundry. The large furnaces ran constantly because once cooled, it took days for them to reach the temperature necessary to melt metal.

The older men recognised Samuel immediately, even though his hair was white, and he was leaning heavily on a walking stick. In no time at all, all the men gathered around him.

"We haven't seen you for some time, Sir," said Archie Burns, who had worked at the foundry for thirty years.

"I miss this place, Archie. I hope that Shilling has you on light duty."

"Yes, Sir," said Archie.

"Miss Shilling has insisted that I work in the office, but I still ruffle some feathers and offer my advice from time to time," he laughed.

"They can't keep me off the factory floor for very long."

"Good man. Things have changed, Archie. The machines may have changed, but the rules of physics have not changed. They still need you, Archie," Archie laughed.

"Yes, Sir, I couldn't have put it better myself."

Before long, Samuel took off his tie. He removed his jacket and gave it to Socrates, then rolled up his sleeves. Samuel walked around the foundry and spoke to all the workers, asking them what they did and showing interest in all the new engineering techniques.

"And Shilling understands all of this?" Samuel asked Archie.

"Oh, yes, Sir. In the beginning, we thought she'd lost her mind introducing all these new things. Between her and Mr Lee, we are the best foundry in the country."

Samuel eventually made his way up to Shilling's office. He had to climb two flights of steel stairs, and by the time he got to the top, he was breathless.

"I'll get you some water, Sam," said Socrates.

When Samuel didn't argue, Socrates was concerned.

Samuel sat down in Shilling's office and looked around. It was still filled with books, files, and drawings. While he waited, he began reading and realised that he was more than capable of understanding all the new concepts. It pleased him to know that his old brain could still solve complex problems. Shilling and Baxter arrived while Samuel had his nose in a book.

"Papa!" she exclaimed, and Samuel stood to greet her. He took her into his arms and kissed her on the forehead.

"I'm so happy to see you," she smiled and kissed
him on his cheek.

The first thing that Samuel noticed was the sparkling
diamond on Shilling's ring finger. He took in the large
perfect stone, and the twinkling emeralds that surrounded
it. He looked from the jewel to Baxter, unsure of what to say
or feel.

All that Samuel could manage to say was –
"When?"

Samuel knew that Shilling would never have committed to
Baxter if she didn't love him.

"Papa," she said to Samuel as her eyes searched
his for acceptance.

"I love you, Shilling. You have never disappointed
me, and you never will. I'm glad that you have
found somebody who makes you happy."

Shilling threw her arms around her father. When she finally
let him go, Samuel walked across the room to Baxter and
put out his hand.

"You have worked very hard to win her back,
"said Samuel. "I admire that. Very few of us get a
second chance at love."

"Thank you."

"We need to celebrate."

"Yes, Papa, we do."

As soon as they left the factory, Samuel spoke to Socrates.

"So, what do you think of that, Socrates? Will he
be good to her? I'm sure there is somebody in her
household that can keep you updated?"

"Stop it, Sam. I'm not spying on Shilling, and you
are not going to interfere."

Samuel shook his head. He felt like an old lion who was
losing his teeth. Within a few minutes, he discarded his self-
pity and was planning his afternoon.

"Let us go riding this afternoon," Samuel said,
displaying his usual zest for life.

"That is a better idea than interfering with
Shilling's nuptials," responded Socrates.

Samuel put his head back and laughed loudly.

He told Annabelle all the news with great gusto.

"I was wondering if you would talk to Shilling on
my behalf," asked Samuel, testing the waters.

"No."

Annabelle was emphatic.

"There is a conspiracy against me," grumbled
Samuel.

Samuel and Socrates took a slow ride across the meadows. It was relaxing to do something in the fresh air. Samuel longed for the bustle of the factory, but when he was there, he longed for the peace of nature. Perhaps the contrast was good for him. It kept him appreciative of his surroundings.

"Socrates, what is that?" called Samuel as they trotted over the crest of a hill.

Socrates craned his neck to see what Samuel was looking at.

"Over there, I see a movement. It's an animal."

Samuel nudged his horse forward, and they descended into the valley. As they neared the animal, they realised that it was shot. Tired from being on horseback, Samuel dismounted slowly and was panting as his feet touched the ground. He could hear the pitiful sound of the deer in pain.

"It's wounded, Sam. It wasn't a kill shot."

"Who do you think is responsible for this? What person with a conscience allows a deer to lie suffering to death?"

Samuel was furious.

"How dare someone hunt on my land. I've forbidden it, and our blood-thirsty neighbours know it."

"Unfortunately, it can't be saved, Sam. We need to dispatch it."

Begrudgingly, Samuel walked to his horse and collected his rifle. He hated hunting, even for the pot.

"Someone will know who did this," said Samuel, "and when I find him—," the sentence tapered off because Samuel couldn't think of a suitable punishment to fit the crime.

Samuel put the rifle to his shoulder. *I'm so sorry*, he thought as he looked at the animal, 'you were on my land, in my safekeeping, and I've allowed someone to hurt you. Please forgive me.'

Samuel pulled the trigger and fired a shot into the animal's brain, and the noise echoed through the valley. As the rifle fired, Samuel collapsed to the ground. Socrates thought that it was the recoil that knocked Samuel off his feet, then remembered Samuel normally stood rock solid while holding a gun. Socrates rushed over to Samuel, who was now writhing on the ground clutching his chest.

"In my pocket," gasped Samuel.

Socrates searched every pocket, but he couldn't find the tablets that Samuel used to put under his tongue. It was a catastrophe.

"Can you sit up?"

"I don't know," said Samuel gasping for air.

"We have to get you home. Do you think you can sit on the horse?" asked Socrates.

"I won't let a little bit of pain get in my way," answered Samuel, then doubled up in agony as his heart went into another spasm.

Socrates knew that it was all false bravado, and Samuel knew that he was in trouble.

Socrates dragged Samuel to a tree trunk. He didn't know if he was strong enough to lift Samuel onto the horse. It was a miracle that he managed to get Samuel onto the big log. Then, he used all his strength to lift him from the log into the saddle. Samuel wasn't strong enough to sit up straight. The pain was stabbing through his chest like a hot knife. He flopped forward on the horse. He was almost unconscious, and Socrates had to be very careful not to panic the horses. The loyal valet longed to go faster but knew that Samuel would die if he fell off the horse.

The groomsman was the first person to see the horses approaching the stables. They were walking so slowly that the young man knew that something was wrong. As Socrates reached the stables, young Davy went tearing toward them.

"Did one of them lose a shoe?" he shouted to Socrates.

"No, it's Mr Hudson. He has had a heart attack."

"Heavens be!" gasped the groomsman, springing into action.

"We have to get him off," shouted Socrates, "And not drop him."

The staff heard the noise and rushed into the courtyard. Annabelle ran across the cobbles to the stables.

"What's the commotion all about?" she yelled over the noise.

She pushed herself through the crowd of servants and saw Samuel lying on the cobbled stones. Socrates took charge.

"Fetch his tablets, Lizzy. They're on his desk in the study. He forgot to take them with him. Davy, to the village and get the doctor. Cook, some water, please, and be quick about it."

Only when Socrates had finished giving orders did he look for Annabelle and tell her what happened.

"Let's get him inside," ordered Socrates.

The men found an old door in the stable, placed Samuel on it and carried him to his and Annabelle's room.

Samuel lay on his bed, exhausted. His eyes were closed, and he'd difficulty breathing. Annabelle held the glass of water to his lips, and he managed to take a few sips. Perspiration ran off his body. It drenched his shirt and soaked the sheets.

"Socrates, send someone to fetch Shilling and Baxter, but not you—don't leave me alone."

Socrates knew that Annabelle was devastated, but so far, she'd done a good job of hiding it.

"I'm right here, Miss Annabelle. I'm not going anywhere. Let's undress him and get him comfortable."

The doctor arrived within half an hour. He pushed through the crowd of servants standing outside the open bedroom door.

"Get a move on! Get a move on. Let me through," he barked.

Once in the room, he walked directly to the bed, thankfully with his bedside manner improving with each pace.

"Hello, Mrs Hudson. Please move aside and give me some space."

Annabelle and Socrates moved to the other side of the bed and watched the doctor examine Samuel. The doctor took his time and remained well into the evening to ensure that Samuel was comfortable. Then, he nodded towards the door as he planned to share Samuel's prognosis with them in private.

"I know Mr Hudson's medical history," he told Annabelle. "Today, his heart has suffered irreversible damage. There is nothing that I can do. Keep him in bed, and as calm as possible."

"I should've checked that he had his tablets," cried Annabelle.

"The tablets would not have saved him, Mrs Hudson. With Samuel's history, it was just a matter of time. It's a miracle that he didn't die on the spot."

Shilling and Baxter arrived as the doctor was leaving, and they confronted him in the library.

"What is the situation with my father-in-law?" asked Baxter.

"He has irreparable damage to his heart, Mr Lee. There is very little anybody can do for him—."

"There has to be a doctor who can help him in London. I've read about new techniques in medicine. For heaven's sake, doctor, you must have a solution," interrupted Shilling.

"Your father has had a better life than many men his age. He has been a fit man, well into his late eighties. He has lived a long life," The doctor told her.

"I'm afraid that he will not survive a trip to London, and even with all the modern methods available, surgeons cannot replace a damaged heart."

Shilling nodded. Baxter took her hand. He could see that she was in shock.

"He has not got long to live, so make the best of the time you have left."

Shilling couldn't believe that this was happening. Her emotions were out of control. She didn't know what to do or say. She was a woman who could solve any problem, and now she was stuck. There were no options available to save her father. She burst into tears and fled up the stairs to Samuel and Miss Annabelle's bedroom.

Annabelle stopped her at the bedroom door.

"I want to see Papa now," Shilling cried hysterically.

"No!"

"Don't you dare say no! I must see him right this minute."

Baxter reached Shilling's side and listened to what Annabelle saying.

"Your father is weak but conscious. He will be deeply distressed if he sees you in this condition. Go downstairs and have a drink, wash your face, and calm down. Then come back and see him. I'm sure that he will perk up when he sees you."

"She's right," said Baxter softly.

Shilling burst into tears again.

"Come here," Baxter took her in his arms and encircled her, drawing her tightly to his chest.

"I know that you are sad, my love, but Samuel must see you at your best."

Annabelle observed Baxter's tenderness and Shilling's absolute reliance on him for support. The sight warmed her aching soul.

"I'll stay with Samuel, "said Socrates, "go and
have something to drink and calm down."

Shilling drank two whiskeys in great haste. Eventually, she felt calm enough to see her father, but by then, he was sleeping. Annabelle and Shilling kept vigil over Samuel throughout the night. Socrates set himself up in the room next door. When the sun rose, the two women were so tired that they collapsed onto their beds exhausted. Baxter put his arm over Shilling as she climbed into bed next to him.

"I love you, Shilling."

Baxter watched her close her eyes and fall asleep immediately. She still looked young, like the girl he fell in love with, but Samuel's illness had made her vulnerable. He pushed his body up against hers. He wanted to be as close to her as he could be. He wanted her to know that he was there and that he would never leave her again.

Socrates was put in charge of Samuel while Annabelle and Shilling slept. At eight am Samuel woke up bright as a button.

"Get me out of this bed, Socrates," he said,
panting for breath.

"The doctor said that you must rest."

"I've very little time to live. Do you think I'm
going to waste it in bed?"

"You can't walk, Sam. You'll lose your breath. Then what?"

"Hurry up then, find a wheelchair. I've things to do."

Socrates laughed out loud.

"Samuel, you exasperate me, but I love you all the same."

"You know, "said Samuel, "I didn't think that we would still be friends after all these years."

"Neither did I," said Socrates.

"You saved my life, Sam."

They sat in silence for a while. Socrates got up and propped some pillows behind Samuel's back, allowing him to sit up. Then he poured them both a cup of tea.

"Did you ever long for a family, Socrates?"

"I've a family. This household was my family."

"I mean, a real family. A wife and children."

"Ah, it was so long ago, Sam. I grew up in Whitechapel. My mother was Greek, and my father was English. A sailor. The two met when he was docked in Athens. When I was a little child, my mother, Dimitra—well, she was a real beauty. Her looks didn't last long, though. Poverty seems to age people before their time, don't you think?"

Samuel nodded.

"Greece was poor as well, of course, but I think the people are happier there. It's warm, and the people are cheerful. Family means everything to them, and they all live together and support each other. It's a different culture."

Samuel listened carefully.

"But she fled and came here. Whitechapel finished her, she died of tuberculosis. When she died, I became a hooligan. That is when you found me. I would have been strung up or deported if it had not been for you. I never really wanted children. The idea of raising them in the dirt and filth of Whitechapel appalled me."

"And love, have you ever been in love?" asked Samuel.

"Of course, for many years now."

In a reflex action, Samuel sat bolt upright, winced, then looked at Socrates with a sneaky smile.

"With whom?"

Socrates laughed.

"Just this once, I'll gossip. With Lizzy. We have been in love for many years."

"And you have managed to keep it a secret from me?"

"You—and her husband."

"What?" roared Samuel, and then began to cough until the bed rattled.

Socrates got up and gave him some water.

"He was a cruel man, her chap. Ended up deported to Australia for some sort of misdemeanour. She never saw him again."

Samuel laughed.

"Good for you, Socrates. I would've done the same."

The two men chuckled and finished their tea.

"I've left you something in my will," advised Samuel solemnly.

"Thank you, Sam, but you didn't need to do that."

"Now, I'll have none of your backchat, my good man. Do you remember the neat little farmhouse where my mother lived, near Solihull?"

Socrates nodded.

"Well, you aren't as young as you used to be. You'll need a pension, and a place to retire. Take Lizzy and go and live in peace. Make the best of your time. You deserve it."

"Sam, I've never wanted anything from you. Just trusting me was good enough."

Samuel ignored him.

"Will you take care of Miss Annabelle when I'm gone?"

"Of course."

"What am I going to do without her?" Samuel asked with tears in his eyes.

"You're going to be patient and wait for her, Sam."

"Do you really believe in all of that nonsense?"

"Of course, I do," answered Socrates. "Our souls are always searching for the love we left behind."

"How will I know where she is? How will I know where to find her?"

"That's easy, Sam, just study the heavens. Miss Annabelle has always dazzled you. She'll be the brightest star in the sky."

21

THE END OF A LEGEND

Tanner arrived at the Manchester Herald full of energy. Nobody could have guessed that she only had two hours of sleep. Nor could anyone have guessed that she'd received help from one of the most dangerous men in the city.

Her reputation was everything to her, and word would never reach Johnny Bocelli that she had ever dropped his name in public. It was a matter of trust.

She was pondering going to see Sean Carlyle to discuss the next steps of their plan, but before she'd time to unpack her satchel, a messenger boy came tearing through the office and shoved a brown envelope into her hand.

"A telegram for you, Miss Fischer."

"Thank you, Cecil."

Tanner ripped open the envelope, expecting it to be something related to Emmy's story. Instead, it was a telegram from Shilling. Tanner threw down the telegram and raced up the steps to the mezzanine. She rushed into Sean's office, and without greeting him, she began to talk.

"My grandfather had a heart attack, he is very ill,
and I've to go home immediately."

Sean took a moment to digest the news. He knew that Tanner wasn't prone to over-exaggeration, so it was serious.

"Are you going to London?" he asked her

"No, Birmingham. I'll take the first available
train."

"I'm coming with you."

"No, Sean, you need to be here. You need to be in
court when the judge announces the date of the
trial."

"If you need me, I'll travel to Birmingham."

Tanner gave a brave and grateful smile. Sean stood up and walked around the desk. He wanted to kiss her goodbye, but she was already halfway down the staircase, and on her way to Samuel's bedside.

Tanner stopped at her apartment, packed a small suitcase then headed for the train.

Tanner arrived at the station and ran down the platform, fearing that she was late. As she ran towards her coach, she saw Sean.

"What are you doing here?" she asked.

"I'm going with you."

"Don't be ridiculous."

"Besides, I like Samuel," he ordered.

Sean and Tanner reached Birmingham on the midday train. Socrates was waiting for them on the platform.

"Socrates," shouted Tanner over the crowd and waved.

"Ah, Tanner, I'm so glad that you are here. Your grandfather is lucid but very tired."

"I'm sorry to hear that," said Sean and shook Socrates's hand.

"He refuses to stay in bed. I'd to get the carpenters to build wooden ramps all over so that we can wheel him around the house."

"That sound just like Grandpa," she smiled.

Sean laughed.

"I wish that I'd known him when he was young."

"Yes," laughed Socrates.

"He was quite a character back then. A force to be reckoned with. He started out as poor as a church mouse, but everyone respected him. Let's hurry now. We don't want to miss our connection."

Thirty minutes later, having disembarked into scenic countryside, they turned down a narrow lane lined with hedges. Eventually, they reached a wider road lined with oak trees. A quarter of a mile further, they turned into an overgrown driveway. They rode through what resembled a tunnel of leaves until they reached a magnificent house with a small garden overlooking a river.

The first person to come rushing out of the house was Shilling as soon as she heard their footsteps crunch on the gravel.

She flung her arms around her daughter and kissed her face.

"Mama, mama! Stop!" whimpered Tanner.

Annabelle followed close behind. Regardless of her age, Sean thought she looked lovely.

"Grandpa's in the library," she told them.

"Lizzy has made tea and scones. Let's celebrate your arrival."

Everyone cheerily agreed despite feeling there was nothing to rejoice about. Sean wondered how everyone could be so cheerful at such a sad time. His question was answered when he saw Samuel sitting in a high-backed wheelchair.

Every movement he made was slow, his breathing was laboured, and his countenance was pallid. Yet, his eyes remained bright, his mouth smiling.

"Shilling! "he called to his daughter, "Please design a better wheelchair than this. It's so uncomfortable. Far too tiny for a fellow like me. It belongs in a doll's house!"

"Papa! Tanner is here," called Shilling.

Tanner rushed over to Samuel's side and kissed him on the cheek.

"Grandpa, I've missed you so much!"

"Ah, Tanner, here you are," he looked past her and saw Sean.

"Oh, and you've brought that handsome fellow who is going to marry you."

Sean laughed, and Tanner blushed. Shilling shook her head.

"Enough, Papa. We all know that you are a hopeless romantic."

Annabelle seated herself next to Samuel, and Lizzy poured the tea.

"Can I help you with your scone, Papa?" sked Shilling.

"I can manage, my darling. The day I can't feed myself is the day I stop eating."

"You're so stubborn," whispered Annabelle.

"It's my job to look after you Annabelle, I'm the man of the house, and you are not here to look after me, my darling."

His reply made Annabelle sad because she knew that he meant it sincerely but could no longer fulfil the promise.

"Socrates!" called Samuel, "Did you find the bugger who left that animal for dead."

"No, Sir," replied Socrates.

"Drag him in here as soon as you find him."

"Grandpa, are you are on the warpath again," laughed Tanner.

Samuel began to quieten down. The tiny bit of exhilaration exhausted him, and in a short time, he dozed off in his chair.

"We should get him up to bed before it gets cold," suggested Annabelle.

Tanner found it strange to have dinner without her grandfather at the head of the table. That evening, Annabelle was sat in his seat, fidgeting uncomfortably with her crisp white napkin. Halfway through the meal, she burst into tears and excused herself. Shilling followed to the parlour and watched as Annabelle sobbed silently.

"Miss Annabelle," said Shilling gently.

Annabelle turned around, and Shilling put her arms around her.

"He is acting so bravely," said Annabelle.

"He is a brave man. Always has been. He won't change now."

"He loves us all so much, Shilling. He doesn't want
to leave us behind."

Shilling got a lump in her throat, but she suppressed her
tears to console Annabelle.

"How am I going to live without him, Shilling?"

"I don't know, Annabelle. I only know that there
is nothing duplicitous in his nature. He loves you,
and he is enjoying every day he has left with you."

Four days later, Samuel couldn't get out of bed. Try as he
might, he didn't have enough strength to sit up. His breath
was shallow, and he longed to sleep. When Socrates told
her the news, Shilling was furious, and Baxter followed her
as she ran up the stairs to Samuel's bedroom.

"Shilling, come back."

"I must speak to him," said Shilling.

"What do you want to say to him?"

"He must get up, Baxter. He must get up and fight.
If he fights, he will live."

Baxter could see that Shilling had false hope Samuel would
recover.

"Darling, don't humiliate him by demanding
something that he can't do."

Shilling looked into Baxter's eyes, and she could only see
kindness in them. He was helping her as gently as he could,
but the news still cut deep.

"Your Papa is very sick, Shilling. He is the strongest man that I've ever met, but he cannot resurrect himself for you. Don't let him die feeling that he couldn't fulfil your last request. You need to meet him on his terms."

"How do you know this?" she asked quietly.

"Because I experienced it with Kate. There comes a time when you just need to be next to him, hold his hand and love him. You must accept, it's the time to accept that he cannot get better."

"I love him so much, Baxter. I can't imagine him gone."

"I know, but you don't have to think about that when you are with him. Go sit next to his bed, and talk to him. Stop focusing on his death, focus on the little bit of life still left in him."

Baxter put his arms around her.

When Shilling calmed down, Baxter opened the door for her. She crossed the room and pulled a chair up against Samuel's bed.

"Hello, Papa," Shilling said, trying to behave normally.

"Hello, my Shilling," smiled Samuel.

"I'm buying a new milling machine for the factory, Papa."

"Yes?"

"It'll be three times faster than the ones we have."

"I hope you have chosen the most advanced one."

"Of course."

"Where is it made?"

"America," answered Shilling.

"Go to New York City, and have a holiday."

"Oh, Papa, only you would think of a holiday right now."

Samuel gave a small smile, and Shilling laughed. Then he became serious.

"I would've paid anything for you, Shilling. Maggie Carrot didn't realise that I would've bought you for a million pounds if she demanded it. When I saw you dangling from that filthy woman's hand, I knew that I was destined to be your father."

"Oh, Papa," cried Shilling.

A tear ran down Samuel's cheek.

"You have given me happiness every single day of your life," said Samuel softly.

"Even when I was difficult?"

"Especially when you were difficult. It gave me confidence that you were a woman who would live life on her own terms, with no regrets."

"Oh, Papa, I'm going to miss you. I know I should not say it, but I love you, and I cannot make peace with you leaving."

"Shilling, I've had a truly remarkable life. I believe that the saddest thing that can happen is to die a bitter person. I'm dying with joy, love, and appreciation for the blessing of having you in my life."

Shilling held Samuel's hand and cried. Her heart was broken. Eventually, she wiped her eyes and blew her nose.

"I want to be buried in the churchyard in the village. I like it there," Samuel said, changing the subject.

"Why not here, on the estate?"

"Because I don't want Annabelle to look out at my grave every day, being reminded that I'm being eaten by the worms."

Shilling smiled. Even on his deathbed, Samuel was trying to make life better for someone else.

"I thought you may want to be buried with Catherine."

"No, Shilling, that was a different life, only a fond but faded memory now. I'm with the people I love, and I want Annabelle buried next to me. She won't be happy sharing me with Catherine, will she?"

Shilling smiled.

"Of course. Whatever you wish, Papa."

Shilling held Samuel's hand, and they sat quietly.

"Papa."

"Yes?"

"What would you have called me if I cost a million pounds?"

Samuel wanted to laugh loudly, but he began coughing instead.

"I would've called you Milly Quid."

Baxter heard Shilling burst into giggles. Samuel was still doing his magic.

Another telegram arrived at ten o'clock in the morning. It was addressed to Sean Carlyle, and it was from Keith Downs.

Court assembles in three days stop

Sean threw the telegram down, wishing that he could tear it up and throw it away.

There was no easy way to tell Tanner that the trial date had been brought forward and that he needed to go back to Manchester.

Sean darted up the staircase and went looking for Tanner, who was exiting Samuel's room.

"What's wrong?" asked Tanner when she saw his face.

"The trial begins in three days."

Tanner was speechless.

"I've to go back immediately," said Sean.

"How can this happen?" yelled Tanner in fury.

"I'll go back and report on the proceedings. You don't have to be there."

"Emmy is counting on me. Send a message to Mr Schulz, and ask him if he can postpone it somehow."

"It doesn't work like that Tanner, the judge has the final word."

"I cannot leave my family at a time like this," Tanner yelled.

"I know, I'll take over."

Tanner went to her bedroom and slammed the door.

"What the hell is going on out there?" Samuel asked Socrates. "It sounds like a riot."

"It sounds like Mr Carlyle has to go back to Manchester immediately."

"What else did you hear, Socrates?"

"Oh, Sam, you are still so inquisitive."

"Something about a trial, and a court date."

"Is Tanner in trouble?"

"No, Sam, I think it has to do with a murder case in Manchester."

"Bring Tanner here."

"Rest, Sam, you don't need to worry about Tanner."

"Fetch her, Socrates. I want to speak to my granddaughter!"

"Yes, Sir," said Socrates, knowing that Samuel was giving a command, even though he could barely speak.

Tanner touched Samuel's hand.

"How are you today, Grandpa?"

"I'm doing very well," said Samuel, both eternal optimist and sneaky old fox.

"Are you and that man you will marry arguing?"

"Oh, Grandpa, you always say that!"

"You wait and see," he told her with a weak smile.

"Now, tell me about this case in Manchester."

Tanner was taken aback.

"How do you know about that, Grandpa?" she
asked with a smile.

"You were kicking up a right royal rumpus
outside my door. I can't speak very much, but my
ears still work," he rasped.

Tanner had to laugh.

"A girl has been accused of murder."

"Did she do it?" asked Samuel.

"Yes."

"Oh, dear, "said Samuel, "that is a pickle."

Samuel closed his eyes, and Tanner relayed the story to
Samuel, sparing no details.

"Oh, dear God, Tanner," said Samuel under his
breath.

"I would kill the blithering idiot too."

"Grandpa, this young woman will never lead a
normal life, but she has a wonderful family who
can look after her."

Tanner went on to tell the story of how Emmy became a
watchmaker and that she and Tilda ran the little shop
together.

"You would love the Weiners, Grandpa. They're
kind and generous. They aren't rich, but they go

out of their way to care for Emmy and Tilda. And Rachel makes the best brisket in Salford."

"I wish I could meet them," said Samuel.

"So, do I."

Samuel closed his eyes and dozed off for a moment.

As Tanner was about to leave, Samuel called out to her.

"Come here Tanner."

Tanner went and stood next to the bed.

"Listen to me, my angel, I've lived my life. I've a few days left. That girl, Emmy, she has a life ahead of her. Go back to Manchester now, go and help her."

"Oh, Grandpa," cried Tanner, "I can't leave you alone."

"Tanner, I've loved you since I held you in my arms, maybe even before that. Your mother has raised you to be a fine, caring woman. You have given me many years of joy, my darling. Nothing will make me happier than you saving that girl's life."

"I've to be here."

"Well, Tanner, I'm not going to be here."

Tanner was puzzled.

"I'm here now, fully aware of what is happening. I would rather you contribute to my life by making me proud of you than have you stand at my grave and mourn, where you can't change anything."

"Look around, Tanner. I'm not alone—but that girl is."

"I love you, Grandpa. I won't see you again if—."

"Don't count on that Tanner, who knows what happens beyond here."

Tanner gently embraced Samuel, and they cried in each other's arms.

"Go!" Samuel said bravely. "Go now. Go and save Emmy's life."

*

Samuel passed away peacefully, surrounded by the people he loved and loved him. Shilling sat in a chair holding his hand, and Samuel died in his wife's arms. Earlier that evening, Annabelle climbed onto the bed with him, and for the last time, she lay in his arm, with her head against his chest.

Shilling looked from Annabelle to Samuel and realised how powerful and intimate their marriage was. As the daughter of Samuel and Annabelle, she'd never taken time to examine or observe her parents need for each other. It was taken for granted that they loved each other. She took it for granted that they would always be together.

Annabelle didn't cry. There would be plenty of time for that later. She wanted Samuel to leave this world knowing that he'd fulfilled her every dream of love. She'd no shame talking to him in front of Shilling.

Annabelle ran her hand over his arms and his chest. She touched his face and kissed him gently. She examined his hands that touched her with so much tenderness, and she told him their love story, like she was reading it from a book.

She began when she first saw him in the cab after he'd bought Shilling. He was handsome, commanding, driven and gentle. She touched on his most tender and funniest moments. And she ended their story with her lying in his arms, still as in love with him as when they met. Shilling listened to their life story. Sometimes she commented. Sometimes Samuel gave a weary smile, sometimes he sighed or moved a finger to assure her that he was listening.

Then with the greatest effort, he took Shilling's hand.

"Do you know how much I love you?" he asked
her gently.

Shilling nodded, and tears began to stream down her face.

"Did I tell you enough?"

"Yes, Papa, always."

"I'll always be your Papa, and no matter what
happens, I'll be there, right next to you."

"And I'll always be your Shilling, Papa. I love you.
I always will."

Samuel tried to say something to Annabelle as she lay with her head on his chest.

"Sam, "she smiled, "Rest, my darling. I know what you want to say."

Samuel's mouth moved but in vain.

"You're going to tell me that you can't live without me, aren't you?"

Samuel gave her a dazzling smile.

"I'll find you, Annabelle. I'll look for you until I find you again."

There was no death rattle, no gasp for breath, no cries of pain.

Samuel simply closed his eyes and fell asleep, loved and cherished to the end by his beloved wife, with his treasured Shilling at his side.

Samuel was buried in the little churchyard in the village. There were no dukes, duchesses, lords, ladies, sirs or madams in attendance. All the people who came to pay their respects were honest, hard-working people he mentored and cared for. The house staff were overcome with grief. Socrates couldn't bear to watch Samuel being rendered to the earth. It was the first time in his years of service and friendship that he couldn't stand to be at his master's side.

Eventually, Shilling found him sitting on the church's front steps, his head in his hands, weeping. She sat down on the pavement next to him, put her arm around him and pulled him towards her, cradling his head with her other hand.

"We still have each other. We'll look after each other," she said tenderly.

Socrates couldn't reply. Shilling sat with him, sharing his pain. She didn't leave him alone when he needed comfort—how could she? He was as responsible for saving her as was Samuel.

22

SEAN'S REVOLUTION

Tanner was tired of trains and telegrams, as she was starting to associate them with bad news. The trip from Birmingham to Manchester was tedious. It seemed that everything was moving at half the speed.

Sean sat opposite her, and for a large part of the journey, both were too tired to talk. He tried to lay down and sleep, but the bunk was too small. Sean's head was sore and his brain felt foggy. Tanner was too tired to sleep. Every time she closed her eyes, her mind was a jumble of frenetic thoughts.

Eventually, Sean sat up. He leaned forward, put his elbows on his knees and rubbed his eyes, then he looked at Tanner. Her eyes were red rimmed.

"You need looking after," Sean told her.

Tanner gave a weak smile.

"I feel guilty for leaving my mother behind."

"She gave you her blessing. She's a unique woman."

"I know, but it doesn't make it any easier to leave her behind. And Socrates will be beside himself with sorrow," Tanner's eyes began to water.

"I'm sorry, I wish I could take the pain away," he said, quietly.

"Tell me about your family," said Tanner, trying to distract herself from the sadness.

"Ah, yes. I've four brothers. My father is a shopkeeper and my mother helps him."

"It must be wonderful to come from a big family."

Sean laughed. "I'm the second son. They didn't take much notice of me, and I was a naughty little bugger."

Tanner laughed.

"Are they all married?"

"Yes, and I've four nieces and three nephews."

Tanner nodded.

"It's a full house at Christmas," laughed Sean.

"And you? Did you want a wife and children?"

Sean sat up and ran his hand through his hair.

"I think I'm looking for a woman who has more to offer than children. Until lately I didn't think that I would find one."

"Until lately?" she smiled and raised her eyebrows.

"Yes, Rosie Jones in the editing department is quite attractive."

Tanner frowned, her heart skipped a beat. She didn't know whether he was joking or not.

"I'm teasing," he laughed.

Tanner pretended to think that it was funny.

"Have you ever been in love?" she asked him.

"Yes," he smiled. "Yes, a long time ago."

Tanner put her head to one side and smiled.

"Who was the lucky lady?"

"She was beautiful and we were best friends, and every day was a new adventure."

"What was her name?"

"Erica," he laughed "She lives in Surrey, has three children, and is married to a nice bloke."

"Did she break your heart?"

"No, she was six, and her father owned the shop next to ours. We'd a wonderful time together.

When I was older, I realised that I wanted a wife who would also be my best friend."

Tanner shook her head and laughed.

He bent forward and took her hand. "You're clever, passionate and stubborn." He kissed her hand. You are the only interesting woman I've met in a long time."

Tanner didn't know what to answer, so she looked out of the window.

"What do you want Tanner?"

"I do not want to be like other women. The idea of having babies does not enchant me yet, and I want to see more than dreary old England."

"Why not just take your inheritance and go from country to country, see the world? You have enough money to travel for a lifetime."

"I need purpose."

"You could write a book."

"I'll do that when I'm old," she laughed.

"Perhaps you could work as a foreign correspondent. There is a lot to report on throughout the empire."

Tanner nodded her head.

"I really like that idea, but I don't think anyone would publish my articles, I'm not enthralled by the Empire."

"That is why I love you," smiled Sean. "Do you think that you will want to marry one day?"

"I don't want to be owned by a man."

"My word, Shilling has raised a monster," Sean laughed loudly.

Tanner smiled.

"I didn't know Samuel very well, but I liked him a lot."

"He wanted my mother and me to follow our dreams."

"Are you?" asked Sean.

"Yes."

"What are your plans going forward?" asked Sean.

"I'm going to join the suffragettes in their cause," Tanner said determinedly.

Sean laughed loudly. "It was just a matter of time. Yes, you do that. Just do not riot, I'm not spending my well-earned wages bailing you out of gaol."

"How many times have you been arrested?" asked Tanner.

"More than I can count on my fingers, and I've spent a couple of nights in gaol."

"Is it frightening?" asked Tanner.

"Of course, you never know who will bail you out. I'm lucky, and Keith always rescued me."

Tanner laughed loudly.

"Keith told me I was the most expensive editor he'd ever employed. And now we pay a very competent lawyer to keep me out of trouble."

"Do you laugh at everything?"

"Yes," he looked into her eyes, "except at you Tanner, I'm beginning to take you very seriously."

The train reached Manchester at eight o'clock at night. As soon as Tanner got into the cab, she fell asleep on Sean's shoulder. When they reached his apartment, he woke her up.

"Do you want to come in?"

She yawned and nodded.

"I want to talk about the trial."

Sean took her hand, and led her up the stairs to his apartment.

"I'll boil the kettle," he told her, but when he went to serve the tea to her, he found her fast asleep on his bed."

He covered her up, then lay down next to her looking at the ceiling.

Tanner got the fright of her life when she woke up in the early hours of the morning, and at first didn't know where she was. She was lying under a blanket, in a strange bed, and somebody had their arm over her. She threw the covers off and shot to her feet. It took a few moments to realise that she was in Sean's apartment.

Sean's eyes fluttered open, to see a silhouette of a woman speaking down at him.

"I slept in your bed."

"What? Yes," he rolled over and closed his eyes.

"What happened?"

"You fell asleep, and I felt sorry for you," he mumbled.

"What did you do?"

"I covered you up. You looked cold."

"What else did you do?"

"Nothing we both have our clothes on."

"Oh, yes. Why did you get under the blankets?"

"Oh, dear God. Must I go through this so early in the morning? I was bloody cold, that's why. Should I've rather frozen to death?"

"I've never slept in a man's bed before."

"I know. Can I make you some tea?"

"What if the neighbours see me? I'll have the worst reputation in Manchester."

"Nobody is watching you," Sean yawned.

"What will the neighbours say?"

"Since when did a granddaughter of Samuel Hudson care what the neighbours thought?"

"I still like my privacy."

"Well, Mr Brown on the left has a lot of female visitors. Usually colourful characters, and never the same woman twice. Mr Cartwright on the other side is very private, he is also very spiritual, there is a priest who comes to pray for him every Thursday night after ten o'clock. Mr Silverstone across the hall has a very sick wife, she contracted malaria in India. He nurses her with so much gin and quinine water, it must be a severe disease because she does not seem to recuperate."

Tanner huffed in the dark.

"So, as long as you don't kick up a fuss, and keep your voice down, nobody will notice you."

Tanner couldn't believe that he was fobbing her off.

"When we have had our tea, you can wash and change your dress. You must have something clean in that suitcase," he said. "We have to be in court by eleven o'clock."

Tanner gave in with a long sigh.

Sean stood up, already fully clothed. He headed for the door, but as he walked past he pulled her into his arms and kissed her hard and passionately. She knew he was aroused, and she would've continued if he wanted to. Instead, he let her go.

"That was worth publishing," he said, without smiling and walked away.

23

THE INHERITANCE

Rachel and Yakov had not slept for a week. The Jewish community supported them in the only way they knew how: they didn't stop praying for justice, they provided Emmy with the best legal counsel, and the Jewish women provided meals. There was a constant flow of visitors through their little apartment. The community was determined that the Weiners would not go into battle alone.

"We can only pray that the judge is merciful, and that nobody gives false evidence," Yakov told Rachel.

"If only Emmy would speak," lamented Rachel. "Surely, she knows that it'll save her life."

"I've visited Emmy twice," said Mr Schulz, sitting at the kitchen table. "I'm preparing for an outcome where she is declared mentally unfit."

"But that will be mean she will stay in the asylum. She'll be deemed dangerous, and live with the depraved," shouted Rachel, there must be more you can do than that.

"Now, Rachel," soothed Mr Schulz, "we are still claiming her innocence, but I cannot carry the final judgement. Surely you would rather have her in an asylum than hung?"

"Living in that place will be an eternal torture. She'll remain there until she is an old woman. Death may be more merciful," Yakov told Mr Schulz.

"Yakov, I can do my best, no more."

"Have you had situations like this before?"

"Yes," mumbled Mr Schulz.

"What is it Arnie, tell us everything. I must know the truth."

"The court must see—the truth is the truth," interrupted Rachel.

"The article that Tanner Fischer wrote on Tilda, was very powerful. I've heard comments that it has cast new light upon Emmy's character. The fact that she is a watchmaker has won her a lot of respect."

"Must the courtroom be open to the public given the nature of the subject?" asked Yakov.

"Yes, even in the light of the subject."

"We are glad that you can help us Arnie. Any other person would've thrown her at the mercy of the court and put little effort into defending her."

"It's a pleasure, Yakov. I've also waived the fee that the Jewish community has collected. This will be my gift to you."

"May Hashem be with you Arnie," said Rachel.

"Thank you. I'll see you in the courtroom tomorrow."

The corridors of the old building which housed the courtroom were cold and dirty. People milled around the hall, lost and confused as to where they should to be. Witnesses stood in the corridors and were summoned to give testimony at a moment's notice. Pompous lawyers and barristers paraded by in white wigs and black capes. They treated the people around them abominably, believing that they were their client's only salvation. Many them would arrive in court unprepared, not able to remember the name of the person they were to defend.

Arnie Schulz was always surprised by the cross section of the public that were in attendance during the procedures. The more ghoulish the crime, the more demand for a seat in the court room. If a poor member of the public secured a seat, they would sell it to the highest bidder. It amused Arnie that the onlookers were comprised of all classes, and the irony was that class didn't matter while everyone was enjoying themselves. Of course, the elite stood on the peripheries, their coaches parked at a distance, but they were as inquisitive as the poorest of the poor whom they deplored. When it came to death, everyone was equal. The street sellers were doing a roaring trade, everybody was hungry, and on busy days they made (excuse the pun), a killing.

The courtroom was dirty. It seemed that the floor had not been washed or swept in months. The robes and uniforms of the authorities around Arnie were stained, and their wigs were knotted with pieces of hair unglued and hanging about their faces. Arnie Schulz stood out among the shabby bunch; he'd a pride in his work, accompanied by a keen sense of responsibility. One of the earliest instructions that his people had received from God was to set up courts of law, and he respected that command. Other than that, Evie Schulz would've had a heart attack if he ventured into public with even a spot on his shirt. He had to look impeccable at all times. His wife was very proud of him, he was a man of integrity and faith.

> "The law isn't perfect Evie," he would lament,
> "but thankfully this country does not hang
> children any longer. If I was born fifty years
> earlier, I surely would've lost my mind."

> "There are still a lot of injustices Arnie, the poor
> need you, never give up."

It had been no easy feat for Arnie to practise law in England. If it had not been for his tenacity, he would never have become a barrister. He had to fight tooth and nail for every appointment, but he believed that the Jewish fraternity needed representation as they were ostracised. It took him five long years, of much debate and argument, to eventually earn the right to represent his clients in front of a British judge.

"Go home Jews," shouted a group of Irishmen in the crowd.

Yakov and Rachel looked straight into the faces of the people who were heckling them. The Irish Catholic community had never accepted them, and the chants were familiar, but had become less over time.

"Ignore it," said Yakov, who knew that Rachel would lose her temper at any time. "If we react, we will play right into their hands. "It'll be better in the courtroom."

"But there are so many people here, Yakov, and they're all aggressive. Do these people want Emmy to hang?"

"Rachel, when people are in a big group like this, they tend to forget their values and beliefs. We have seen this many times before. The nicest men or women can become unrecognisable monsters. Trust me, there are Jews in that crowd as well," answered Yakov.

This time, Sean and Tanner were able to circumvent the mob, and snuck into the damp old building through a side door.

"How did you know about the side door?"

Sean laughed.

"Experience," he answered.

"Can we get into trouble?" asked Tanner.

"Only if they catch us," Sean laughed.

Sean seemed to have recovered from their argument, and was in a good mood. She'd been thinking about the way he'd kissed her. Tanner was beginning to understand that the man wasn't a labrador, although he was kind and loving, he knew how to say no. He wasn't going to roll over at her every whim, and she respected him for it.

The court was infested by the press. Everybody watched Tanner when she arrived. This was the woman who had beaten the law by writing an article about Emmy's sister Tilda, outlining the Weiners role in raising her, and her sister, highlighting the young women's skills and achievements, without once mentioning her sister's name, Embeth Sterling. It was a stroke of journalistic genius.

The Manchester Herald, and Sean Carlyle's bold action had been discussed in parliament. The liberals thought that he was brilliant, and the conservatives wanted him put away, never to raise his head in the publishing world again.

"Well, done, my boy," said Keith Downs. "We are the centre of nationwide attention. I must congratulate you."

"Tanner came up with the suggestion," said Sean truthfully.

"Good for her. But you took a great chance publishing it. We can only change the world if we are brave."

"The government may rap us over the knuckles," said Sean. "They may fine us."

"Indeed, they may, but likely not, they won't want bad press," laughed Keith. "Besides, I'm old. What can they do to me? I've no wife or children. If I die in gaol I can say I'd an interesting life."

Sean laughed. He loved the old man's spirit.

"We need to discuss succession Sean. I want you to have this old rag."

"What?" asked Sean.

"I want you to own it, have it. You're an honourable man. You'll use it to serve the greater good."

"Keith, I can buy it from you, I've savings."

"What must I do with the money, stuff it in my coffin? No, Sean, you have been the son I never had. I want you to use it for good."

Sean hugged the old man.

"I'll make you proud, Keith."

Keith slapped him on the back, "You have already my boy."

24

JUSTICE IS MINE

It was day three of the trial. The prosecutor was a lazy man, but he'd managed to dig up some of Jimmy's friends to testify to his fine character, and Emmy's insanity.

"The girl is out of her mind, always has been," said Stuart Brown.

Roy Faure had only experienced the best of Jimmy.

"He was the perfect father to that girl, generous to a fault. He looked after em lil uns like thems were golden treasures, he did."

John Lewis told the court how Jimmy was of sober habit.

"He was hardly in the pub Sir, he was home early, never missed a day of work, yes, was never shy of work, our Jimmy."

Tanner was having difficulty listening to the lies. Sean put his hand on hers, "calm down or they'll put us out," he warned her.

"Jimmy Sterling is dead," said the prosecutor, "we are trying his daughter for murder, and she is the one who needs to answer for her murderous deeds, not Jimmy Sterling."

The common people roared in support. Murder cheered them up.

Arnie Schulz didn't spend much time examining Jimmy's friends, nothing they said could incriminate Emmy. The truth was that she did murder Jimmy; all that Arnie Schulz could do was tell the court why, and pray that the jury would be sympathetic toward his client.

Arnie Schulz went through witness upon witness who testified to what a terrible father Jimmy Sterling had been, but it was Mary's testimony that stunned the court, and the jury.

"Who told you that Jimmy Sterling was having physical relations with his daughter?" asked Arnie Schulz.

"Emmy did."

There was a collective roar from the onlookers, and the journalists eagerly noted this fact in their jotters.

Mary told the court the circumstances of the birth, then Sheila, and the midwife gave details of Emmy's suffering, and horrendous injuries.

Even though the story was horrific, the men in the courtroom didn't seem to be affected by the details; there was very little sympathy for a woman that murdered a man. And a lot of sympathy for a man who was having intercourse with his daughter, because after all, it happened all the time.

When Martin Blackburn took the stand, the men all sat at attention. Martin told the court that because he'd daughters of his own, he felt compelled to speak up for Emmy. He explained how Jimmy had bragged about his doings and how disgusted Martin had been when he heard what was happening.

Tanner almost fell of her chair when Arnie Schulz called up Johnny Bocelli. This time, the court was in a true uproar. Nobody had ever anticipated this gangster to testify on behalf of Emmy.

Johnny told the court that on the night that Emmy had the baby, Jimmy Sterling had come to ask him for a loan. He said that he needed a midwife to deliver his daughter's baby at the rows. Johnny was so disgusted, that he refused to give him the loan. Johnny asked who the father was, and in a panic, Jimmy said that he was the father. Then Jimmy realised that he'd made a mistake admitting it and tried to change his tune, but it was too late, the story was out.

Sean squeezed Tanner's hand.

"Johnny Bocelli would never have done that if not for you," he whispered.

"He is still a bad man," Tanner answered, but he may have redeemed himself a little."

The last person that Arnie Schulz called to the stand was Embeth Sterling. Everybody craned their necks to see the beautiful young woman who had killed her father.

Embeth Sterling stood in the dock, and looked like a serene angel. She stood dead still and stared at nothing, in a world of her own. Arnie Schulz asked her question after question, but she didn't reply to any one of them. Arnie shook his head and shrugged his shoulders at Yakov and Rachel. He couldn't force Emmy to speak if she refused.

The prosecutor jumped to his feet.

"I insist upon interviewing Emmy Sterling," he shouted, "I want to be satisfied that the court has seen her defiant attitude."

"That is unacceptable, the woman is mental," shouted Arnie.

"Order, order," shouted the judge banging down the gavel time, and again. "The prosecution may question the witness."

"I've to go and sit next to Rachel," said Tanner.

Before Sean could complain, Tanner was down the steps, and running toward the first bench where Yakov and Rachel sat.

"You're disrupting my courtroom," the judge shouted at her, "sit down or I'll put you out."

Some people jostled to make space for her, and she squeezed onto a bench, and as fate may have it, it was directly in front of the dock where Emmy was standing.

Emmy's eyes were roaming around the courtroom, void of any emotion or awareness of what was happening around her, she'd shut out the world. As her vacant eyes wondered, she saw a woman dashing down the aisle and squashing onto a bench. There was something familiar about the woman, and for the first time all day, her eyes lit up, she recognised Tanner Fischer.

As Tanner Fischer looked up into the dock, she looked straight into the eyes of Embeth Sterling. Emmy's eyes were full light and intelligence, then she gave Tanner a small smile, Embeth Sterling knew her. Tanner held her arm up and pointed at her wrist. Embeth looked down at her own wrist and touched the delicate watch. Tanner nodded at her, and Embeth nodded back. Sean watched the magic unfold between Tanner and Emmy. It was a miracle.

The prosecutor stood up, his wig was untidy and his cape was shoddy. He looked at Emmy with disdain.

"You're a murderess," he shouted at Emmy. "You must hang."

"Bullying, your honour," yelled Arnie Schulz.

Tanner was terrified that Emmy would withdraw again, if she did, there was no telling what the verdict would be. Tanner kept eye contact with Emmy, willing her to be brave. Emmy kept her hand on the watch, as if it was anchoring her to reality.

"Why did you murder your father?" shouted the prosecutor.

"Jimmy Sterling who is my father was going to rape my sister, and I'd to stop him," It was the first full sentence that Emmy had uttered in years. The words were as clear as a bell.

The prosecutor turned around and looked at Tilda. "Is that true?"

Tilda nodded.

Tanner could see the disappointment on the prosecutor's face.

"Did your father impregnate you?"

"Yes, Sir," answered Emmy.

"How old were you at the time?"

"Thirteen years old."

"Were you happy to have relations with him?"
The Prosecutor gave her an intimidating stare.

"No, Sir, I begged him to stop every night."

The courtroom was in chaos. Everyone was on their feet. This woman had not only claimed that her father had committed incest, but it was non-consensual. The jury had to rule in her favour.

In the noise and stress, Emmy felt herself floating in and out of reality. Her fingers touched the watch, she looked into Tanner's eyes, *I must be brave*.

The jury didn't have to leave the chambers to make their decision, it was unanimous, and Emmy Sterling was innocent.

Rachel burst into tears and rushed to embrace Emmy. Yakov followed, but Tilda reached her first. The bailiff removed Emmy's shackles and for the first time in years Emmy spoke to her sister.

> "I'm going to be brave Tilda, it's hard, but I'm going to be brave, nobody will hurt us ever again."

There shouts of Mazel tov, congratulations and jolly good show, from every corner of the courtroom. The press were on their feet applauding. It was one of the most important trials in the history of the country.

> Tanner went up to Emmy, and smiled at her. "I knew that you would do it, you were so brave."

Yakov and Rachel beamed.

Emmy looked at her wrist and touched the gold watch. With something akin to reverence she took it off her arm. She reached out and took Tanner's arm and fastened the watch onto her wrist.

> "Thank you," smiled Emmy. "You saved my life."

Tanner flung her arms around Emmy.

"What are you going to do now?" Tanner asked.

"We are going to do what all good Jews do when they have been blessed," laughed Rachel, "we are going to give thanks and we are going to eat."

Tanner laughed.

"Thank you, Tanner," said Yakov.

"It was in God's hands Yakov."

"Indeed, it was Tanner, Baruch Hashem."

As Tanner walked through the crowds of people and looked for Sean, she remembered Samuel's words 'Go save that girl Tanner, go.' Tanner got tears in her eyes, it felt as if she'd completed a very long, tiring journey and was relieved to have survived it. She felt a hand on her shoulder, and turned around, it was Sean. In the mayhem, he bent down and kissed her passionately. Sean and Tanner walked hurriedly to work, there was a lot to write about, and the story would be covered in an early edition.

Tanner and Sean left the offices of the Manchester Herald when the last newspaper was printed. Both were exhausted.

"Can I make you a cup of tea?" asked Sean.

"Yes, please."

They climbed the stairs and reached his apartment.

Once in the apartment, he took her in his arms and kissed her.

"I love you," he whispered.

Tanner felt his beard against her skin, once again she was crushed to his chest. She realised that she'd wanted this man from the day that he'd picked her up and rescued her from being trampled by the riotous mob.

"I love you too."

The kettle whistled, and Sean made them tea.

"We should be drinking something stronger," he laughed.

"Sean, I know what I want to do with my life."

"Tell me," he said with a smile as he grabbed her hand, "you want babies, and a nice man to cook dinner for every night."

"Definitely not," she laughed.

"I've inherited a lot of money. I want to start my own newspaper."

Sean frowned.

"Where?"

"London."

"Why London?"

"It's the seat of the government, our publications will be noticed, and we can influence decisions."

Sean became solemn.

"You'll need a highly experienced editor, until you develop the right skills."

"I'm asking you to come and help me."

He looked at her for a moment, and then turned away, torn.

"I don't want to move to London, Tanner. I've a newspaper to run here in Manchester. Keith hasn't got long to live, he has no family to pass it on to, and he wants me to have it. And to tell the truth, I've built it to where it's today, I'm not leaving."

Tanner was shocked, furious, and heartbroken all at once.

"What about me?" she demanded.

"I think you will make a fine newspaperwoman. You're talented, influential and people like you. You're a lot like Samuel."

"And us? Is it over?"

"I love you. It's not going to change whether you live here or in London. I'm always going to love you," Sean answered.

"But we will not be together."

Sean frowned, nodding that she was correct.

"I'm sorry Tanner. I'm not leaving Manchester."

18

TOGETHERNESS

London was as bleak as ever. Tanner Fischer climbed the worn steps of a medieval style building on Fleet Street. She felt both apprehension and elation as she looked up at the façade, yet she was determined to overcome her nerves and to savour the moment.

Tanner could have sworn she smelled paper and ink where she was standing outside, yet it was all her imagination. Those smells would only reach her senses when she passed through the imposing wooden doors and entered the lobby, which teemed with reporters frantically meeting deadlines. Tanner couldn't wait to hear the thundering clickety-clack of the enormous printing press as it spat out newspaper after newspaper. She would watch as they were baled and put on carts to be delivered all over England.

Tanner paused at a plaque screwed to the wall beside the grand front doors. The brass was tarnished here, and there, so she polished it with the cuff of her shirt sleeve. Tanner looked down at her leather satchel for the umpteenth time to confirm that it was still by her side.

Shilling watched Tanner from the coach. Tanner turned around and looked at her with large eyes, willing Shilling to join her. Shilling alighted from the cab and walked briskly toward Tanner, but the ever-loyal Socrates reached Tanner first.

"Go ahead, Tanner," Socrates told her softly. "It's all yours."

"It's a significant responsibility," Tanner answered.

"I know, but we trust you. The public trusts you."

"Yes, they do. That is what makes it more difficult. They'll rely on me for the truth. There will be no room for error," Tanner answered.

"What did my mother do on her first day at the foundry?" she asked him.

"Samuel gave her no choice, she had to run the business, and she had to face the challenges that it brought. It'll be the same for you. Shilling stepped into the foundry with confidence and never looked back."

Tanner smiled.

Shilling reached Tanner and put her hand on Tanner's shoulder.

"Do you know how proud I'm of you?" Shilling asked her.

"Thank you, Mama," she smiled at her.

"I know how intimidating it can be. You have to trust yourself," said Shilling.

Socrates nudged Tanner lightly.

"The time has come. You cannot be late on your first day,"

Socrates smiled and looked at his pocket watch. He stepped toward her and hugged her affectionately.

Tanner returned the smile. She stood up straight, pushed back her shoulders, and lifted her chin.

"What do you plan to do today?" asked Shilling.

"I'm going to change the world, Mama, I'm going to change the world," she took a deep breath and opened the door.

Tanner stood tall; she was the proprietor of a newspaper- 'The London Beacon.'

"Will you go with her, Socrates?" asked Shilling, as she watched Tanner walk away.

Socrates put his hand on Shilling's arm.

"No, Shilling, let her do this by herself."

"What if—?" mumbled Shilling.

"Are you behaving like Samuel?" asked Socrates.

Shilling laughed.

"Now, you know how he felt about you," chortled Socrates.

Shilling blinked away her tears. How she missed her father.

Tanner's secretary, Mr Hodges, opened the large front door. He'd gathered the entire staff in the foyer to welcome Tanner Fischer. A lot of the men thought that she was too young to run a newspaper, and also criticised her decision to hire young journalists, but she'd ignored their criticism.

Mr Hodges greeted her with respect and shook her hand.

"Good morning Miss Fischer."

Tanner walked toward the staircase, she knew that she would be required to say a few words. With each step she took she became more emboldened, convinced that this was her destiny.

She climbed the staircase until she was in a position where she could see the staff below her.

"Good morning," said Tanner.

She remembered Sean telling her not to smile for at least six months or the staff would never take you seriously.

"Thank you for the warm welcome," she said sincerely.

"My name is Tanner Fischer. You may refer to me as Miss Fischer, whether you are the editor-in-chief or the mail boy. We'll serve the public, and I

hope that we can do a better job than the
government."

Chuckles rippled round the room.

"We'll report accurately and responsibly. We'll
petition for justice, and we will be a voice for the
people who need one. By reporting our findings,
we can change this nation, and improve the lives
of those around us. We'll have many challenges,
but we will face them bravely."

"Miss Fischer," shouted someone from the back
the crowd, "will you be the new editor in chief."

This was the only question that Tanner dreaded. She knew
that they would criticise her ability and inexperience; she
took a deep breath.

Somewhere at the back of the group was a shuffling, and a
mild commotion, and she watched somebody pushing their
way through group. It was a man, his coat was unbuttoned
and his hands were in his pockets. Tanner watched the
crowd slowly part as he walked through them.

As he took his first step up the stairs, Tanner realised that
it was Sean Carlisle.

Tanner was so surprised to see him that she couldn't
muster a smile. She dared not ask what he was doing there
in fear of looking stupid and unprepared in front of her
staff. Sean gave her a casual roguish smile as he reached her
side, and at that moment, he was the most attractive man
she'd ever seen.

"Good morning," he smiled down at her.

Tanner nodded in greeting.

Sean turned around and faced the staff confidently.

"My name is Sean Carlisle, and I'm your new editor-in-chief. I'm also the owner of the Manchester Herald, and Miss Fischer and I'll be running them as sister companies."

The employees gasped when they heard the names. This was one of the most famous editors in the country, and the Manchester Herald was one of the most successful newspapers. Suddenly, they felt a surge of confidence, and they cheered.

Sean smiled.

"I answer to Miss Fischer, and she will be disappointed if I dilly-dally on the staircase."

A rallying cry followed.

"Back to work everybody," he shouted. "Let's get the first London Beacon onto the streets."

The response was immediate, the employees were eager to work for this man, and they rushed off to their stations in anticipation of building the most powerful newspaper in the country.

Tanner marched to her office, with Mr Hodges on her heels.

"Please give Mr Carlisle, and I a moment," she asked Mr Hodges.

The instant that the door was closed, she spun around and began to speak.

"Not now," he shushed her.

He took a determined step forward and took her face in his hands and kissed her. She tried to pull away from him, but Sean would not stop. Eventually, he let her go.

"You're not fighting with me today," he instructed.

Tanner nodded, breathless.

"Why are you here?" she asked him.

"A few things."

Tanner looked at him quizzically.

"You need a good editor so that you don't get arrested every other week," he winked at her, "and I love you," he added nonchalantly.

"But—."

"No buts, Tanner. We can fight every day, but we are going to sleep together every night. We are going on adventures, not only to change the world, but to see it too. You're the most challenging woman I've ever met, but I don't ever regret falling for you."

Tanner laughed out loud.

Sean put his hand behind her head and bent to kiss her again.

"Are you going to say, yes?" he asked her.

"Of course," she whispered.

Tanner and Sean were married in Shilling's small garden in Birmingham. Tanner looked beautiful in a snow-white gown. The dress was silk, the lace collar reached to below her chin, and the sleeves to her wrists. Her hair was a mass of loose black curls held back with large white roses. Tanner didn't wear a veil, she wasn't a possession to given away. Baxter escorted her down a flower lined path, to a quaint gazebo under tall trees, where Sean was waiting for her. Shilling and Miss Anabelle stood next to each other, and they both became tearful when they saw Tanner.

"She's almost as beautiful as you," Baxter whispered in Shilling's ear. "I love you," he kissed Shilling on the cheek.

Shilling looked up into his rugged good-looking face; she was so in love with him.

Tanner vowed herself to Sean Carlisle. As Tanner spoke, a single tear ran down her face. With the utmost display of tenderness, Sean lifted his hand and wiped the tear away. Then he bent forward and whispered:

"I'm never going to make you cry again," he smiled as he looked into her adoring eyes.

"Uhm," the official cleared his throat.

Socrates gave the man a stern look, annoyed at his impatience.

Sean became very serious when he said his vows, he was committed to every promise that he made. It was his turn to become emotional, not that anyone watching would've guessed.

With great joy Sean and Tanner were declared man and wife.

The official made a hasty retreat. These were the strangest people he'd ever met. Although they were a very wealthy family, the small congregation was comprised of servants and working- class families, who behaved as if they were family. He made this observation to Socrates as he was being escorted to the door.

"That is a great compliment to the late Mr Samuel Hudson, thank you, Sir."

The man was even more baffled than before.

Mr and Mrs Carlisle boarded the train at Calais. As the train left the station behind them, the sunset cast a soft romantic light over the countryside. The compartment was lavish, with exquisite walnut finishes. It was spacious; with two club chairs, and a table under the windows, and a sumptuous double bed.

"We won't need all of this for such a short trip to Paris," said Tanner.

"We aren't going to Paris," laughed Sean, "I thought we would just trundle along to Nice."

Tanner laughed.

> "I've hired a little villa for us. It's going to be a
> longer journey than usual," he said, seriously.
> "We have only associated train journeys with
> tragedy, I need to change your perception,"

He'd a twinkle in his eye.

Sean walked toward and kissed her. Instead, of embracing
her, he began to remove her dress.

Anxiously, she began to undress him as well.

Sean remembered, the night in Mayfair when Tanner had
descended the stairs wearing the emerald dress, he'd
longed to touch her perfect skin. This time, there was so
much more to see, so much more to touch. He lay Tanner
on the bed gently, this time he didn't have to stop himself,
Tanner Carlisle was his wife.

Author's Note

Proposals to criminalize incest in England and Wales, which was formalised in several Incest Bills from 1899 to 1907, met considerable resistance from the Lord Chancellor who thought the subject too repulsive for public debate. Concerned that the issue would be greatly magnified if such crimes were prosecuted through the criminal courts, he believed that the press couldn't be trusted to report it responsibly.

.

Printed in Great Britain
by Amazon